Cosmo Monkhouse

**Life of Leigh Hunt**

Cosmo Monkhouse

**Life of Leigh Hunt**

ISBN/EAN: 9783337056384

Printed in Europe, USA, Canada, Australia, Japan

Cover: Foto ©Raphael Reischuk / pixelio.de

More available books at **www.hansebooks.com**

# LIFE

OF

# LEIGH HUNT.

BY

COSMO MONKHOUSE.

LONDON:

WALTER SCOTT, Ltd.,

24, WARWICK LANE, PATERNOSTER ROW.

1893.

# CONTENTS.

5

## CHAPTER IV.

## CHAPTER V.

## CHAPTER VI.

## CHAPTER VII.

## CHAPTER VIII.

## CHAPTER IX.

## CHAPTER X.

## CHAPTER XI.

## CHAPTER XII.

# LEIGH HUNT.

## CHAPTER I.

IN that most desultory but delightful book — the Autobiography of Leigh Hunt—among the few facts which it is not difficult to find are some relating to his ancestors.  It is evident that at the first start he proposed to write his life in a manner more in accordance with custom in such matters, and to state events in their due order with some approach to particularity ; and it may be that, having strong views upon heredity, he judged it of special importance to account for those elements in his own composition which he was wont to trace to what he called the "tropical blood" in his veins.  However that may be, we learn that both his parents came of families long settled in the New World, and we may believe, if we choose, that he was descended, on the father's side, from " Tory Cavaliers," (which, as he truly says, is "a wide designation "), who fled to the West Indies from the ascendency of Cromwell ; and, on the mother's side, " amidst a curious mixture of Quakers and soldiers . . . not only from the gentry,

but from kings, that is to say, *Irish* kings." As
Leigh Hunt himself treats these prehistoric traditions
but half seriously, and they have not passed unchal-
lenged by others, they may be regarded, perhaps, as
matters of speculation more fit for the antiquarian than
the biographer. At all events, in this small volume
which cannot afford to be discursive, we may be content to begin with his grandfathers and grandmothers.

His father's father was the Rector of St. Michael's, in
Bridgetown, Barbadoes, whose wife was "an O'Brien,
or rather Bryan, very proud of her descent from the
kings aforesaid (or the kings from her)." His mother's
father was Stephen Shewell, "a merchant of Philadelphia, a vehement man, both in public and in family
matters," who married a lady of the name of Bickley.
Her family is said to have come from Buckinghamshire,
and to have borne three half-moons on their coat of
arms. "On that [his mother's] side of the family," wrote
Leigh Hunt, "we seem all sailors and rough subjects,
with a mitigation (on the female part) of quakerism ; as,
on the father's side, we are creoles and claret-drinkers,
very polite and clerical."

The Rector of St. Michael's spoilt Leigh Hunt's
father, whose name was Isaac, and then sent him to
school and college on the American continent, where
he took the degree of M.A. at both Philadelphia and
New York. "When he spoke the farewell oration on
leaving college [at Philadelphia], two young ladies fell
in love with him, one of whom he afterwards married.
He was fair and handsome, with delicate features, a
small aquiline nose, and blue eyes. To a graceful

address he joined a remarkably fine voice, which he
modulated with great effect. It was in reading, with
this voice, the poets and other classics of England, that
he completed the conquest of my mother's heart."
The other young lady who fell in love with this
West Indian Adonis, was the aunt of Mary Shewell,
his future wife, and married Mr. Benjamin West, the
young American artist, who was afterwards to become
the President of the Royal Academy. The two ladies
were about the same age.

Miss Mary Shewell was " a brunette with fine eyes,
a tall lady-like person, and hair blacker than is seen of
English growth," so that Leigh Hunt's father was fair
and his mother unusually dark, notwithstanding that,
according to his own view just quoted, the creole blood
was on his father's side. In another place he ascribes the
dark complexion of himself and his brothers to the
influence of climate, which " Anglo-Americans had already begun to show." He further describes his mother
as having " no accomplishments but the two best of all,
a love of nature and a love of books," as " diffident of
her personal merit," but possessed of " great energy of
principle." She was too bashful to accept Dr. Franklin's
offer to teach her the guitar, yet, when her husband's
life (or at least freedom) was in danger, she refused to
save him by a sacrifice of principle. For at the time
the Revolution broke out, her husband, then practising
as a lawyer in Philadelphia, " entered with so much zeal
into the cause of the British Government, that, besides
pleading for loyalists with great fervour at the bar, he
wrote pamphlets equally full of party warmth, which

drew on him the popular odium." After a narrow escape of tar and feathers, if not of worse, he was got on board one of his father-in-law's ships, and taken to Barbadoes.

Thence he came to London, where he exchanged the law for the Church. He was ordained by Lowth, Bishop of London, and soon became a popular preacher, much in demand for charity sermons. His ministrations at Bentinck Chapel, Lisson Green, Paddington, appear for a time to have drawn crowds of fashionable admirers, and it was here that his wife found him officiating, when, after some two years' separation, she and her children rejoined him in England. When precisely all these events took place the Autobiography does not tell us ; perhaps the writer did not know himself. He was not born till afterwards, and his dislike of anything connected with figures probably deterred him from any resolute research for dates, when, in middle life, he took up his pen to record, not only the events of his life, but those which happened before his entry into the world. Such outline as he has drawn of the latter, though softened by his cheerful optimism and his genius for apology, suggest little less than a long domestic tragedy.

The sudden removal of a semi-tropical family to a more moderate clime, the no less sudden conversion of a colonial lawyer into a London clergyman, were dangerous ventures, and succeeded about as well (or ill) as might have been expected. The position of the family in Philadelphia was presumably comfortable and

honourable. They at least were surrounded by friends
and relations, and the conditions of their existence were
those in which they had been born and bred. But Mrs.
Hunt, on her arrival in London, found her husband on
the verge of bankruptcy, and pledged to a profession
for which he appears to have had few qualifications but
a fine voice and a charming delivery. Though there
were crowds of carriages at the door when he preached,
the chapel speculation proved a failure, and his wife
found him "horribly in debt." Fortunately they were
not without friends, many of them fellow-refugees.
Three of the boys were sent to school, the other (there
appear to have been four living at this time ; the firstborn, called Benjamin, after Dr. Franklin, was dead)
went to live for some years with a Mrs. Spencer, who,
Leigh Hunt "thinks," was a sister of Sir Richard
Worsley ; and the father and mother were taken in by
Mr. West, the painter, who lived in Newman Street,
and, as has before been stated, had married an aunt of
Mrs. Hunt.

Nor was Mrs. Hunt to see any very good times again.
And her troubles were aggravated by her own delicate
health, the result of a violent attack of jaundice which
had seized her on the day of her husband's arrest in
Philadelphia. Reading between the lines of pious
euphemism in which Leigh Hunt tries to soften, without concealing, the faults of his father, it may be seen
that he was too fond of society and the claret bottle, was
idle and self-indulgent, and that he grew worse rather
than better as years went on. "He should have been
kept in Barbadoes," wrote his son. "He was a true

exotic and ought not to have been transplanted.  He might have preached there, and quoted Horace, and been gentlemanly and generous, and drunk his claret, and no harm done."   Ah, if things had only happened differently, what fine fellows we all might have been ! Unfortunately for such as poor Mr. Isaac Hunt, a London clergyman, who wishes to make his home happy, and to bring up a family in repute and comfort, needs something more than a fine voice and a large stock of good intentions.

"The power of making sacrifices for the sake of a principle," is a quality which Leigh Hunt claims for his family, and there is no doubt that both he and his brother John showed that they possessed it.  Whether his father was capable of any great conscious act of noble self-denial, may be open to question ; but it is a matter of fact that he was ruined by his loyalty.  And it is further related, that if it had not been for his zealous efforts in favour of a fellow-refugee, Colonel Trumbull, the celebrated American painter, he might have been a bishop.  The argument is in this wise.  Trumbull had come over to study painting under West, and was arrested as a spy.  Isaac Hunt assisted West in his effort to obtain his release.  Hunt at this time was tutor in the family of the Duke of Chandos.  To be tutor in a ducal family was to be on the road to a bishopric, and the chances in Hunt's favour were increased by the fact that his duke was also a state officer (Master of the Horse), for whom the king had a personal regard. Hunt was informed by Mr. Thompson (afterwards the celebrated Count Rumford, and then Lord George

Germaine's secretary) that " he made himself very busy
in this affair, and very little to his own reputation," and
Trumbull records that his effort was " pushed so far as
almost to endanger his own safety." *Ergo* Hunt lost
his bishopric. At all events, there is sufficient proof
that Hunt's action in the matter was generous and un-
selfish, and it deserves to be recorded in his honour.

After leaving West's house, Isaac Hunt went to live
in Hampstead Square, whence he used occasionally to
go and preach at Southgate; and thus it happened
that he attracted the attention of the Duke of Chandos,
who had a seat in the neighbourhood. His Grace was
so pleased with Hunt's sermons, that he asked him to
become tutor to his nephew, Mr. James Henry Leigh.
It was at Southgate, at a house called Eagle Hall, that
James Henry Leigh Hunt was born (October 19, 1784),
and it was to his father's pupil that he owed not only
his familiar Christian name Leigh, but the two others
as well.

Although Leigh Hunt could have no very early
memories connected with the place, he tells us : " It is
a pleasure to me to know that I was even born in so
sweet a village as Southgate. I first saw the light there
on the 19th of October, 1784. It found me cradled, not
only in the lap of nature which I love, but in the midst
of the truly English scenery which I love beyond all
other. Middlesex in general . . . is a scene of trees and
meadows, of ' greenery ' and nestling cottages ; and
Southgate is a prime specimen of Middlesex. It is a
place lying out of the way of innovation, therefore it
has the pure, sweet air of antiquity about it."

How long Isaac Hunt retained his engagement in the Duke's family is not recorded ; but it must have ceased before his youngest son could have had any knowledge of Southgate, for Mr. Leigh was married two years after his godson's birth, and the first room of which Leigh Hunt had any recollection was one in the King's Bench Prison.

From the time, however, that Leigh Hunt's impressions fixed themselves on his memory, they appear to have been vivid. He records the " strange lively air " that a game of rackets gave to the prison ; his " astonishment and horror at a song sung, as he tottered along, by a drunken man," the words of which appeared to him " unspeakably wicked "; and gives a striking description of one of the prisoners who " was veritably wicked enough." This was Andrew Robinson Stoney Bowes, Esq. (whose career is supposed to have suggested much of Thackeray's " Barry Lyndon "), then undergoing a sentence of three years for attempting to extort by cruelty the property of his wife, the Countess of Strathmore.

A loyalist pension of £100 a year, gained by the good offices of West, did not greatly improve the affairs of Isaac Hunt. His son writes : " Small as it was, he was obliged to mortgage it ; and from this time till the arrival of some relations from the West Indies, several years afterwards, he underwent a series of mortifications and distresses, not always without reason for self-reproach. . . . My poor father ! He grew deeply acquainted with arrests, and began to lose his graces and (from failures with creditors) his good name. He became irritable with the consequences, and almost took hope of better days out of the heart [his wife's] that loved him, and was too often glad to escape out of its society. Yet such an art had he of making his home comfortable when he chose, and of settling himself to the most tranquil pleasures, that if she could have ceased to look forward about her children, I believe, with all his defects, those evenings would have brought unmingled satisfaction to her, when, after brightening the fire and bringing out the coffee, my mother knew that her husband was going to read Saurin or Barrow to her, with his fine voice and unequivocal enjoyment." "We thus struggled on," he continues, "between quiet and disturbance, between placid readings and frightful knocks at the door, and sickness, and calamity, and hopes, which hardly ever forsook us."

Notwithstanding all things, the elder sons were educated and started in life, and, in course of time, Leigh, who was nine years younger than the youngest of his brothers, was sent to school also. Incapable as he was of helping himself, Isaac Hunt appears to have been always ready to help others, and to have been a kind if not a judicious father. "As to his children," says the Autobiography, in a passage of which the candour sounds strangely like satire, "he was healthy and sanguine, and always looked forward to being able to do something for them ; and something for them he did, if it was only in grafting his animal spirits on the maternal stock, and setting them an example of independent thinking. But he did more.

He really took care, considering his unbusinesslike habits, towards settling them in some line of life." In other words, he probably used his influence with his many friends and relations. " One of my brothers went to sea—a great blow to my poor mother. The next [1] was articled to an attorney. My brother Robert became pupil to an engraver, and my brother John was apprenticed to Mr. Reynell, the printer, whose kindly manner and deep, iron voice, I well remember and respect."

His brother Stephen, who when a child in Philadelphia had been saved by his uncle, Stephen Shewell, from being kidnapped by Indians, married one of the relations from Barbadoes. This was his cousin, Christiana Dayrell, and it was her rich and generous mother, the sister of Isaac Hunt, who, from her arrival in England till her death, made " the West Indian sun " to shine again upon her luckless brother. Stephen used to delight in terrifying his little brother Leigh in the dark, especially by personating that terrible beast the Mantichora, of which Leigh had seen a representation in a picture-book. " In vain my brother played me repeated tricks with this frightful anomaly. I was always ready to be frightened again. At one time he would grin like the Mantichora ; then he would roar like him ; then call about him in the dark. I remember his asking me to come up to him one night at the top of the house. I ascended, and

---

[1] This was Stephen, to whom he refers as his *eldest* brother afterwards. Of the brother that went to sea nothing more is recorded.

found the door shut. Suddenly a voice came through the keyhole, saying, in its hollowest tones, ' The Mantichora's coming.' Down I rushed to the parlour, fancying the terror at my heels." "These tricks," he adds, "helped to morbidise all that was weak in my temperament, and cost me many a bitter night."

Save a few passing notes, as of the tenderness of Robert to their mother in her last illness, the Autobiography contains few references to any of his brothers except John, side by side with whom he was to fight the battles of his life. Besides the firstborn, Benjamin, two daughters, Eliza and Mary, died young. " My little sister Mary," he says, " died not long after [after 1789 or 1790]. She was so young that my only recollection of her, besides her blue eyes, is her love of her brother, and her custom of leading me by the hand to some stool or seat on the staircase, and making me sing the song with her favourite burden, [' Dans vòtre lit.'] We were the two youngest children, and about of an age."

So at least there was music in this not very happy household. His mother, though she had refused the instruction of Dr. Franklin, was "fond of music and a gentle singer in her way," and she listened with admiration to her little weakly boy as he sang his show-song, "Alone by the light of the moon," to the accompaniment of Miss C. on the piano. Leigh Hunt was always fond of music, and some of the pleasantest pages of his autobiography are devoted to the recollection of the songs which were sung in the home of his childhood. One of his mother's favourite songs was,

"Encompassed in an Angel's frame," by Jackson, of
Exeter. She was charmed also with "The Hardy
Tar" and "The topsails shiver in the wind"; but
these nautical songs made her sad, too, for thinking
of that son at sea, of whom we at least hear no
more. Leigh Hunt never mentions his mother but
in a tone of sadness. The gleams of comparative prosperity which shone awhile upon the household from
their rich relations, seem to have had but little cheer
for her. There was "a mixture of tenderness and
anxiety always in her face," and her son never forgot
it, as it used to appear when she was "coming up the
cloisters with that weary hang of the head on one side,
and that melancholy smile." One can only hope that
Leigh Hunt's picture of his mother's sadness is a little
overdrawn, but there seems to be no doubt that it was
not to her, but to his father, that he owed his perennial
fund of "animal spirits." In one passage he contrasts
the temperaments of his parents with a terrible dis-
tinctness. "Indeed," he says, "as I do not remember
to have ever seen my mother smile, except in sorrowful
tenderness, so my father's shouts of laughter are now
ringing in my ears."

Leigh Hunt himself seems to have been not the least
of his poor mother's anxieties. She had been told
that, if he survived to the age of fifteen, "he might
turn out to possess a more than average amount of
intellect," but that, otherwise, "he stood a chance of
dying an idiot"; and during childhood he "hardly
recovered from one illness before he was seized with
another." Once, to assist his recovery, he was sent to

France, which must have been a strain on their slender resources, unless Mrs. Dayrell, or " Aunt Courthope," (Ann Courthope Hunt, his father's and Mrs. Dayrell's sister) came to their aid. For the anxieties there were doubtless some maternal consolations—the visits with her little boy to their friends the Wests in Newman Street, or the Thorntons in their fine city house ; the pride in his voice, and, later, in his juvenile verses, which she hoarded in her pocket-book with a mother's care.

Even at the risk of making this chapter too long in proportion to the rest of this small book, I cannot resist the inclination to add a few more of those scattered touches with which Leigh Hunt has given us perhaps the most tender and faithful portrait of a mother that ever was painted by a son. He loved her even for the weaknesses, physical as well as mental, which she transmitted to him. From her, if we may trust his belief in this matter, he inherited a tendency to jaundice, which permanently affected his health. "I doubt, indeed," he writes, "whether I have passed a day during half my life without reflections, the first germs of which are traceable to sufferings which this tendency once cost me " ; and then he adds, with that filial special pleading which he always employs in writing of his father, "My prevailing temperament, nevertheless, is my father's ; and it has not only enabled me to turn these reflections into sources of tranquillity and exaltation, but helped my love of my mother's memory to take a sort of pride in the infirmity which she bequeathed me."

It is not every one who could feel such a sentiment as this, and fewer still who would have chosen to express it ; but it was doubtless genuine enough, and thoroughly characteristic of Leigh Hunt, who could moralise and sentimentalise on anything personal— even a bilious attack.

But the influence of Mrs. Isaac Hunt on her son did not end here. From her he derived his dislike of violence, and his sensibility to the least show of pain and suffering. She "inoculated him with timidity," not only physical, but moral ; not only of fights in the streets, but of strong language, whereby hangs one of the most amusing of the tales of his childhood. "She," he relates, "had produced in me such a horror, or rather such an intense idea, of even violent words, or of the commonest trivial oath, that being led one day, perhaps by the very excess of it, to snatch a 'fearful joy' in its utterance, it gave me so much remorse that for some time afterwards I could not receive a bit of praise, or a pat of encouragement on the head, without thinking to myself, 'Ah ! they little suspect that I am the boy who said d—— it.' "

But this sad woman, broken in health and spirits, still "retained her energy of character on great occasions," and remained to the last "a little too peremptory in her opinions," one of which was that the madness of George III. was a judgment of Providence for being the cause of unnecessary bloodshed. But her will showed itself most beautifully in actions of sympathy, as when, one severe winter, she took off her petticoat in the street and gave it to a poor woman.

"It is supposed that a cold which ensued, fixed the rheumatism upon her for life." "Saints," adds her son, "have been made for charities no greater."

Not from her apparently did Leigh Hunt derive his literary tastes. Her favourite books were Mrs. Rowe's "Devout Exercises of the Heart," and Young's "Night Thoughts," which was a pity, adds Leigh Hunt, who preferred a more cheerful religion than that of the bereaved doctor. Mrs. Hunt's religious opinions were, however, cheerful enough ; both her husband and she for years before her death held the broadest of views. They became Unitarians, and afterwards Universalists, believing in the salvation of all created things, including the " puir de'il " himself. Leigh Hunt would appear, from a passage of his biography, to have arrived at much the same opinions independently, and very early in life ; but it seems probable that he inherited or imbibed them from his parents. Whether they were right or wrong, there is no doubt that they encouraged great tranquillity of mind, and that they were very congenial to the temperament of Isaac Hunt, who, according to his son, had "an irresistible tendency to seize on a cheering reflection." They do not seem to have had such a potent charm for his mother ; but even she, when her husband sat down of an evening and read her sermons or the Bible, of which he was always fond, or talked divinity and politics, or smoked his pipe (it is strange to read now that "he was one of the last of the gentry who retained the old fashion of smoking"), while he related anecdotes of my Lord North and the Rockingham Administration—even she, when she saw or heard her husband do any of these pleasant things, must have derived some solace from the thought that not all the most unpleasant things he had ever done would prevent him from being as happy as she could wish him to be hereafter. This wife's love for him never faltered, nor apparently that of his children. " What a kind man he was ! " said his son Robert to his other son Leigh, after his death.

Mrs. Isaac Hunt died some years before her husband. Her last illness was long, and she was tormented with rheumatism ; but she was tenderly cared for, especially by her son Robert. Leigh Hunt regrets that he did not pay her all the attention he should, "being more giddy than he was young," and tells us that " her greatest pleasure during her decay was to lie on a sofa looking at the setting sun. She used to liken it to the door of heaven, and fancy her lost children there waiting for her. She died in the fifty-third year of her age, in a little miniature house which stands in a row behind the church which has since been built at Somersham ; and she was buried, as she had always wished to be, in the churchyard of Hampstead."

Isaac Hunt lies in the churchyard in Bishopsgate Street. He died in 1809, at the age of fifty-seven.

# CHAPTER II.

AFTER Leigh Hunt begins his school reminiscences, the reader of the Autobiography will find few references to his parents and family, with the exception of his brother John. Both parents lived for several years after he left school. His mother did not die before Leigh was engaged to be married, and his father survived to see him the editor of the *Examiner;* but he has thought fit to exhaust nearly all he has to say about them in the early chapters of his book, and it is convenient to follow this arrangement here, as it is impossible to assign with exactitude the dates of most of the records of his home life, although it is plain that some of them relate to his schooldays.

The conditions of his life at Christ Hospital (for this, says Leigh Hunt, is its proper name, and not Christ's Hospital) was such as to encourage the natural independence of his mind. When he entered he appears to have had no friend nor relation at the school, and though, no doubt, whole and half-holidays gave him frequent opportunities of paying short visits to his family, he was prohibited from sleeping out; and during the whole of the period he remained at school, he

was only allowed one vacation of three weeks, which
he spent with his Barbadian relations, then living at
Merton, in Surrey.

At Christ Hospital there appears to have been little
to interfere with the natural development of Leigh
Hunt's character, except the discipline of the school
and the principles which he imbibed from his parents.
The latter were of a somewhat indefinite character,
but they included a strong belief that everything would
come right in the long run, and that the Hunt family
had a special gift for martyrdom, which should never
be neglected when an occasion offered for its display.

His autobiography contains many evidences of his
pride in this "spirit of martyrdom," and the lessons of
endurance and resistance of a passive kind which he
had learnt from his mother. "I went to Christ Hospital," he writes, "an ultra-sympathising and timid
boy. The sight of boys fighting, from which I had
been so anxiously withheld, frightened me as something devilish, and the least prospect of corporal chas-
tisement to a schoolfellow (for the lesson I had learned
would have enabled me to bear it myself) affected me
to tears." At first he "went to the wall," but afterwards "dared everything from the biggest and
strongest boys" on account of his schoolfellows. In
other words, he "stood up" with his tongue (not his
fists) against bullies, and took his thrashing quietly.
He records more than one "moral" victory so obtained,
and tells us that he " gained, at an early period of boy-
hood, the reputation of a romantic enthusiast, whose
daring on behalf of a friend or a good cause nothing

could put down." He employed his powers of endurance on his own behalf also, and successfully resisted
all attempts at making him a "fag," or "boy" (which
was equivalent to "fag" at Christ Hospital); but he
tells us, "I could suffer better than act," and "I never
fought with a boy but once, and that was on my own
account; but though I beat him, I was frightened, and
eagerly sought his good will." It would be interesting to know the size of this boy, but that he does not
tell us. It would also be interesting to know how
this small, stammering, black-haired, "ultra-sympathising," West Indian child appeared to his ruder,
rougher, less sentimental English schoolfellows; but
it may be accepted that his determination to "undergo
any stubborn amount of pain and wretchedness"
rather than submit to what he thought wrong, earned
their respect, if not their sympathy, and that he was
left pretty much to himself, as a curious boy whom
nobody could quite "make out." They had probably
much experience of boys who would fight and boys who
would run away, but one who would do neither was a
puzzle. In fact, not only at school, but in after life,
his was a personality not easy to "make out"; for he
took little colour from his surroundings, but proceeded
steadfastly on a few elementary principles, out of which
he manufactured a simple code of conduct, without
regard to the customs and prejudices of the society in
which he lived. Though very sociable and very
human, he seems never to have been quite "in touch"
with any man; even Keats and Shelley are doubtful
exceptions.

Nevertheless, if he did not much share that "intelligence in common," or gain much of the knowledge "boy gets from boy," which Charles Lamb reckons among the chief advantages of Christ Hospital, he was not a solitary recluse. He was full of animal spirits, and if not fond of boyish sports, he at least bathed and boated. He "played antics, and rioted in fantastic jests" with his ordinary schoolfellows, and he entertained ardent friendships for a selected few. With regard to these friendships, it may be remarked that they were founded rather on a romantic ideal than on a true insight into character or reciprocity of feeling, and that his method of kindling attachments, by imputing to others perfections which they did not possess, clung to him afterwards, and was the cause of much misunderstanding and disappointment, especially in the case of Lord Byron. "If ever," he writes, "I tasted a disembodied transport on earth, it was in those friendships which I entertained at school, before I dreamt of any maturer feeling. I shall never forget the impression it first made on me. I loved my friend for his gentleness, his candour, &c., &c. . . . . I thought him a kind of angel. . . . . With other boys I played antics and rioted in fantastic jests; but in his society, or whenever I thought of him, I fell into a kind of Sabbath state of bliss; and I am sure I could have died for him."

It is somewhat disappointing to find that these transports (more like those of a school-girl than a school-boy) were not only short-lived, but were experienced "towards three successive schoolfellows;" but they were evidently founded on imagination, and not the result of any community of tastes—even for those books which soon began to be a "never-ceasing consolation" to him.

For a boy with such strong literary proclivities, he arrived at Christ Hospital too late—a day, so to speak, after the fair. "Charles Lamb had lately been deputy-Grecian, and Coleridge had left for the University." Lamb used to come and see the boys, but Leigh Hunt "did not know him as Lamb," but "took him for Mr. Guy," the nickname by which Lamb was called by the boys. "Coleridge I never saw till he was old." The only boys who then, or afterwards, had literary tastes were, "Wood, whom I admired for his verses, and who was afterwards Fellow of Pembroke College, Cambridge, where I visited him"; Mitchell (the translator of "Aristophanes"), and Barnes (afterwards editor of *The Times*). It is of the last that he has left the most agreeable reminiscence. "What pleasant days have I not passed with him and other schoolfellows, bathing in the New River and boating on the Thames. He and I began to learn Italian together; and anybody, not within the pale of the enthusiastic, might have thought us mad as we went shouting the beginning of Metastasio's 'Ode to Venus,' as loud as we could bawl, in the Hounslow Fields."

This was probably towards the end of his time at Christ Hospital, when he had begun to take in Italian literature an interest greater than he had ever felt for that of ancient Rome. The method of teaching at Christ Hospital (probably not more there than at other public schools), was not calculated to make boys greatly interested in the classics or other subjects of study. In the under grammar school, where Leigh Hunt was first placed, the discipline was lax. The master was the Rev. Mr. Field, described by Leigh Hunt as "a good-looking man, very gentlemanly, and always dressed at the neatest. I believe he once wrote a play. [Charles Lamb gives more information about this play.] He had the reputation of being admired by the ladies. A man of more handsome incompetence for his situation perhaps did not exist." He was so absent that when the boys had a request to make they would put to him the most absurd and impertinent questions. "We would say, for instance, 'Are you not a great fool, sir,' or 'Isn't your daughter a pretty girl,' to which he would reply, 'Yes, child.'"

The upper grammar master, Boyer, was as strict as Field was lax, a stern "disciplinarian" of the old school, not content even with the use of the birch, but using his hands freely. On one occasion he knocked out one of Leigh Hunt's front teeth with the back of a Homer in a fit of impatience at his stammering. Both Coleridge and Lamb have left pictures of this school tyrant, doing more willing justice to his better qualities as a schoolmaster. Leigh Hunt admits that he was laborious and conscientious, but this amiable view was the result of "age and reflection," and it is evident that while at school Boyer was to him the impersonation of cruelty and injustice, and that he did not profit greatly by his instruction. Indeed, it is scarcely possible to imagine a worse master for such a weakly and sensitive boy, who needed all the sympathy and encouragement he could get.

"What a bit of a golden age was it," he writes, "when the Rev. Mr. Steevens,[1] one of the under grammar masters, took his place on some occasions for a short time. Steevens was short and fat, with a handsome, cordial face—you loved him as you looked at him, and seemed as if you should love him the more the fatter he became. I stammered when I was at that time of life, which was an infirmity that used to get me into terrible trouble with the master. Steevens used to say, on the other hand, 'Here comes our little black-haired friend who stammers so. Now let us see what we can do for him.' The consequence was I did not hesitate half so much as with the other. When I did, it was only out of impatience to please him."

Not, however, did the occasional kindness of this master avail to interest the boy in the classics, verse or prose.

"How little did I care for any verses at that time, except English ones. I had no regard even for Ovid. I read and knew nothing of Horace, though I had got somehow a liking for his character. Cicero I disliked, as I cannot help doing still. Demosthenes I was inclined to admire, but did not know why, and would very willingly have given up him and his difficulties altogether. Homer I regarded with horror, as a series of lessons I had to learn by heart before I understood him. . . . The only classic I remember having any

[1] Or Stephens. The Rev. L. Pepys Stephens, under grammar master of Christ Hospital, is among the subscribers to "Juvenilia."

love for was Virgil, and that was for the episode of
Nisus and Euryalus. [On account of its picture of
devoted friendship, which made him tolerant of the
butchery of sleeping foes. He afterwards translated
the similar episode of Medoro and Cloridano from
Ariosto. See Poems, 1860, p. 354.] But there were
three books which I read in whenever I could, and
which often got me into trouble. These were Tooke's
'Pantheon,' Lemprière's 'Classical Dictionary,' and
Spence's 'Polymetis,' the great folio edition with the
plates."

But if Leigh Hunt did not enjoy his classical studies,
and never became much of a "scholar" at school or
afterwards, he was from an early age very fond of
"books," and his reading at school was extensive and
various, especially of English poetry.

"In those days Cooke's edition of the British
Poets came up. I had got an odd volume of Spenser,
and I fell passionately in love with Collins and Gray.
How I loved those little sixpenny numbers containing
whole poets! I doted on their size; I doted on their
type, on their ornaments, on their wrappers, containing
lists of other poets, and on the engravings from Kirk.
I bought them over and over again, and used to
get up select sets, which disappeared like buttered
crumpets; for I could resist neither giving them
away, nor possessing them. When the master tormented me—when I used to hate and loathe the sight
of Homer and Demosthenes and Cicero—I would
comfort myself with thinking of the sixpence in my
pocket, with which I should go out to Paternoster

Row, when school was over, and buy another number of an English poet."

He loved the " Arabian Nights" also ; Chaucer, who was not included in Cooke's edition, was a later favourite. He knew only one play of Shakespeare— " Hamlet "—for which he had a "delighted awe "; he read " Hudibras " " at one desperate plunge," when he was in bed with two scalded legs. Milton's " Paradise Lost " he read, "with little less sense of it, as a task," and paying more regard to the pictures than the text. Then, as afterwards, the cheerful but indolent optimism of his mind seems to have rejected everything that was distressing or tiresome. For him Adam and Eve were always happy in Paradise, and he derived a similar impression from " Rasselas." " The Happy Valley was new to me, and delightful and everlasting ; and there the princely inmates were everlastingly to be found." No doubt he also indulged in fiction of a less edifying character than Dr. Johnson's famous apologue, for he subscribed to " the famous circulating library in Leadenhall Street," and became " a glutton of novels."

English literature was the one thing which interested him during his school life, and English verses were the only exercise which he performed with satisfaction. He does not seem, however, to have gained much credit by these, and as for his prose essays, Boyer treated them with contempt, crumpling them up in his hand, and "calling out, ' Here, children, there is something to amuse you.' Upon which the servile part of the boys would jump up, seize the paper, and be amused accordingly."

There is no trace of mortification, or a sense of injustice, in his account of this treatment of his early prose efforts. His heart was not in them, for they were set tasks on subjects of no interest to himself personally ; nor did he then probably care about writing prose at all. For his own pleasure the boy wrote, not prose, but verses. "I was already fond of writing verses," he says. " The first I remember were in honour of the Duke of York's ' victory at Dunkirk,' which victory, to my great mortification, turned out to be a defeat. . . . Afterwards, when in Great Erasmus,[1] I wrote a poem, called ' Winter,' in consequence of reading Thomson ; and when deputy-Grecian I completed some hundred stanzas of another, called ' The Fairy King,' which was to be in emulation of Spenser ! I also wrote a long poem in irregular Latin verses (such as they were) entitled ' Thor ' ; in consequence of reading Gray's ' Odes,' and Mallett's ' Northern Antiquities.' " No doubt these verses, or some of them, were among the signs of genius which his mother treasured in her pocket-book and showed to her friends. His love of poetry was not unnoticed by Boyer, who put into his hands the " Life of Pope," by Ruffhead, and " Irene, and other poems," by Doctor Johnson, actions which were of a kindly character, and deserved to be recorded without the sneer which accompanies their mention in the Autobiography.

The houses which he most frequently visited were those of the Wests and the Thorntons before mentioned : " Mr. West's (late President of the Royal

---

[1] A form at Christ Hospital called by that name.

Academy), in Newman Street, and Mr. Godfrey Thornton's (of the distinguished city family) in Austin Friars." It was at the former house that he perhaps first learnt to take an interest in art, and it is characteristic of him that in the house full of casts of antique statues, prints from the old masters, and West's "historical" pictures, he should have selected for special admiration certain prints of the Loves of Angelica and Medoro,[1] which gave him a love for Ariosto before he knew him. His picture of the old house is full of his best touches. "The talk was very quiet ; the neighbourhood quiet, the servants quiet ; I thought the very squirrel in the cage would have made a greater noise anywhere else " ; and of its master he says, " The two rooms contained the largest of his pictures ; and in the farther one, after stepping softly down the gallery, as if reverencing the dumb life on the walls, you generally found the mild and quiet artist at his work ; happy, for he thought himself immortal."

But his favourite house was the Thorntons', where, besides quiet, " there was cordiality, and there was music, and a family brimful of hospitality and good nature, and dear Almeria," with whom he would have fallen in love if he had been old enough. There was cranberry-tart also. " I have been told, that the cranberries I have met with since must have been

---

[1] He afterwards translated this episode from Ariosto, and in a note to the collected edition of his poems (Routledge, 1860), he says, "the lovely combined names of Angelica and Medoro" have become almost synonymous with "a true lover's knot."

as fine as those I got with the T——'s ; as large and
as juicy, and that they came from the same place.
For all that I never ate a cranberry-tart since I dined
in Austin Friars."

To these two "Paradises" a third was added in
Great Ormond Street, after the arrival of his aunt,
Mrs. Dayrell, with her two daughters and a sister from
Barbadoes. When precisely this happened it is difficult
to say. The nearest approach to a date is afforded by
Leigh Hunt's statement that he was not more than
thirteen when he fell in love with his younger cousin
Fanny, " a lass of fifteen, with little laughing eyes, and
a mouth like a plum."

Mrs. Dayrell (*née* Elizabeth Hunt), was " a woman of
a princely spirit, and having a good property, and every
wish to make her relations more comfortable, she did
so. My mother raised her head, my father grew young
again ; my cousin Kate (Christiana rather, for her
name was not Catherine ; Christiana Arabella was
her name) conceived a regard for one of my brothers
and married him." This brother was Stephen, the
lawyer, and the marriage was kept secret for a time.
But Leigh " became acquainted with it by chance,
coming in upon a holiday, the day the ceremony took
place," and was bound over to secrecy, to which circumstance he traced " the religious idea " he ever after
entertained of keeping a secret. He benefited also in
pocket-money, and by a holiday spent in the country
—his one vacation of three weeks before mentioned.

The holiday was spent at a house taken at Merton,
Surrey, by his aunt, Mrs. Dayrell, in August, of some

year not stated. "Imagine a schoolboy passionately fond of the green fields who had never slept out of the heart of the City for years. It was a compensation even for the pang of leaving my friend, and then what letters I would write to him ! And what letters I did write ! what full measure of affection pressed down and running over ! I read, walked, had a garden to run in, and fields that I could have rolled in to have my will of them." There are not many boys (about thirteen or less) turned out into the country for the first time in their lives for three weeks, who would place reading in the front of all their pleasures ; and in another place he says of the same visit, "My strolls about the fields *with a book* were full of happiness." Even in after life he seems to have regarded nature chiefly as a reading-room out of doors, a place to lie down in, under a tree or a haystack, for the better enjoyment of a book.

What with "strolls with a book," writing letters to his friend, and adoring his cousin Fanny, the three weeks at Aunt Dayrell's must have passed very quickly and pleasantly, and not the less pleasantly for the change of diet. After being accustomed to meat (boiled unsalted beef, with the fat tabooed) only every other day ; roast beef once a month ; no vegetables and no puddings, except the pease pudding which accompanied the pork twice in the year, Aunt Dayrell's Barbadian (and perhaps a trifle barbarian) hospitality must have added not a little to the sum of happiness of even so sentimental and studious a young gentleman as Master J. H. L. Hunt. Altogether he had a good time, and considering the benefits he and his family received from these generous West Indian relatives, it cannot be said that his picture of them errs on the side of panegyric. If he has set down naught in malice, he certainly has extenuated nothing, especially with regard to his maiden Aunt Courthope (Ann Courthope Hunt), the sister of Mrs. Dayrell and his father. He has done little less than "gibbet" her for posterity, as "an elderly maiden who piqued herself on the delicacy of her hands and ankles, and thought slavery indispensable." Nor is this the worst hit he aims at her peccadillos, over which he might have been expected rather to draw a veil, especially as he thought fit to address her as "a nymph" in some verses suggested by her decease.

At his aunt's he met Dr. Callcott, who gave him a Schrevelius (for it was long before the days of Liddell and Scott), and it was about the same time that his father took him to Wimbledon to see Horne Tooke, who patted him on the head. Leigh Hunt had a sense that he was a patriot, and says : "I felt very differently under his hand and under that of the Bishop of Lincoln, when he confirmed a crowd of us at St. Paul's. . . . My head only anticipated the coming of his hand with a thrill in the scalp, and when it came it tickled me." Charles Lamb reckons a tendency to superstition as among the characteristics of the Christ Hospital boy, but Leigh Hunt and his schoolfellows, from this and other passages in his Auto-biography do not appear to have been very different from other boys in this respect. He was not, however, without serious thoughts or spiritual sympathies. He had a great respect for the Jews, and got up imitations

of religious processions in the schoolroom, persuading
his coadjutors to learn even a psalm in the original
Hebrew, in order to sing it as part of the ceremony;
and elsewhere he finely says : " If I met a Rabbi in
the street he seemed to me a man coming not from
Bishopgate or Saffron Hill, but out of the remoteness
of time." But the most deeply rooted of his religious
convictions (and he had not many), and that which
had the greatest effect in the formation of his character, was what he calls " the impiety of the doctrine
of eternal punishment." This conviction, no doubt,
was the result of his parents' teaching, indeed he says
so, but it appears, nevertheless, to have flashed upon
him with some suddenness.

"I remember," he says, " kneeling one day in the
school church during the Litany, when the thought
fell upon me, ' Suppose eternal punishment should be
true.' An unusual sense of darkness and anxiety
crossed me, but only for a moment. The next instant
the extreme absurdity and impiety of the notion
restored me to my ordinary feelings, and from that
moment to this—respect the mystery of the past as I
do, and attribute to it what final good out of fugitive
evil I may—I have never for one instant doubted the
transitoriness of the doctrine and the unexclusive
goodness of futurity." This sentence is a key to
much of Leigh Hunt's " criticism of life," and not
the least characteristic part of it is the sanguine bound
from " eternal punishment " to " exclusive goodness
of futurity." He did not trouble himself with refine-
ments of logic where a " cheering reflection " was

concerned, any more than his father, who no doubt, by example and precept, throughout his son's school-days, encouraged a view of the Christian virtues, in which Hope was certainly not the least in favour of the " sisters three."

These schooldays came to an end in 1799. He was then first deputy-Grecian, and as a Grecian was expected to deliver a public speech before he left school, and to go into the Church afterwards, and as Hunt stammered in his speech and had no clerical in-tentions, a Grecian he could not be. He had, he tells us, the honour of going out of school in the same rank, at the same age, and for the same reason, as his friend Charles Lamb. This sentiment was born of reflection years afterwards, for he did not know Lamb then, and he had no such proud thought to cheer him on leaving school, and he was sad at going.

"I had now a vague sense of worldly trouble, and of a great and serious change in my condition, besides which, I had to quit my old cloisters, and my play-mates, and long habits of all sorts, so that what was a very happy moment to schoolboys in general was to me one of the most painful of my life. I surprised my schoolfellows and the master with the melancholy of my tears. I took leave of my books, of my friends, of my seat in the grammar school, of my good-hearted nurse and her daughter, of my bed, of the cloisters, and of the very pump out of which I had taken so many delicious draughts, as if I should never see them again, though I meant to come every day. The fatal hat was put on—my father was come to fetch me.

" We, hand in hand, with strange new steps and slow,
    Through Holborn took our meditative way."

It is to be observed that his conduct at school was directed by the four principal motives of his after life—spreading the pleasures of literature, resistance to tyranny, the diminution of superstition, and love of writing poetry.

# CHAPTER III.

FOR some time after Leigh Hunt left school he did "nothing but visit his schoolfellows, haunt the bookstalls, and write verses. His brothers were all started early in life ; but the Rev. Isaac Hunt does not appear to have been as active, or at least as successful, in finding a career for his youngest son. Perhaps that (West) Indian summer in which he was basking made him less alive to the urgencies of circumstance. That life, once passed between "placid readings and frightful knocks at the door," had been for some time more free from disturbance. Perhaps also Master J. H. L. Hunt was a lad not very easy to "place." He never (according to his own account) had any ambition in his life whatsoever, "but that of adding to the list of authors, and doing some good as a cosmopolite." He had no leaning towards any profession, and for commerce he was peculiarly unfitted, as he had little sense of either time or money. His ineptitude for accounts, which is almost as notorious as his literary gift, he was inclined to trace to a defect in his education. Owing to the curious arrangements (since altered) of the school, "a boy," he

44

says, "might arrive at the age of fifteen in the grammar school, and not know his multiplication table, which was the case with myself." But this can scarcely be admitted as a full explanation of a financial careless-ness which was almost phenomenal. A good deal can be done with a knowledge of simple addition if well employed, and that a man may make a large fortune without learning much arithmetic, we have proof in the history of Richard Thornton, who, to enhance the comparison, was also a Bluecoat boy. In a speech he made at Christ Hospital (June 23, 1859, when he was eighty-three years old), he is reported to have said : " I say I was edikated at the school ; but I was never at this school. I was thought such a rude specimen that I passed through all my time at Hertford. I re-mained there till I was fifteen as an infant. They did not teach me much. I only learnt two rules in arith-metic, addition and multiplication. They tried me at subtraction, but I could not learn that. Addition and multiplication were enough for me. They have made me, from a poor Bluecoat boy, the richest merchant in the City of London." [1]

But then, it may be urged, Thornton learnt his multiplication table, and it may also be urged, perhaps with more force, that he learnt little else.

But if the boy had no talents of a very practical kind, he was clearly a poet : there could be no doubt of that, at least in the minds of his parents, and, pend-ing more substantial arrangements, the Rev. Isaac Hunt soon began to canvass his still numerous friends

[1] " Richard Redgrave, a Memoir," p. 217.

for subscriptions for a volume of poems by the youthful genius. The book was published in 1801 under
the title of " Juvenilia," and in the same year a poem
by him, called " Melancholy," appeared in the *European Magazine*, and another, " Retirement, or the
Golden Mean," in the Juvenile Library. The latter
was reprinted in " Juvenilia," but not the former.
About the same time also appeared an article (at
present untraced) in the *Monthly Preceptor*, which
occupies almost a more important place in the history
of Leigh Hunt, for it was the means of introducing
him to Miss Marianne Kent, his future wife. According to his eldest son, they became engaged when
Hunt was about seventeen, and Miss Marianne about
thirteen, which leaves it uncertain whether the publication of " Juvenilia," or the engagement, was the
former of these two important events. At all events
the personality of Leigh Hunt began to put forth
leaves about 1801.

Leigh Hunt tells us that in his after years he was
as much ashamed of " Juvenilia " as he was proud of
it at the time ; but there was no reason for him ever to
have been ashamed of the book, even though it was
" a heap of imitations." It was a clever book for a
boy of his age, and showed a faculty for catching the
style of the authors he most admired, and what more
could be expected of " a Collection of Poems, written
between the ages of twelve and sixteen " ? The " imitations " of Gray, Thomson, Collins, Milton, Dryden,
Pope, and Spenser, are indeed obvious enough, as in
such lines as these from " The Palace of Pleasure "—

" High on a glorious couch, which far outshone
   The Pomp of Kingly Pow'r and Royal Show."

" Eternal sunshine beams before my gate."

" Lead, lead along! I go, I leap, I fly."

But the book, if containing little that was original,
showed promise of at least as great a master of verse
as Leigh Hunt ever became. Such a stanza as this,
for instance, despite the amusing Cockney touch of the
canary, is far above the average of schoolboy rhymes.
It is part of the description of " Temptation's Isle " :—

" And right aloud the joyous birds did sing,
   With melody confused that fill'd the sky;
   The soaring Lark with tawny dappled wing,
   And humbler Linnet with his gentle eye,
   And gorgeous Finch with breast of golden dye;
   Ne feared the bright Canary there to dwell,
   Ne chattering Thrush that peeps with glancing sly ;
   But ne sad Nightingale mourned o'er the dell,
   Ne owl with flapping wings shrieking the notes of Hell."

But the interest of the book is mainly biographical.
It is dedicated to his godfather, the Hon. J. H. Leigh,
" as the small tribute of an *enlarged* gratitude," an
early instance of a habit constant through life of using
words in an unusual if not mistaken sense, which
spoils much of his best work, especially in poetry.
Here, too, we find, in an " Advertisement," the first
of those many prefaces in which he was wont to take
the reader into his confidence. Master J. H. L. Hunt
" thinks it necessary to inform his readers, as they will
undoubtedly perceive how much superior some of the

following Poems are to the others, that a few of the
first pages, all the translations but one, the two
first Odes, and the first Hymn, were written at a
very early age ; that the Poem on Retirement, the
Pastorals in imitation of Pope and Virgil, Elegy
written in Poets Corner, Westminster Abbey, Ode
to Truth, the Progress of Painting, Wandle's Wave,
the Hymns for the Seasons, the Palace of Pleasure,
and the Funeral Anthem, were the production of his
present age (sixteen) and the rest of his intermediate
years."

A confidence, it may be observed, like many of his
later ones, quite unnecessary, and anticipating a lively
interest by the readers in the progress of the young
poet's genius between the ages of twelve and sixteen,
which few of them were likely to take ; but a confidence natural to a youth who took his poetical
powers very seriously indeed, and not only then, but
through life, desired to enter into familiar relations
with all his readers.   The volume had a frontispiece
engraved by F. Bartolozzi after a picture by R. L.
West, in illustration of a quotation from " Retirement, or the Golden Mean."

> " And ah ! let Pity turn her dewy eyes,
>   Where gasping Penury unfriended lies."

The artist was no doubt Raphael Lamar West, the
son of the Hunts' old friend, the President of the Royal
Academy.   The names of both Wests appear in the
list of subscribers, which is by no means the least
interesting part of the volume to the present admirers
of the author.

The Rev. Isaac Hunt seems to have worked very hard in getting subscribers, many of whom belonged to his old congregations. They numbered no less than 807. The scheme must have been put in hand shortly after Leigh Hunt left school, as the dedication is dated 1800, and both sides of the Atlantic were canvassed. There is an Edmund Bidwell, of New Providence, a Joseph Gilpin, and a J. Hunt, of Philadelphia, and Rufus King, his Excellency, Ambassador of the United States of America, who appears to have borne no malice to the quondam Royalist. The Thorntons appear in force, and were doubtless very useful, and the Wests brought a large contingent of artists, which included many Academicians : Banks, Beechey, Copley, Cosway, Fuseli, Hoppner, Lawrence, Smirke, Stothard, Cipriani, and West, with Colonel Trumbull, James Barry, J. Heath (the engraver), R. K. Porter, Alderman Boydell, the great print publisher and patron, and R. Bowyer, painter to the King. A large number of clergymen and Government clerks swell the list, which comprises several M.P.'s, including Horne Tooke, Thomas Erskine, and Sir Francis Baring, and one lord, the Earl of Guildford. Among other well-known names will be found those of Pye the Poet Laureate, and of William Gifford, the future editor of the *Quarterly Review*, and one of Hunt's bitterest enemies. Two of the masters of Christ Hospital, Stephens and Trollope, took copies, as did also George Dyer the poet, an " old boy," and Christopher Papendieck, the father, probably, of the schoolfellow to whom Hunt dedicated one of his pastorals, and to whom he paid a visit at Oxford some time after " Juvenilia " was published.

A second edition (in duodecimo, the first is in octavo), was published the same year with a list of 158 sub- scribers, among whom were the Bishop of Rochester and Governor Penn, who is indexed as "Penn, Governor, formerly of Pennsylvania, the colony founded by the venerable modern Lycurgus, William Penn, and the Friend of Man." Yes, and was not Master J. H. L. Hunt going to be the Friend of Man also, as well as a great poet? Assuredly. Liberty and Literature for ever !

But Art as well as Literature engaged his thoughts, and inspired his muse. It was not only for poets, but for artists that he sought (but failed) to find fitting epithets.   If he sung of

> " Collins bard sublime,
> Hyblæan Pope, or Dryden's stately verse ; "

or

> " The gentle Gay, trim sonneteer ; "

or

> " Bold Dyer and the plaintive Coleridge ; "

he also sang of—

> " The Star of Italy, expressive Raphael,
> The strict Corregio (*sic*), Titian's glowing hand,
> Fus'li's gigantic fancy, or the fire
> Of Britain's fav'rite West."

In his " Ode to Honour " he does not forget either his good friend West nor " Fus'li," and so impressed is

he with the power or the reputation of the President
that, in the "Progress of Painting," he forecasts the
terrible moment when History shall weep "her dying
West," and tear "her variegated vest, at every
streaming tear." Time probably modified the ardour
of his admiration for this chosen Apelles of George
III., but his interest in art never ceased.

Other painters he also hymned, "R. K. Porter
[afterwards Sir R. K. Porter], the rising painter of
the Storming of Seringapatam," being one of them,
and another, T. Kirk, the illustrator of his dear sixpenny poets, of whom he records, with no doubt
a stern sense of youthful duty, that he died young—
"a victim to licentiousness."

Altogether a great deal about the boy can be
gathered from "Juvenilia," which, while disclosing no
distinct poetic gift, witnesses to considerable reading
and appreciation of many poets, as well as a literary
pasturage unusually wide for a schoolboy. If it
contains quotations from Horace, Virgil, and
Thomson, which might have been expected, it has
others from Sappho and Petrarch, which are more
out of the way, and there are translations from
Spanish as well as from Greek and Latin, and an
epitaph on Rabelais, as well as one on Beattie. It
shows also much facility in versification, and a wide
range of theme, a love of flowers and birds and trees,
a great self-assurance, strangely mixed with modesty,
a love also of locality and of friends, all of which we
shall meet again.

But perhaps there is nothing more characteristic

in the book than the love verses. The name of the object of his affections, real or ideal, was Eliza,—if real she may have been the sister of a schoolfellow, mentioned in the Autobiography as his second love, if ideal it was a strange choice. Still more strange is the epithet by which he fondly called her, for that was "soft."

"Say, soft Eliza, good as thou art fair,"

he sings in joy ; and he moans in anguish—

"Low on the bed of sickness, pale and weak,
Ah, Pity, see the soft Eliza lies."

Now "soft Elizas" may be very nice no doubt, and possess all the virtues, but they are scarcely suggestive of "the grand style" in either love or poetry.

The christian name of his future wife, with whom about this time he fell in love, was not Eliza, but Marianne, and her surname was Kent. She lived in Titchfield Street, or Little Titchfield Street, with her mother who had been a Court milliner, and her sister Elizabeth, who had literary aspirations, afterwards to some extent fulfilled. It was Elizabeth who was the cause of Leigh Hunt's introduction to Marianne, for she had read an article in the *Monthly Preceptor*, which inspired her with a wish to see the author; and John Robertson, a friend of both, brought Leigh Hunt to the house. An intimacy with the family ensued, and one night Leigh Hunt was taken ill at their house with St. Anthony's fire, and had to be nursed for some weeks, all which ended in his becoming a lodger of Mrs. Kent, and the accepted suitor of Marianne. The lover appears from his son's account to have been a little too dictatorial at first, and a rupture ensued about the end of September in the same year (probably 1801, but nobody gives the date). The rupture, according to the same authority, had consequences which affected Leigh Hunt throughout the remainder of ·his life ; but what these consequences were nobody knows. Leigh Hunt himself omits all reference to his courtship from his Autobiography, except in one paragraph in which he tells us that the lady was a good daughter, and completed her conquest by reading verses better than he had ever yet heard. The rupture was not of long duration, the engagement being renewed some time at least before April, 1803, and in the meantime Mrs. Kent had married Mr. Hunter, the nephew and successor of Johnson, the well-known bookseller in St. Paul's Churchyard. At the time of his re-engagement Leigh was acting as clerk to his eldest surviving brother, Stephen, an attorney, and not long afterwards (according to Thornton Hunt) he was placed in the War Office by Mr. Addington (afterwards Lord Sidmouth), who knew his father. So within four or five years after his leaving school he was provided with a wife and a career, and completely "settled in life," or at least he might have been if he had not thrown up his Government appointment shortly after he became editor of the *Examiner.*

The history of these years (1799–1808) is not a little confused in the Autobiography, which testifies most

convincingly to the writer's want of "faculty for
noting the lapse of time." There was first a period
when he was chiefly occupied with his poems and
their success, which, he says, made him a kind of
"Young Roscius" in authorship. "The writer of
'Juvenilia,'" says his son, "found himself famous in
his eighteenth year. His school associations, his
personal qualities, his animated nature, attracted
attention and conciliated liking wherever he went."
He paid visits to his old schoolfellows at Oxford and
Cambridge, where his fame accompanied him; and in
London he "was introduced to *literati*, and shown
about among parties." Kett, the Professor of Poetry
at Oxford, "a good-natured man with a face like a
Houyhnhnm (had Swift seen it he would have
thought it a pattern for humanity)," expressed a hope
in the garden of Trinity that he would feel inspired
by the muse of Warton; Dr. Raine, Master of
Charterhouse, was very kind and pleasant, though
he warned him that "the shelves were full." His
grandfather sent him word that if he would come out
to Philadelphia, "he would make a man of him," and
the conceited youngster sent the old man back the
ungracious message that "men grew in England as
well as America." In fact, he was spoilt to the
content of his parents' hearts and his own.

The most credible testimony, however, to what he
was in these years is contained neither in his own
account of those days written in later life, nor in the
account by his son, but in his own letters written at
the time to the "little black-eyed girl," whom he

vows he loves with his whole heart and soul. Never was there a more model young man, nor a more model letter writer. He apologises in the style of Sir Charles Grandison for writing on coarse paper; he has scruples as to offering her parents admissions to theatres. He treats his *inamorata* to the most elegant descriptions of Oxford, with "its swelling lawns, venerable shades in profusion, silver streams winding wherever you turn, and all the charms of rural magnificence"; he spends his days there in playing on the harpsichord and boating and reading, and his evenings in "conversing very gravely on literary subjects with the students of his friend's college." He sends her (when *she* is out of town) accounts of the theatres, moral reflections, sallies of facetious humour, and poems, of course; for as he wisely remarks, "lovers can no more help being poets than poets lovers." At the conclusion of one of these poems he writes, "There, Miss Kent; I need not tell you to put this letter under your pillow," and adds that his next song will be upon the subject of eyes—"You know whose. Indeed all my amatory effusions are upon one person," &c., &c. From these passages, and from many others, it is delightfully obvious that this young gentleman is quite satisfied with his choice, and feels that his choice ought to be extremely well satisfied with hers. The general tone of ardent affection is not unmixed with advice to the object of his affections.

Apropos of his conscientious scruples against acting as godfather to the child of Mr. Robertson, he cautions her against entering into engagements of the kind.

He expresses a wish that she will cultivate her taste for the pencil, and will read as much as she can, " with such a headache as hers," and write "a fair, even-minded, honest hand, unvexed with desperate blots, or skulking interlineations." On the other hand, his self-complacency is occasionally disturbed by modest misgivings as to his power to preserve her affection, and once (in 1805) he seems to have felt he had lost them for the second time, but it was not for long. What girl could bear to part with a lover so constant, clever, studious, and correct in his behaviour, and of such punctilious manners, and of so scrupulous a conscience! How could she hope to find another who could write her such beautiful verses, or even such prose as this : " Affection, like melancholy, magnifies trifles ; but the magnifying of the one is like looking through a telescope at heavenly objects ; that of the other, like enlarging monsters with a microscope."

What was the source of attraction on the other side, is more difficult to ascertain. We have her son's evidence, given with a candour worthy of the family, that her attainments and faculties were not of a high order. She had fine hair and eyes and a pretty figure, but she was " the reverse of handsome," and except for a knowledge of arithmetic, superior to her husband's and a certain very mediocre talent for art, especially sculpture, she seems to have been devoid of tastes and accomplishments. But this problem may be left to others to resolve. The fact remains that she was capable of inspiring an affection which withstood the siege of an engagement of some seven or eight years, and lasted without suspicion of the least rift through over forty-seven years of married life.

It weighs little against these solid facts that from a passage in the comments of Thornton Hunt in the Correspondence, Leigh Hunt would appear to have had, " independently of his special admiration for Marianne," a desire (quite unintelligible) to form an alliance with the Kent family ; and that, in the Autobiography, Leigh Hunt describes himself as vacillating between the attractions of many beauties during years in which he was engaged to Marianne. He says in a passage which would seem to refer to the years occupied by the most devoted letters to his future wife :—

" I never ceased to be ready to fall in love with the first tender-hearted damsel that should encourage me. Now it was a fair charmer, and now a brunette ; now a girl who sung, or a girl who danced ; now one that was merry, or was melancholy, or seemed to care for nothing, or for everything, or was a good friend, or a good sister, or good daughter. With this last, who completed her conquest by reading verses better than I ever yet heard, I ultimately became wedded for life."

Who would think that Leigh Hunt had been, with only one short interruption, engaged to " this last," from the age of seventeen, till he married her at the age of twenty-five !

In these years Hunt won for himself a conspicuous position as a writer, though he did not much increase his fame as a poet, nor show much signs of those special qualities as a literary critic and genial essayist, which form his truest claim to be included in the present series of Great Writers. He continued to publish poems, especially in "The Poetical Register and Repository of Fugitive Poetry," published by F. and C. Rivington, the first volume of which appeared in 1802, and contained, beside several contributions from Leigh Hunt, a review of "Juvenilia," and an announcement that Mr. J. H. L. Hunt is engaged on the composition of a tragedy called "The Earl of Surrey." He also contributed to the volumes of the *Register* for 1805, 1806–7, 1808–9, and 1810–11, where the curious may discover many pieces which have never been reprinted. In the interval of his departure from school and getting out of his teens, he wrote "two farces, a comedy, and a tragedy." This tragedy was probably "The Earl of Surrey" just mentioned. "I forget," he tells us, what the comedy was upon. The title of one of the farces was the "Beau Miser," which may explain the nature of it. The other was called "A Hundred a Year," and turned upon a hater of the country, who, upon having an annuity to that amount given him, on condition of his never going out of London, becomes a hater of the town.

It was probably one of these farces to which he refers as the cause of an introduction to Mr. Kelly of the Opera House, with a view to its being brought out by some manager with whom he (Mr. Kelly) was intimate. The introduction was given by his "Spring

Garden friends," the family of a schoolfellow for whom
he had one of his devoted attachments which was
afterwards transferred to the schoolfellow's sister.

"Forty or fifty years ago people of all times of life
were much greater playgoers than they are now,"
wrote Leigh Hunt about 1850, and certainly he seems
to have been a great playgoer himself. "The first
time," he tells us in another place, "I ever saw a play
was in March, 1800 ; it was the 'Egyptian Festival,'
of one Mr. Franklin : the scenery enchanted me, and
I went home with the hearty jollity of Mr. Bannister
laughing all the way before me." But though
devoted to the theatre, and fond of writing plays,
he never cared for reading them. His studies were
devoted to other classes of literature. After leaving
school he seems to have continued his education as
a literary man by the study of Italian and of some
English poets not read before like Chaucer, or not
fully appreciated like Pope (he wrote a long mock-
heroic poem called "The Battle of the Bridal Ring," in
emulation of the "Rape of the Lock") and Dryden.
He also read every history that came in his way—
"Good old Herodotus, ditto Villani, picturesque
festive Froissart, and accurate and most entertaining,
though artificial Gibbon." But his greatest delight
was in Voltaire, and in a set of British classics, of
which his father made him a present one day, "with
his usual good-natured impulse." For the finer style
of Addison he had been spoilt by having to take him
for his model at school, and he was specially attracted
by the far inferior papers in the *Connoisseur*, by

Colman and Bonnell Thornton. "They possessed great animal spirits, which are a sort of merit in this climate," he says. With Goldsmith he was "enchanted," and these, with Fielding and Smollett, Voltaire, Charlotte Smith, Bage (the author of "Hermstrong"), Mrs. Radcliffe, and Augustus Lafontaine (the German romancist), were his favorite prose authors ; but the writer who made the greatest impression on him was Voltaire—"The greatest writer on the whole that France has produced ; " "the most formidable antagonist of absurdities that the world has seen ; " "the discloser of lights the most overwhelming, in flashes of wit, a destroyer of the strongholds of superstition, that were never to be built up again."

"He did not frighten me," he adds. "I never felt for a moment, young as I was, and christianly brought up, that true religion would suffer at his hands." Nor indeed would it have been easy to "frighten" Leigh Hunt at this or any other time with attacks on orthodox Christian doctrine. He had been taught at home to look for reforms in religion, and had already privately accustomed himself to doubt and reject every doctrine and every statement of facts that went counter to the plainest precepts of love, and to the final happiness of all the creatures of God. Leaving aside, at least for the present, all questions of opinion, it is at least remarkable, as an instance of the independence of Leigh Hunt's mind at this early age, and his sure eye for literary merit, that he should have perceived the greatness of Voltaire, especially as he read him only in translations. On January 18, 1805, he writes to Mr. Hunter: "I heartily thank you for Voltaire's 'Sequel.' He is an author that perpetually delights me, and has the felicitous art of uniting profound philosophy with the most lively wit." He loved the wit, and he was not discouraged by the philosophy, for he always felt that if this is not "the best of all possible worlds," the next one will be.

Infected with the "animal spirits" of the *Connoisseur*, and taking the "Philosophical Dictionary" as a text-book both for opinion and style, Leigh Hunt began (in 1804) his career as a prose writer, by "a series of papers called 'The Traveller,' which appeared in the evening paper of that name (long since incorporated with the *Globe*), under the signature of ' Mr. Town, *junior*, Critic and Censor-general,'—the senior Mr. Town, with the same title, being no less a person than my friend of the *Connoisseur*." It is to be observed that this "Critic and Censor-general" was not above being delighted with his perquisite of five or six copies of the paper.

He soon afterwards became a critic in earnest—the theatrical critic of a paper called the *News*, which was set up by his brother John. His brother had, it will be remembered, been apprenticed to Mr. Reynell, the printer. He was a strong Liberal in politics and social questions, an avowed Deist, and a thoroughly honest man, so that, though John does not appear to have had any great literary talent, or to have been very companionable, the two brothers had much in common, and for many years enjoyed intimate relations, the one

as proprietor and printer of periodicals, and the other
as contributor and editor.   These relations began with
the *News* at the beginning of 1805, when Leigh went
to live in Brydges Street with John, who was much
his senior, and a married man.   He was now a clerk
in the War Office and twenty-one years old, and he
entered on his extra-official labours with a high ideal
of the duty of a critic to the public, and a steady determination to resist all attempts to influence his opinion.
No doubt he had also plenty of self-confidence in his
own powers, was indeed not a little of a prig morally
and intellectually ; but then, as ever, he had the courage
of his opinions, and stuck to his principles like a man.
To his old schoolfellows it might have seemed that his
days of passive resistance were over, that he no longer
merely maintained a siege, but took to the field ; the
truth was that the situation and the weapons were
altered.   He was bolder with his pen than with his
fists, and the change of *rôle* from physical martyr
to moral Quixote was one not of character, but of
circumstance.

He found plenty to attack.   He attacked the play-
writers of the day (Reynolds, Dibdin, Cherry, Arnold,
Lewis) for their " miserable productions ;" he attacked
the managers for their want of taste, the critics for
their corruptness.   For the latter he drew out a set of
satiric rules.   Nor did he spare the actors, least of all
John Kemble, ridiculing him for his affected pro-
nunciation, or " vicious orthoepy," as he called it, and
condemning him very severely for requiring an actress
(Mrs. St. Leger) to act like a dummy in a love scene

so as not to divert the audience from himself. These attacks, made with all the vigour and confident judgment of two or three and twenty, certainly " wanted finish " ; but they made many " palpable hits," and these produced all the greater effect for the manifest honesty of the writer. It was known also that he would not receive tickets, or be acquainted with actors and managers, and kept himself sternly aloof from all those pleasant festivities, privileges, and perquisites, with which censorship was liable to be corrupted in those (and not only those) days. He was determined that it should not be said of him that "what the public took for a criticism on a play was a draft upon the box office, or reminiscences of last Thursday's salmon and lobster sauce." One of the results of his plain speaking was a letter from Dibdin, which Hunt published with an answer, and another was an attack by Colman in a prologue, but neither had the effect of disheartening the young critic or diminishing his self-esteem.

Part of these criticisms appear as notes in the appendix of a volume of " Critical Essays on the Performers of the London Theatres, including general observations on the practice and genius of the Stage ; by the author of the Theatrical Criticisms in the weekly paper called the *News*," which was printed and published by John Hunt in 1807. That at least is the date on the title-page, but its actual publication seems to have been delayed to the following year, for the book contains an " Advertisement " in which the reader is informed that " it was not till after the title-

page of the present work had been engraved that the
author had any intention of quitting the NEWS ; but
he now writes exclusively for the paper called the
EXAMINER, of which the reader may see a prospectus
at the end of the volume. It was necessary to state
this, that he might not commence his work with an
utter falsehood."

Only those who are very curious about the history
of the stage will care to consult the opinion of Leigh
Hunt, at the age of twenty-three, upon the merits of
actors long deceased; but the book is not without
value as a document in the history of Leigh Hunt
himself. It may well be classed under the title of
Juvenilia—as it is almost as immature as his poems ;
but it has much more individuality, and is full of
characteristics good and bad, which he never outgrew.
It is not easy to decide under which head should be
classed his readiness to form opinions, and his facility
in expressing them, for this faculty was often employed
upon subjects with which he was insufficiently acquainted ; but his opinions were his own, the result
of honest inquiry and conviction, neither prompted by
others nor biassed by venal considerations. He " professed " his honesty too much, as in the " Advertisement " just quoted, but he acted up to his profession.
A greater defect in taste was perhaps the personal
manner he wrote of the actresses—of Mrs. H. Siddons,
for instance, of Miss Duncan, and especially of Mrs.
Jordan. If he was pert to the men, he was impertinent
to some of the women, and in after years, whether his·
subject were an actress, his own wife, or the Queen·

herself, he was liable to adopt a tone of familiarity
which is out of accord with conventional taste. But
he evidently did his best to be just, and of Mrs. Jordan
he has left at least one picture which is wholly charming. "Her laughter is the happiest and most natural
on the stage ; if she is to laugh in the middle of
a speech it does not separate itself so abruptly from
her words as with most of our performers. . . . Her
laughter intermingles itself with her words as fresh
ideas afford her fresh merriment ; she does not
so much indulge as she seems unable to help
it ; it increases, it lessens with her fancy, and when
you expect it no longer according to the usual habits
of the stage, it sparkles forth at little intervals as
recollection revives it, like flame from half-smothered
embers." This is a paragraph worth including in any
book of "Extracts from Leigh Hunt," and it is not
the only one in the book. Here, for instance, is a
lively picture of a true *laudator temporis acti :—*

"You may be amused for a whole evening, not
merely with the vivacity of ELLISTON in *Archer* and
*Sir Harry Wildair*, but with his variety of countenance, the complete occupation with busy pleasure,
and the dry humour so peculiarly his own, and then
an old gentleman sitting next you, with two flaps to
his waistcoat, shall tell you that DODD or GARRICK was
the only man who could *do* that sort of character ;
that PEG WOFFINGTON, the finest breeches figure that
ever was seen, played *Sir Harry* much more *correct ;*
and then, offering you his snuff-box to secure your

attention, he exclaims with a sigh, 'The last time I saw GARRICK—let me see—ay—was it or was it not in *Don John?* Yes, it must have been *Don John*, because he wore slashed breeches,—ay—in Don John— and a very noble performance it was. I watched the eyes of the women, sir, all the time he was playing, and, egad, they followed him about as if they were jealous.' Here the old gentleman looks round to the side boxes, and shakes his head with a sort of triumphant pity: 'Hah! the boxes are very different things from what they were in those times—some pretty women, to be sure—but no wits, sir, nobody knows or reads about—now there was DOCTOR JOHNSON used to be in the boxes when GARRICK played—a very great man— I recollect seeing him when GARRICK did *Lear*—he was fast asleep all the last act, and I couldn't keep my eyes off of him—he was a very great man to be sure— I recollect offering him a pinch of snuff once—allow me, sir,—the true Macabaw, I assure you—pray, sir, isn't it your opinion that this theatre has a certain vile hugeness, as a man may say, in its appearance ;— I often tell Jack Wilkins—"Ah, Jack!" says I, "it's a long time since you and——"' At this instant the stage bell luckily rings," &c.

But, after all, the most important part of the book is the prospectus of the *Examiner*, a new Sunday paper, with which it concludes.

# CHAPTER IV.

THE first editor of the *Examiner* was a young gentleman of four-and-twenty, whose mind was made up on nearly every subject of interest to himself both here and hereafter. He was as honest as the day, and almost as careless, but that he had a lurking suspicion that he was a coward. Of a very nervous temperament, and with a horror of violence, and indeed of any physical discomfort, he was surprised and delighted whenever he found himself come creditably out of any position of danger, and already his opposition to tyranny at school, an encounter with some fishermen on the Thames, and an almost complete drowning at Oxford, had given him occasion for reassurance in this respect, not without a little patting of his own back. Although he did not share in the scare of invasion from France, he had indulged his sense of patriotism in serving as a volunteer in the St. James's Regiment, had paraded in the courtyard of Burlington House, and marched to Acton on field days; he had been himself a "young Roscius" of poetry, and had done not a little to demolish the "young Roscius" of the stage; he had been to a public school, and seen something of college life at both Universities; he had read widely in English literature, had a fair knowledge of Latin and Greek, and a smattering of some modern languages, especially Italian ; he was fond of music, could sing and play on the harpsichord; he had made many friends besides schoolfellows. Among these were the Robertsons, three brothers, one of whom had introduced him to his future wife, and another (Henry) was treasurer of Covent Garden Theatre, and a third was in the Commissariat. He had belonged to a club which they set up, called the "Elders," because they drank elder wine, and also to a debating society, whose members included his friend Barron Field (who calls Leigh Hunt his "dearest friend" in a letter of 1807), Thomas Wilde, afterwards Lord Chancellor, and the future Lord Chief Baron Pollock, who was to remember his old acquaintance in his last years. He had written for the *Times* (probably as a temporary substitute for his friend Barnes, afterwards the editor, or for Barron Field). He had been in a lawyer's office, was now in H.M. Civil Service, and had long been engaged to be married. In short, the young editor of the *Examiner* was no common young man.

That he did not think himself one we have his own warrant. Indeed, no one is a severer critic of young Leigh Hunt than old Leigh Hunt. "The new office of editor," he says, "conspired with my success as a critic to turn my head. I wrote, though anonymously, in the first person, as if, in addition to my theatrical pretensions, I had suddenly become an oracle in politics ; the words philosophy, poetry, criticism, statesmanship, nay, even ethics and theology, all took a final tone in my lips ; " and in following passages he speaks of his " spirit of foppery and fine writing," and of the "nonsense and extravagance" of his assumptions, in no measured terms. But old Leigh Hunt does not fail to give young Leigh Hunt credit for his literary equipment, his honesty, and that spirit of martyrdom "which had been inculcated in him from the cradle."

But there was no more reason for the old Leigh Hunt to be ashamed of the first editor of the *Examiner* than of the writer of "Juvenilia." If the young Leigh Hunt was a prig he could not help it. Circumstances had conspired to make him one, and in no case was ever the child more father of the man. And besides other good qualities which the young editor had even in the time when he was most conceited and pugnacious, was his readiness to admit merit wherever he saw it, and to praise it with warmth and generosity. When an actor or a writer pleased him (and he had always an appetite and a taste for good things) he felt the pleasure keenly, and endeavoured to convey not only the amount but the exact quality of. his pleasure to his readers. There is, however, more of the moral Jack the Giant Killer than of the literary Lucullus in the prospectus of the *Examiner.*

It announced itself as "a new Sunday paper, upon Politics, Domestic Economy, and Theatricals," printed by John Hunt, No. 15, Beaufort Buildings, Strand, nearly opposite Southampton Street. Its peculiar

merits are to consist in keeping its promises, and in
its impartiality, and its bright particular star is to be
a young gentleman who is not named.

"The Proprietors, who will be the Writers of the
EXAMINER, cannot entirely deceive the town, for
they are in some degree already known to the Public.
*The Gentleman, who has hitherto conducted, and is at
present conducting the* THEATRICAL DEPARTMENT *in the*
NEWS, will criticise the Theatre in the EXAMINER ;
and as the Public have allowed the possibility of
IMPARTIALITY in that department, we do not see
why the same possibility may not be obtained in
POLITICS."

After citing the opinions of Swift and Voltaire on
the subject of Party, against those of Solon, the prospectus declares that—

"A wise man knows no party abstracted from its
utility, or existing, like a shadow, merely from the
opposition of some body. Yet in the present day we
are all so erroneously sociable that every man, as well
as every journal, must belong to some class of poli-
ticians ; he is either Pittite or Foxite, Windhamite,
Wilberforceite, or Burdettite ; though at the same time
two-thirds of these disturbers of coffee-houses might
with as much reason call themselves Hivites, or Shuna-
mites, or perhaps Bedlamites."

The *Examiner* "will seat himself by the wayside
and contemplate the moving multitude as they
wrangle and wrestle along." As to the language
and style in which his advice will be given, "it would

be ridiculous to promise that which haste or the
headache might hinder him from performing." As to
THEATRIC CRITICISM, the Critic trusts that he has
already proved in that paper [the *News*] "that he
has no respect for error however long established, or
for vanity however long endured. He will still admire
Mr. Kemble when dignified, but by no means when
pedantic." The department of FINE ARTS will be
conducted by an artist. [Probably Robert Hunt, his
brother. The articles are signed R. H.] "The little
attention" which newspapers pay to this subject "is
no little proof of a very indifferent taste, especially
when we consider that this country possesses its own
school of painting ; that we have artists like WEST,
who claim every merit so much admired in the old
masters except indeed that of being in the grave ; and
that a youth, named WILKIE, has united HOGARTH
with the Dutch school by combining the most delicate
character with the most delicate precision in drawing." The paragraph on DOMESTIC ECONOMY is the
most vigorous and scathing. The "man, however
high his rank may be, or profuse of interest his
connexion, who dares to take advantage of his eleva-
tion in society to trample with gayer disdain on the
social duties" ; the "selfish and vulgar cowards,"
whether jockeys (who will run a horse to death), or
cock-fighters, or "those miserable ruffians, whether
the ornaments of a gaol or the disgracers of a noble
house," who encourage or practise prize-fighting—are
not to be spared. Finally, there are not to be any (or
hardly any) Advertisements or "Markets," for, "as

there are fifteen daily papers that present us with advertisements six days in the week, and as there is perhaps about one person in a hundred, who is pleased to see two or three columns occupied with the mutability of cattle and the vicissitudes of leather, the proprietors of the *Examiner* will have as little to do with bulls and raw hides as with lottery-men and wigmakers." Above all, no quack doctors. "If the paper cannot be witty or profound, it shall at least never be profligate." What magnificent promises, what fine sentiments are these ; what very "superior persons" must the "Proprietors " be or think themselves ! Never perhaps was preface penned more "obnoxious" to sneers. But the worst of it was that the promises were kept, the sentiments were genuine, and the Hunts were really "superior persons," for their principles were founded on the most elemental canons of truth and justice, and they stuck to them in spite of the most powerful and virulent persecution, ending in obloquy, imprisonment, and something like ruin, social and financial.

In its first years the *Examiner* showed its teeth on the subjects of reform, Catholic emancipation, cant and corruption generally, and spared neither Court nor Cabinet, but its chief object of attack was the war policy of the ministers. Be content, it said, in a word, with being mistress of the seas, defend our island and our commercial fleet, and don't waste your money in bribing allies to crush Napoleon. It's a difficult job, and won't do England any good even if you succeed. Napoleon is unscrupulous and rapacious, but he is purging the Continent of the feudal system, and besides he is a born conqueror, and the less you meddle with him and the balance of Europe the better. After all, why should you hold up hands of righteous indignation against him? Is he doing worse than England has done in India, Ireland, and America? So, without exactly defending or championing Napoleon, the *Examiner* sharpened its tools on him against the ministers, who soon began to watch for an opportunity to crush it.

The prefaces to the first and second volumes of the *Examiner* both record attempts at prosecution—the former with defiance (and exultation also because the attempt had failed), the second with not less defiance, although the Court was undecided. The first prosecution of the *Examiner* was instigated by an article in October, 1808, commenting on the case of Major Hogan, who compromised the Duke of York by the disclosures he made in a pamphlet as to the manner in which promotion in the army was obtained by bribes to his mistress, Mrs. Clarke. But the prosecution fell through, as the whole matter was investigated on a motion by Colonel Wardle in the House of Commons. The cause of the second prosecution was a passage in an article called "Change of Ministry," in October, 1809, after the retirement of the Duke of Portland from the premiership. The continued incapacity of George III. and the probability of a regency, excited the hopes of the Whigs and the *Examiner*. The Prince of Wales was expected to favour the Foxites and the removal of Catholic disabilities in Ireland, and this opened out to the *Examiner* a vista of reforms. "What a crowd of blessings," it wrote, "rush upon one's mind that might be bestowed upon the country in the event of such a change! Of all monarchs indeed, since the revolution, the successor of George the Third will have the finest opportunity of becoming nobly popular." Here was a chance for the ministers. Was not this a shameful libel against his sacred .Majesty? This was the view which it suited them to take, but it was unjust, for the *Examiner*, though patronising, was never unkind to George III. These passages were quoted by the *Morning Chronicle*, and the Government chose to prosecute that paper first. Mr. Perry, the proprietor, who conducted his own case, was acquitted by Lord Ellenborough, and so the *Examiner* escaped again.

The next prosecution (1811) was for quoting an article against flogging, written by John Scott for a country newspaper, but this also was unsuccessful.

The next and last prosecution was successful, but that we must leave for the present.

Meanwhile this rebel of an editor, this firebrand of a reformer, whose main object in life seemed to be to arouse animosity in powerful places, was far more of a moralist than a politician, of a Voltairean than a Radical, and in private life was a quiet, harmless young man, whose chief delight was to write verses and shut himself up with his books. On this point, as in most others where he speaks of himself, he may be trusted. He writes :—

"In the course of its warfare with the Tories, the

*Examiner* was charged with Bonapartism, with Republicanism, with disaffection to Church and State, with conspiracy at the tables of Burdett, and Cobbett, and Henry Hunt. Now Sir Francis, though he was for a long time our hero, we never exchanged a word with ; and Cobbett and Henry Hunt (no relation of ours) we never beheld ;—never so much as saw their faces. I was never even at a public dinner ; nor do I believe my brother was. We had absolutely no views whatsoever but those of a decent competence and of the public good ; and we thought, I dare affirm, a great deal more of the latter than of the former. Our competence we allowed too much to shift for itself. Zeal for the public good was a family inheritance ; and this we thought ourselves bound to increase. As to myself, what I thought of, more than either, was the making of verses. I did nothing for the greater part of the week but write verses and read books. I then made a rush at my editorial duties ; took a world of superfluous pains in the writing ; sat up late at night, and was a very trying person to compositors and newsmen. I sometimes have before me the ghost of a pale and gouty printer whom I specially caused to suffer, and who never complained. I think of him and of some needy dramatist, and wish they had been worse men."

He was nevertheless fully alive to the importance and responsibilities of his position. In December, 1808, he resigned his appointment in the War Office with comical self-assurance.

" To THE RIGHT HON. SECRETARY - AT - WAR.
" WAR OFFICE, MR. STUART'S DEPARTMENT,
. " *Monday,* 26th *December,* 1808.

" SIR,—An employment which I pursue in my extra hours, and which demands a greater duty to the public than any I can perform in the War Office, induces me to retire from a situation in which a sound freedom of thinking and speaking is liable to mistrust and misre-presentation ; and I do hereby accordingly resign my situation as clerk in the War Office into the hands of the Secretary-at-War.

" By this proceeding, sir, you will do me the justice to believe, that my motives are exactly as I describe them, and that every petty consideration is incompatible with their purity and public ends. I beg leave to subscribe myself, sir, your very obedient servant,

" LEIGH HUNT."

In a letter dated March 31, 1809, after the first prosecution of the *Examiner,* he was asked by John Murray to write for the *Quarterly Review,* just started ; but if this was intended as a bait for the clever young Radical, it was ineffectual, and he showed a much greater fastidiousness afterwards in declining to visit Lord Holland, so determined was he to keep himself entirely free from any influence which might in the remotest degree affect his independence as a public writer.

On July 3, 1809, Leigh Hunt married Marianne Kent, and went to live at Beckenham. Though the engagement had been such a long one, the bride still wanted a month or two of her majority, and the bride-groom was not yet five and twenty. Although he had given up his appointment in the War Office, his prospects were sufficiently good to warrant the step. In November, 1808, he states the circulation of the *Examiner* as 2,200, and going up, and he tells his future wife that his brother John says they will be making eight or ten guineas a week a-piece in a year's time. To this prophecy of flowery future he adds :—

"I can anticipate what your love might prompt you to say—that we could live on little ; but I have seen so much of the irritabilities, or rather the miseries arising from want of a *suitable* income, and the best woman of her time was so worried, and finally worn out with the early negligence of others in this respect, that if ever I was determined in anything, it is to be perfectly clear of the world, and ready to meet the exigencies of a married life before I do marry, for I will not see a wife, who loves me and is the comfort of my existence, afraid to speak to me of money matters ; she shall never tremble to hear a knock at the door, or to meet a quarter day ; she will tremble, I hope, with nothing but love and joy in the arms of her husband."

So, in marriage, as in everything else, Leigh Hunt began with the best intentions.

Almost the next published letter of his to her is dated January 4, 1811, and she is "Marianna mia," and he sends a kiss to "Thornton," their firstborn ; it is written from Trinity College, Cambridge, where he had gone on a visit for his health, which was a source of much trouble to him for some years after his marriage, as it had been before. It is not easy to quite characterise the nature of his frequent attacks. They seem to have been due to a naturally bilious temperament and a bad digestion, aggravated by want of exercise and foolish experiments in diet. They affected his spirits as well as his body, and are referred to by his son as attacks of hypochondriacal debility. "For upwards of four years," he tells us himself, "without intermission, and above six years in all, I underwent a burden of wretchedness." The attack in 1811 is said to have been partly due to excessive abstinence.

This visit to Cambridge in 1811 was to an old schoolfellow, Scholefield, Greek Professor, and there he dined with another old schoolfellow, Wood, Fellow and tutor of Pembroke. On his return he quitted his cottage at Beckenham, and went to live at Hampstead. The cottage was too damp, and he would not allow it to be let during the winter, telling his agent "that Mr. H. would rather keep it at the expense of his purse than let it at the expense of his decency." Shortly after his return to London he received his first letter from Shelley (dated University College, Oxford, March 2, 1811), who congratulates him on his recent triumph (the Scott trial), and submits for his considetion, "as to one of the most fearless enlighteners of the public mind at the present time, a scheme of mutual safety, of mutual indemnification for men of public spirit and principle, which, if carried into effect, would evidently be productive of incalculable advantages." Thus began the intercourse between these two " fearless enlighteners of the public mind," which ended in a firm and deep friendship, and permanently affected the whole life and character of Leigh Hunt. It was apparently between the date of this letter and Shelley's first marriage that they met for the first time, *i.e.*, between March and September, 1811, when Mr. R. Hunter sent Shelley to Leigh Hunt for counsel in regard to a MS. poem ; but their intimacy did not commence till 1816, after the suicide of Harriet Shelley, though they had some correspondence, and Shelley's " Hymn to Intellectual Beauty " appeared in the *Examiner* during the interval.

The four years with which this chapter is principally concerned (1808-12), or what may be called the pre-imprisonment period of the first editor of the *Examiner*, was the most successful period of his life. In this short time he firmly established for the first time a paper which fought, and fought effectively, with prejudice and privilege, with superstition and tyranny, which was a beacon of light to all men of Liberal principles in the country, and set the example of that independent thought and fearless expression of opinion, which has since become the very life and power of the press.

This was no small thing for a very young man to accomplish mainly by his own effort and his unflinching principle—sufficient to condone many mistakes and faults in the doing of it. Personally he achieved notability, a result no doubt gratifying to his vanity,

but a notability of which he could be justly proud.
He had earned the friendship of many distinguished
men, and the respect of many more. He had married
happily, and had increased his boyish reputation as a
critic and a writer of verse. His position not only
gave him reason for content with the past and the
present, but for hope of a prosperous career in the
future, for he had shown himself the possessor of
varied gifts, and extraordinary energy in their exercise,
even in uncongenial fields. For the post of editor and
leader-writer of a paper that was bound to be political
before all things, was not congenial to a man whose
tastes were essentially literary ; and this was no doubt
partly the cause of another venture of this time which
has not yet been mentioned.

After two years of the *Examiner*, to which he
contributed political and critical articles and a series
of essays on the " Folly and Danger of Methodism,"
he started his first magazine, the *Reflector*, written by
himself and those literary friends who had now collected around him. " Lamb," he says, " Dyer, Barnes,
Mitchell, the Greek Professor Scholefield (all Christ
Hospital men), together with Dr. Aikin and his
family, all wrote in it." Not that politics were
excluded from the *Reflector*, which of course took
the same line as the *Examiner* in this respect, but it
afforded greater scope for literary efforts, especially in
the shape of longer essays on literature and the fine
arts. It was not a brilliant success, nor was it a very
brilliant magazine. Only four quarterly instalments
were published, and it contains little that is now worth

reading, except a few of Charles Lamb's best essays, the " Genius and Character of Hogarth," " Bachelor's Complaint of the Behaviour of Married People," and " Farewell to Tobacco," and two compositions of Leigh Hunt—the first version of the " Feast of the Poets," and an essay, " A Day by the Fireside," in which his special literary quality was first distinctly shown.

The " Feast of the Poets " was suggested by Sir John Suckling's " Session of the Poets." The giver of the feast is Apollo, who selects those poets whom he deems worthy, and rejects the rest. It is written with much spirit, and is far more offensive and amusing than the revised editions of 1814 and 1859, in which, among other alterations, the verdicts on Coleridge and Wordsworth are reversed, that on Scott greatly softened, and other poets admitted to the breakfast table of Apollo. The first persons who present themselves are Leigh Hunt's favourite subjects of ridicule, Dibdin, Cherry, and the rest of the dramatists. Apollo pretends to mistake them for the waiters, and the satirist adds :—

> " 'Twas lucky for Colman, he wasn't there too,
>   For his pranks would have certainly met with their due :
>   And Sheridan's also, that finish'd old tricker ;
>   But one was in prison, and both were in liquor."

The following lines ridicule Rogers, James Montgomery, and Crabbe. Then the " sour little gentleman," William Gifford (whom Leigh Hunt never ceased to detest), is rejected with scorn, and Scott,

6

though accepted, receives a sound lecture and is told that—

"Prose such as yours, is a pure waste of time."

" A singer of ballads subdu'd by a cough,
Who fairly talks on, till his hearers walk off."

" Be original, man ; study more, scribble less ;
Nor mistake present favour for lasting success ;
And, remember, if laurels are what you would find,
The crown of all effort is freedom of mind."

To the lines on Scott was appended a long footnote, in which Hunt abuses Scott as a prose writer (it was before the Waverley Novels), a critic, and a politician ; the prime cause of all this animosity being, as he confesses in his Autobiography, a single word in Scott's edition of Dryden.

But Apollo's, or Leigh Hunt's, special scorn is reserved for Wordsworth and Coleridge. After abusing them roundly he cries—

" What ! think ye a bard's a mere gossip who tells
Of the ev'ryday feelings of ev'ry one else ;
And that poetry lies, not in something select,
But in gath'ring the refuse that others reject ?
Depart and be modest, ye driv'llers of pen,
My feasts are for masculine tastes, and for men."

And then, as they don't go, he drives them from the room by putting on the full glory of his deity, the effect of which is described with vigour and with more imagination than Leigh Hunt often displayed. On the whole, however, the satire shows want of taste and judgment, and although the author was five and twenty must be classed with " Juvenilia."

Not so "A Day by the Fireside," which, though long for so trivial a subject, is kept alive all through by that charming current of personal sensation and thought, small but always moving, which is the life of Leigh Hunt's best work. Who else had written quite like this?

"A single friend, perhaps, loiters behind the rest ; you are alone in the house, you have just got upon a subject delightful to you both ; the fire is of a candent brightness, the wind howls out of door ; the rain beats ; the cold is piercing ! Sit down ! This is a time when the most melancholy temperament may defy the clouds and storms, and even extract from them a pleasure that will take no substance by daylight. The ghost of his happiness sits by him and puts in the likeness of former hours ; and if such a man can be made comfortable by the moment, what enjoyment may it not furnish to an unclouded spirit ? If the excess belong not to vice, temperance does not forbid it when it only grows out of occasion.

"Even when left alone, there is sometimes a charm in watching out the decaying fire ; in getting closer and closer to it with tilted chair, and knees against the bars, and letting the whole multitude of fancies that work in the night silence come whispering about the yielding faculties. The world around is silent : and for a moment the very cares of day seem to have gone with it to sleep, leaving you to snatch a waking sense of disenthralment, and to commune with a thousand airy visitants that come to play with innocent thoughts.  Then, for imagination's sake, not for super-stition's, are recalled the stories of the secret world, and the midnight pranks of Fairyism ; the fancy roams out of doors after rustics lead astray by the Jack-o'-lantern, or minute laughings heard upon the wind, or the night spirit on his horse that comes flouncing through the air on his way to a surfeited citizen, or the tiny morris-dance that springs up in the watery glimpses of the moon ; or, keeping at home, it finds a spirit in every room, peeping at it as it opens the door, while a cry is heard from upstairs announcing the azure marks inflicted by

> " ' The nips of fairies upon maids' white hips ;

or, hearing a snoring from below, it tiptoes down into the kitchen, and beholds where

> " Lies him down the lubber fiend,
> And stretched out all the chimney's length,
> Basks at the fire his hairy strength."

Among the friends he made during these years should be mentioned Haydon the painter, and Bell of the *Weekly Messenger*, and publisher of the well-known edition of the Poets, in which, to Hunt's delight, Chaucer and Spenser were included.  At his house he heard of " politics and dramatic criticism, and of the persons who wrote them," probably saw something of them also.  Haydon's vigorous letters attacking Payne Knight and the Academy appeared in the *Examiner* in January and February, 1812.  They cost him dear, for they alienated the Directors of the British Gallery (of whom Payne Knight was one of the most influential), and probably prevented the award to his picture of "Macbeth" of a prize of three hundred guineas ; money never more needed by the fiery improvident painter, who had been living entirely on credit for two years. Leigh Hunt he says behaved nobly and offered him a plate at his table till his next great picture, "The Judgment of Solomon," was completed. Another much more useful acquaintance was his life-long friend Charles Ollier, the future publisher of Shelley, Lamb, and Procter, then (1810) in a bank, and the writer of a theatrical criticism which he tendered to the editor of the *Examiner.*

# CHAPTER V.

IT was on the 12th of March, 1812, that the article appeared in the *Examiner* for which John and Leigh Hunt were fined £500 each, and suffered imprisonment in separate gaols for two years (3rd of February, 1813, to the 3rd of February, 1815). This famous attack on the Prince Regent has been often reprinted, but it is too important to be altogether omitted here, especially as the comments on it by writers who do not quote it vary considerably. The following are the most notable passages :—

" What person, unacquainted with the true state of the case, would imagine, in reading these astounding eulogies, that this ' Glory of the people' was the subject of millions of shrugs and reproaches !—that this ' Protector of the arts' had named a wretched foreigner his historical painter, in disparagement or in ignorance of the merits of his own countrymen !—that this ' Mæcenas of the age' patronised not a single deserving writer !—that this ' Breather of eloquence' could not say a few decent extempore words, if we are to judge, at least, from what he said to his regiment on

its embarkation for Portugal !—that this ' Conqueror
of hearts ' was the disappointer of hopes !—that this
' Exciter of desire' (bravo ! Messieurs of the *Post !*)—
this ' Adonis in loveliness,' was a corpulent man of
fifty !—in short, this *delightful, blissful, wise, pleasure-
able, honourable, virtuous, true,* and *immortal* prince,
was a violator of his word, a libertine over head and ears
in disgrace, a despiser of domestic ties, the companion
of gamblers and demireps, a man who has just closed
half a century without one single claim on the gratitude
of his country, or the respect of posterity !

" These are hard truths ; but are they *not* truths ?
And have we not suffered enough—are we not now
suffering bitterly—from the disgusting flatteries of
which the above is a repetition ? The ministers may
talk of the shocking boldness of the press, and may
throw out their wretched warnings about interviews
between Mr. Percival and Sir Vicary Gibbs ; but let
us inform them, that such vices as have just been
enumerated are shocking to all Englishmen who have
a just sense of the state of Europe ; and that he is a
bolder man, who, in times like the present, dares to
afford reason for the description. Would to God, the
*Examiner* could ascertain that difficult, and perhaps
undiscoverable point which enables a public writer to
keep clear of an appearance of the love of scandal,
while he is hunting out the vices of those in power !
Then should one paper, at least, in this metropolis
help to rescue the nation from the charge of silently
encouraging what it must publicly rue ; and the
Sardanapalus who is now afraid of none but informers,

be taught to shake, in the midst of his minions, in the very drunkenness of his heart, at the voice of honesty."

Viewed calmly at this distance of time the article appears very forcible, very true, but also very foolish. It was a deliberate challenge to a prosecution in the then state of parties and the law. The Hunts had been made reckless by the failure of former prosecutions, and rushed upon their own ruin. The possible advantage to the public interest was but slight and remote, the consequences to themselves were almost certain to be immediate and serious. The article did not reform the Prince Regent, it did not prevent the triumph of the Tories. So violent and personal an attack upon the private character of the head of the State was politically unjustifiable, and of doubtful efficacy as a moral protest ; and, as Mr. Saintsbury has pointed out in his admirable essay on Leigh Hunt, it would not have been tolerated by the Government of any country at the time.

If the article cannot be altogether excused, it can easily be accounted for. It was part of the profession of the *Examiner* to attack the Government, to expose fearlessly the licentiousness of the aristocracy and the servility of the press — and circumstances occurred which gave an opportunity of doing all three at one blow. Wrath—political wrath—had been long simmering against the Prince Regent. He had disappointed the hopes of the Liberals in retaining the Tory Ministry in power. His opposition to his father while he ruled, and his encouragement of the

Whigs, led them to expect all sorts of good things when the reins of power fell into his hands. In the matter of the Catholics in Ireland, they were especially hopeful. The passage which we have already quoted from Leigh Hunt's article on the future King of England reflected truly the anticipations of the Whigs. The state of feeling was strongly shown at a public banquet on St. Patrick's day. The usual toast of the Prince's health was omitted, and Sheridan while attempting to make a speech in his favour was met with cries of " Change the subject." The occasion called forth a fulsome panegyric of the Prince in the *Morning Post*, and the *Examiner* (or Leigh Hunt) exploded. It is probable that neither political anger nor moral indignation would have caused the catastrophe, but one acted on the other in Leigh Hunt's mind like flint and steel, and produced the spark, which lit the stake, which burnt the Leigh Hunt—the Martyr.

And, as must not be forgotten, it burnt John Hunt, the Martyr, also. To him should be given perhaps the larger share of our sympathy, for he had equal courage, equal if not greater purity of principle, and to him was allotted equal suffering, while the larger share of honour and glory remained with his brother. Our sympathy with both of them would have been more perfect if their martyrdom had been less self-provoked.

The blow was long in falling. It was nearly nine months from the appearance of the article, on March 22, to the day of trial, December 9, 1812. The delay was caused, according to Leigh Hunt, by the non-attendance of special jurors, and it lulled the

Hunts into a false security. In August he paid a visit to a Mr. Marriott, at Taunton, who was connected by marriage with his brother John, and made excursions to Wells and Glastonbury. To this period belong the first of the published letters which passed between him and Brougham, who had already been employed as the advocate of the *Examiner*, and was to defend the Hunts in the prosecution for the libel on the Prince Regent. Brougham sympathised with many of Hunt's political and religious views, and was also much interested in his literary efforts. The " Story of Rimini " was commenced in the summer of 1812, and Brougham took the trouble to look up information about Ravenna in " out-of-the-way " books on Italy, and sent him notes. Leigh Hunt in return sent him bits of " Rimini," and translations from Catullus and other Latin poets, which were duly admired (not without criticism) by the future Chancellor. Brougham also betrayed some anxiety about his friend, and gave him some good advice. In a letter written from Lancaster, on a Saturday in 1812, and very possibly referring to the famous article on the Prince Regent, he writes :—

" I cannot but greatly applaud the boldness as well as the ability of your attacks upon the ruinous and unworthy conduct of our present rulers ; and I am persuaded that the press alone can now be looked to as the saviour of the country, and the discussions in Parliament *through* the press. But this makes me the more anxious that the press should be saved from the strong hand of power, which I fear will be raised

against it. Without at all counselling times or com-
plying measures, I would only recommend to you as
much caution as may be consistent with the bold and
manly expression of your sentiments on men and
measures. One passage in last *Examiner* has somewhat frightened me."

Another very flattering and agreeable tribute to his
character, and the value of the services of the
*Examiner* to the cause of liberty, were the friendly
approaches made to him by Jeremy Bentham, who
wrote to him and asked him to dinner—" a hermit's
dinner at this my hermitage," in Queen's Square
Place. Bentham's house was called The Hermitage.
The first invitation Leigh Hunt was obliged to decline
on account of ill-health, but Bentham then (August,
1812) called on him, and appeared to Hunt "like a
father laughing and talking with one of his children,"
and again asked him to dine. The philosopher
appears to have paid him another visit shortly before
his imprisonment, when Hunt was out of town. Upon
this occasion he was accompanied by Romilly.

The sympathy excited by the imprisonment of the
Hunts was increased by the knowledge that they need
not have gone to prison, or even paid their fines, if they
had undertaken to abstain from commenting on the
actions of the Prince Regent. But they declined all
compromise with the Government, and on the 3rd of
February, 1813, were driven off to their respective
prisons—John to Clerkenwell, and Leigh to Horsemonger Lane. At first Leigh, who was in a bad state
of health, fared somewhat badly. From being a great

deal too thin (in September he was reduced to skin and bone), he had become stout, and jaundiced, owing to "lamentable bodily indolence, brought by long habits of studious lounging, and in-door enjoyment." This indolence, he tells us in the diary, which he commenced shortly after his imprisonment and continued for a few days only, was in the family. He had at that time a grand-aunt in a dying state, who had lost the use of her limbs from taking no exercise. "But," he adds, " nothing could warn me sufficiently. It is true I had lately taken to walking every day, on account of the neighbourhood of the Hampstead fields, which, from various causes, had ever been my delight; but my body might almost as well have been sitting, as moving along with a luxurious leisureliness that shook not a particle in it ; besides, I never stepped out of doors without a book in my hand, mostly a volume of Spenser or Milton ; and whenever I came to a stile, there I sat for a quarter of an hour, with my back dropped round, and my legs dangling, in order to enjoy the complicated luxury of resting limbs, a cooling air, a fanciful passage, and the sense of being wrapped up in a rural landscape."

At first he was lodged alone, in a dismal room with a look out (if you stood on a chair) on the courts where the felons walked. But soon this severity was relaxed through the exertions of Barron Field and others of Hunt's friends. He was removed to rooms in the infirmary, his wife and children were allowed to share his captivity, and visitors were admitted to be with him till ten o'clock. The rooms consisted of a ward on the ground floor, which had never been used, and a smaller room for a bedroom. The former he turned, he tells us, into a noble room—"not very providently (for I had not yet learned to think of money)."

"I papered the walls with a trellis of roses; I had the ceiling coloured with clouds and sky; the barred windows I screened with Venetian blinds; and when my bookcases were set up with their busts, and flowers and a pianoforte made their appearance, perhaps there was not a handsomer room on that side the water. I took a pleasure, when a stranger knocked at the door, to see him come in and stare about him. The surprise on issuing from the borough, and passing through the avenues of a gaol, was dramatic. Charles Lamb declared there was no other such room, except in a fairy tale.

"But I possessed another surprise; which was a garden. There was a little yard outside the room, railed off from another belonging to the neighbouring ward. This yard I shut in with green palings, adorned it with a trellis, bordered it with a thick bed of earth from a nursery, and even contrived to have a grass plot. The earth I filled with flowers and young trees. There was an apple tree, from which we managed to get a pudding the second year. As to my flowers, they were allowed to be perfect. Thomas Moore, who came to see me with Lord Byron, told me he had seen no such heart's-ease. I bought the *Parnaso Italiano* while in prison, and used often to think of a passage in it, while looking at this miniature piece of horticulture :—

" Mio picciol orto,
A me sei vigna, e campo, e selva, e prato "—(*Baldi*).


(" My little garden,
To me thou'rt vineyard, field, and meadow, and wood.")


Here I wrote and read in fine weather, sometimes
under an awning. In autumn, my trellises were hung
with scarlet-runners, which added to the flowery in-
vestment. I used to shut my eyes in my armchair,
and affect to think myself hundreds of miles off.

"But my triumph was in issuing forth of a morning.
A wicket out of the garden led into the large one
belonging to the prison. The latter was only for
vegetables ; but it contained a cherry tree, which I saw
twice in blossom. I parcelled out the ground in my
imagination into favourite districts. I made a point
of dressing myself as if for a long walk ; and then,
putting on my gloves, and taking my book under my
arm, stepped forth, requesting my wife not to wait
dinner if I was too late."

The two years spent by Hunt in the Surrey gaol,
where his eldest daughter Mary Florimel (afterwards
Mrs. Gliddon) was born, were probably not by any means
the unhappiest of his life. He suffered no doubt much
from the sense of restraint, and the depressing atmosphere of the place was unusually trying for a man of
his sensitive and sympathetic temperament with an
almost morbid horror of pain. Gibbets were put in
order outside his windows, and erected in places visible
therefrom. But despite these disadvantages, and "un-

ceasing ill-health," he had many comforts, and his friends rallied round him. His wife and sons—Thornton and John — were with him for most of the time. When his wife was away, his sister-in-law, Elizabeth Kent, devoted herself to his comfort. Among the friends he specially mentions his old schoolfellows, Pitman, Mitchell, and Barnes. Bentham paid him a visit, and played battledore and shuttlecock with him. He also sent him some books. New friends came to him — Thomas Alsager (who then lived opposite the prison, and sent him in his first dinner there), Charles Cowden Clarke (from whose father's house at Enfield arrived weekly baskets with fruit and eggs and other country luxuries), Sir John Swinburne, Thomas Moore, Lord Byron, and William Hazlitt. But the most constant of his visitors were the Lambs, who came " in all weathers, hail or sunshine, in daylight and in darkness, even in the dreadful frost and snow of the beginning of 1814." In his Epistle to Charles Lamb, included in his volume of poems called "Foliage," published in 1818, he recurs to these days.

" You'll guess why I can't see the snow-covered streets,
  Without thinking of you and your visiting feats,
  When you call to remembrance how you and one more,
  When I wanted it most, used to knock at my door.
  For when the sad winds told us rain would come down,
  Or snow upon snow fairly clogged up the town,
  And dun yellow fogs brooded over its white,
  So that scarcely a being was seen towards night,
  Then, then said the lady yclept near and dear,
  ' Now mind what I tell you,—the L.'s will be here.'

So I poked up the flame, and she got out the tea,
And down we both sat, as prepared as could be ;
And there, sure as fate, came the knock of you two,
Then the lanthorn, the laugh, and the ' Well, how d'ye do ? ' "

In the Correspondence we find traces of many
visitors, beside old friends, not mentioned in the
Autobiography, of " Mr. Mill (a Benthamite) " (no
doubt James, father of John Stuart) and a Dr. Lindsey,
of Bow, of Brougham and Miss Edgeworth, of Haydon, " sending those laughs of his about the place
that sound like the trumpets of Jericho, and threaten
to have the same effect;" of Wilkie, and several others.
He entertained freely ; from his letters to his wife
during her absence with the children at the seaside
(April to June, 1813), few days seem to have passed
without one or more friends to dinner. Thus, on
June 5th, he writes, " Mr. Wilkie dines with me
to-morrow at three, in company with Mr. and Mrs.
Scott ; and I shall have quite a party on Friday next,
as it is the last week Mr. Moore will be in town ;
there will be himself, Mr. Brougham, Dr. Gooch, Lord
B[yron], Mitchell, and Barnes ; this, you will allow,
is a company worth something, and you will be sorry
that you did not enjoy it." His friends were not only
constant in their visits, but they came, at least several of
them, with presents in their hands—" small gifts from
large hearts," as he called them in a letter to Cowden
Clarke—some were books, tributes of literary admiration, which he probably appreciated as much as sympathy with his political martyrdom. Among these
givers was Lord Byron, who brought him " the last

new Travels in Italy, in two quarto volumes," to help him with his poem ("Rimini"), and afterwards sent him the "Giaour" and the "Bride of Abydos."

Of all the incidents of his prison life none had a greater influence on his future than his introduction to Lord Byron. Notwithstanding his Radical principles, he was not above being flattered by the notice of a lord, because he was a lord, and in this case the lord was also the most distinguished poet and satirist of the day, the author of "English Bards and Scotch Reviewers," and the first two cantos of "Childe Harold." Moreover, the "noble poet" had sought Leigh Hunt out, and had pleasant things to say about "Juvenilia," and their influence on the boyish author of "Hours of Idleness." In his "Epistle to Byron" on his leaving England in 1816, Leigh Hunt refers to this :—

> "And so adieu, dear Byron,—dear to me
> For many a cause, disinterestedly ;—
> First, for unconscious sympathy, when boys
> In friendship, and the Muse's trying joys ;
> Next for the frank surprise, when Moore and you
> Came to my cage, like warblers kind and true,
> And told me, with your acts of cordial lying,
> How well I looked, when you both thought me dying."

Byron first sent Moore as his ambassador, and made terms as to the food and company to be provided for his lordship, who was not eating meat at that time ; but they appear to have soon approached to a more familiar footing, or rather Leigh Hunt did. He promptly jumped to the conclusion that Byron's courtesy and kindness to a fellow poet in distress would lead to a strong personal attachment. "It strikes me," he writes to his wife, after what was probably their second interview, "that he and I shall become *friends*, literally and cordially speaking ; there is something in the texture of his mind and feelings that seems to resemble mine to a thread ; I think we are cut out of the same piece, only a different wear may have altered our respective naps a little." In this singular misjudgment lay the germ of much of the lamentable misunderstanding which afterwards arose between the two. His son Thornton, in his introduction to the Autobiography, has noted it as a characteristic of his father, that "when he first became acquainted with a new friend whom he liked, he noticed with all his vivacity of ready and intense admiration the traits which he thought to be chiefly prominent in the aspect and bearing of the other ; constructed a character inferentially, and esteemed his friend accordingly. This constructive appreciation would survive the test of years. Then he would discover that in regard to some quality or other which he had ascribed to his friend, 'he was mistaken ;' the whole conception of the admired character at once fell to the ground."

A dinner together, and a present of books given " with an air of one who did not seem to think himself conferring the least obligation," (a manner of giving which was peculiarly appreciated . by Leigh Hunt), convinced Leigh Hunt that his wife should make allowances for Byron's " early vagaries," that his heart was an excellent one, and that they would be mutually pleased at becoming acquainted. This was the man of whom Hunt, according to Lord Houghton, deliberately said in his old age, long after all bitterness of feeling had passed away, that he was never sincere, and certainly not at Missolonghi.

It may seem strange to some that the stern censor of the Prince Regent's irregularities, and generally of the vices of the wealthy and privileged classes, should have been so lenient to a man of Lord Byron's reputation for debauchery ; but Leigh Hunt, though he lived a pure life, and had a strong antipathy to licentiousness, never adopted the ordinary code of morality, nor was inclined to look with severity on what he terms the " vagaries " of others provided they were unaccompanied by any of the less genial vices, such as cruelty and meanness. The conviction that Byron had " a good heart," was sufficient to cover a multitude of " vagaries."

It need scarcely be said that the effect of Byron on Hunt was very different to that of Hunt on Byron. We are able to estimate the latter pretty accurately by a passage in his lordship's diary of Dec. 1, 1813 :—

" *Wednesday, Dec.* 1, 1813.—To-day responded to La Baronne de Stael Holstein, and sent to Leigh Hunt (an acquisition to my acquaintance—through Moore— of last summer) a copy of the two Turkish tales. Hunt is an extraordinary character, and not exactly of the present age. He reminds me more of the Pym and Hampden times—much talent, great independence of spirit, and an austere yet not repulsive aspect. If he

goes on *qualis ab incepto*, I know few men who will
deserve more praise or obtain it. I must go to see him
again ;—the rapid succession of adventure, since last
summer, added to some serious uneasiness and business, have interrupted our acquaintance ; but he is a
man worth knowing ; and though, for his own sake, I
wish him out of prison, I like to study character in
such situations. He has been unshaken, and will continue so. I don't think him deeply versed in life ;—he
is the bigot of virtue (not religion), and enamoured of
the beauty of that ' empty name,' as the last breath of
Brutus pronounced, and every day proves it. He is
perhaps a little opinionated, as all men who are the
*centre* of *circles*, wide or narrow—the Sir Oracles, in
whose name two or three are gathered together—must
be, and as even Johnson was ; but, withal, a valuable
man, and less vain than success and even the consciousness of preferring the right to the expedient
might excuse."

From this it is evident that Byron had a sincere but
cynical respect for Hunt's character, and looked upon
him as an interesting figure, whose acquaintance was to
be cultivated in the intervals of more absorbing pur-
suits ; but there is no symptom of any tendency to a
more cordial friendship. The " love " was all on one
side.

Now that we are able to see Leigh Hunt as a whole
from the distance of time, and know how genuine
and inevitable were his impulses, how guileless his
nature, it is possible not only to pardon but to sympathise with much in his utterances and actions that

must have seemed ridiculous, and worse, at the time, to men of the world who did not know him. In his first leaders in the *Examiner* after his incarceration, he, in a thoroughly characteristic manner, took the world into his confidence, made the most handsome allowances for his prosecutors and judges, only complaining that one of them had accused him of bad motives,—vindicated the purity and patriotism of his own conduct, told his readers what a splendid fellow his brother was, how hard it was to separate such a united couple as John and himself, what a devoted wife and family he possessed (to whom, without him, any paradise would be a prison, and *vice versâ*) ; how bad his health was, how his sensitive nature suffered from the clanking of the prisoners' chains, &c., &c.  To his intimates, like Mitchell, the tone he took seemed to be worthy of praise, sincere, independent, even manly ; but to his enemies, who were made of much sterner stuff than he, it could scarcely fail to be an object of ridicule and contempt—a weak appeal for personal sympathy—if not an unworthy effort to gain political capital out of his sufferings.  In public life, as at school, the style of his heroism was too unusual to be understood of the people.

He edited the *Examiner* regularly during his imprisonment ; he bought and studied the " Parnaso Italiano " in many volumes, from which he made many translations ; he read these and other verses without end, and wrote almost as many (the " Descent of Liberty " and the greater part of the " Story of Rimini " were written in prison), but he wrote no prose of any importance, and seems to have taken things generally as easily as possible. Perhaps unconsciously, his confinement was made an excuse for inactivity, and his ill-health and the constant visits of his friends conduced to the relaxation of his energies. It is certain that his imprisonment did him little good except in increasing his knowledge of literature. It fostered his indolent habits of body by restricting his opportunities of exercise ; it confirmed his habit of self-absorption and self-indulgence ; it flattered his vanity at every point ; and it weakened, if possible, the small responsibility which he felt as to the conduct of his private concerns.

About money, it appears from his own account, he had never yet troubled himself. He left the details of expenditure to his wife, who is said to have been at this time a good manager. His income from the *Examiner* (as he told the world in its pages) had been sufficient to keep up a respectable appearance, and notwithstanding the expenses of the various prosecutions and the heavy fine he had to pay, he looked forward to clear himself from debt and prison at the same time. This was the reason he gave for refusing the offers that were made, shortly after he entered prison, to raise the fines by subscription ; and he subsequently refused similar offers of help, including a "princely" one from Shelley, though whether he was equally sanguine at this time does not appear. As we know that he accepted "princely" offers from the same source on account of private needs afterwards, there seems to be some inconsistency here, especially as he publicly stated that he saw no objection to such subscriptions for persons suffering in the public weal. But in his Autobiography he takes no credit for his refusal, saying that he had not then thought about money. He appears to have been swayed by a mixture of pride and principle; and we can only conclude that he thought it would damage his martyrdom to accept such offers, but that he nevertheless would have accepted them but that he hoped to pull through without assistance.

# CHAPTER VI.

THE Poet-patriot! this is the name given to Leigh Hunt by Charles Cowden Clarke, and it fairly represents the position which he held in the eyes of that part of the world which was friendly to him during the period occupied by the present chapter. The editor of the *Examiner* who had suffered imprisonment in the cause of Liberty, the author of "The Story of Rimini," one of the most original poems of the day, which attained additional notoriety from the exceptionally malevolent and brutal attacks of *Blackwood* and the *Quarterly*—this was Leigh Hunt as he appeared to his very large circle of admirers at the age of 32, and for many years afterwards.

As a patriot there is not much more to say about him, for after Leigh Hunt left prison nearly all interest of a political character dies out of his life. He continued to edit the *Examiner*, indeed, until he left for Italy in 1821 ; but though after Hunt left prison he stuck to his old principles, and kept the pages of the *Examiner* open for the advocacy of all liberal causes, his zeal was more tempered with discretion. He never concealed his animosity to the Government or the

Prince Regent (who became king in 1820), but he had felt the strength of the tiger, and left off pulling his tail.

It is significant, then, in his account of this period of his life, written forty-two years afterwards, how little politics or the *Examiner* enter into his narrative. His sensations on leaving prison, the memories of his great literary friends, Keats, Shelley, Byron, and Lamb, fill up the whole of the canvas, and leave little or no space for even his family. We have to turn to his letters and the memories of others to fill up the meagre record of his existence during a period which was, perhaps, the most eventful and fruitful (at least in quality) of his life ; for it was then he published "The Story of Rimini," and produced the *Indicator*, besides other of his best poems and essays.

In 1815 appeared "The Descent of Liberty," in 1816 "The Story of Rimini," in 1818 "Foliage," and in 1819 "Hero and Leander, and Bacchus and Ariadne." All these, and " The Feast of the Poets," were published together, in three volumes, as " Poetical Works," in 1819, in which year also appeared " Amyntas," a translation of Tasso. It should always be remembered that Hunt's most natural and strongest ambition was to achieve fame as a poet. It began as a boy, it scarcely ceased before his death. While in prison he had no greater solace than writing verses, and when he came out it was his most constant recreation.

"The Descent of Liberty," like the greater part of these poems, was written in prison. The dedication to

Thomas Barnes is dated "Surrey Jail, 10th July, 1814,"
and the poem is called by himself, "the first poetical
attempt of my maturer years." It is in the form of a
Mask, and was introduced by "Some account of the
origin and nature of masks," a charming essay, con-
veying the results of much reading in that light and
pleasant manner which was his own. Nor is one surprised to find that the book has a preface in addition
to the letter of dedication, and that the essay on Masks
in general contains "some account of the origin and
nature " of his own Mask in particular ; in the course
of which he tells us that it was originally written with
a view to its performance on the stage, and that "an
eminent person, who relieves his attention to public
business by looking after the interests of the theatre,
and to whom an application was made on the subject,
gave him reason to expect every politeness, had he
offered it to the stage." He gave up the intention
mainly from his fears (which were indeed well founded)
of the demands its representation would make on the
machinist, and concludes his essay with a turn which
is too thoroughly characteristic not to be quoted :—

"In a word as the present piece was written partly
to indulge the imagination of one who could realise no
sights for himself, so it is more distinctly addressed to
such habitual readers of poetry, as can yield him a
ready mirror in the liveliness of their own appre-
hensions. There is a good deal of prose intermixed,
but the nature of a Mask requires it ; and if the reader
be of the description just mentioned, and shall settle
himself with his book in a comfortable armchair con-

dition,—in winter perhaps, with the lights at his shoulder, and his feet on a good fender,—in summer, with a window open to a smoothing air, and the consciousness of some green trees about him,—and in both instances (if he can muster up so much poetical accompaniment) with a lady beside him,—the author does not despair of converting him into a very sufficient and satisfied kind of theatre."

The Mask was suggested by the fall of Napoleon, but, if it were not for the introduction among "The Persons of the Drama," of the four genii of the kingdoms (the allies, Prussia, Austria, Russia, and England), it would bear little trace of the source of inspiration. Napoleon is conceived as an enchanter, who dwells in a cloud which has long overshadowed a city; to him Liberty in another cloud comes and gives battle. It is needless to say who is the victor. The air is cleared, the inhabitants smile again. Liberty's attendant spirits call down Spring, Peace, and Poetry to prepare the way for Liberty, who gives good advice to the four kingdoms, encourages Painting, Music, and Poetry, Experience, and Education, and promises the abolition of slavery.

The Mask itself contains many graceful and musical passages. In the opening scene, which is charming throughout, there is a beautiful song beginning :—

> " Gentle and unknown delight,
>   Hovering with thy music near us,
> If that our request be right,
>   Lean thee tow'rd the earth, and hear us ;
> And if we may yet rejoice,
> Touch the silence with a voice."

Founded on the Elizabethans and Milton (especially "Comus" and "L'Allegro"), the "Descent of Liberty" has yet much original merit, and though one may smile at an occasional "Leigh-Huntism," as "the nest-resuming bird," and such Cockney touches as the introduction of "the genteel geranium" among the flowers of spring, it may still be read with pleasure, for the lyric level is fairly sustained throughout. One of its best passages is near the close, part of the final speech of Liberty before she reascends to the skies :—

> " There sometimes, when I have ended
> What my daily task intended,
> I sit looking, with still eyes,
> At the many-starred skies,
> Or go pace the central sun
> With his gardens, every one,
> Where the golden light is kept,
> And the winds are music-swept ;
> Or in graver mood take wing
> Beyond the bounds of everything,
> And look in, with half-check'd sight,
> On the unform'd infinite,
> Where with his eternal ear
> Time is listening.—Mortals dear,
> Think on all I've done and said,
> And keep my blessings on your head."

Of course this passage is not without blemish—it would be difficult, except in "Abou Ben Adhem," to find one of equal length in all Leigh Hunt's poems that is. The epithet of "eternal" to Time's ear is particularly unhappy. Yet it has more of the true lyrical note, and is of a higher strain of fancy, than Leigh Hunt ever, perhaps, attained again.

But in the history of literature, and of the author, "The Descent of Liberty" is insignificant when compared with "The Story of Rimini," which, whether we regard its influence on English verse, or the violent storm which its appearance aroused, must be regarded as one of the most notable items of this chronicle. The period of its gestation was considerable ; it was commenced at Hastings a year or two before his imprisonment, and was completed at Hampstead in 1816, so that it was on hand four or five years. During its progress it had formed the theme of correspondence and conversation with his friends, some of whom, like Brougham and Byron, had supplied him with part of its material. It attracted a great deal of attention on its appearance ; but the result was notoriety rather than success. No doubt it was read with avidity and admiration by Hunt's small circle, to some of whom, like the Cowden Clarkes, he was an object almost of adoration ; he was strangely and weakly proud that a lady or so had been melted to tears over its pages, but, notwithstanding the sonnet of Keats and the letter of Lamb, the verdict even of his poetical friends does not appear to have been enthusiastic. Byron called the poem "a devilish good one," and Moore admitted it was "full of beauties" ; but the former thought it disfigured by a strange style, and the latter "could not undertake to praise it seriously in a review."

At all events, whatever may have been the acclamations of his friends, they were drowned by the noisy and violent abuse of his enemies. In Mr. Alexander Ireland's valuable list of writings of Hazlitt and Leigh

Hunt will be found quoted a number of the most virulent of contemporary criticisms. Of its dedication to Lord Byron, the *Quarterly* remarked : " We never in so few lines saw so many clear marks of the vulgar impatience of a low man, anxious and ashamed of his wretched vanity, and labouring, with coarse flippancy, to scramble over the bounds of birth and education, and fidget himself into the stoutheartedness of being familiar with a lord." Of the poem itself, *Blackwood* declares, two years later : " No woman who has not either lost her chastity or is desirous of losing it, ever read ' The Story of Rimini ' without the flushings of shame and self-reproach." And this was by no means the strongest of the passages levelled against the morality of the poem. The fact that Francesca was the wife of Paolo's brother did not of course escape Leigh Hunt's adversaries. The versification and language of the poem met with equal condemnation. But those were days in which it was rare to find a critic who would treat with fairness the poetry of a political antagonist, especially of such an audacious one as Leigh Hunt. The following prophetic passage from the *Quarterly* of January, 1818, is addressed rather to the editor of the *Examiner*, the champion of free-thought, the asperser of the Government and the Prince Regent, the champion of Shelley's devious courses in theory and real life ; but it contains the same *virus* as poisoned the criticisms on " The Story of Rimini " : " He may slander a few more eminent characters, he may go on to deride venerable and holy institutions, he may stir up more discontent and sedition, but he will have no peace of mind within ; he will do none of the good he once hoped to do, nor yet have the bitter satisfaction of doing all the evil he now desires, but he will live and die unhonoured in his own generation, and for his own sake it is to be hoped moulder unknown in those which are to follow."

Poor dear Leigh Hunt ! (surely no one ever deserved these epithets more or in more senses) forced into politics against his inclination, imprisoned for a burst of righteous indignation, and now treated as a monster of immorality for a poem the object of which was to prove the tragical effects of deceit. For, according to his version of the story, the daughter's sin was the natural consequence of her father's duplicity in making her believe that Paolo, who married her as the deputy of his brother, was the duplicate of her intended husband. It is possible that in other hands this false direction of the maiden's imagination might have been used with powerful effect as a cause of the tragedy. But in "The Story of Rimini " it tells only, if it tells at all, as a very weak apology. The husband is not represented as a brute or ill-favoured, but only somewhat stern and careless, reposing too much confidence in his brother and wife. There is positively no excuse for them which might not be made for any two young people who are thrown together. In Leigh Hunt's version the whole episode sinks to the level of a commonplace intrigue scarcely more elevated than that of Don Juan and Julia. The *banalité* with which the catastrophe is described is comic. The critical interview is thus commenced :—

> " ' May I come in ? ' said he ;—it made her start,—
> That smiling voice ;—she coloured, pressed her heart
> A moment, as for breath, and then with free
> And usual tone said, ' O yes,—certainly.' "

The poem as a whole curiously marks the limits of Leigh Hunt's capacity, not only as a poet, but as an appreciator of poetry. It shows much ingenuity and a good deal of fancy, but it fails utterly in higher qualities. Paolo and Francesca are without character, and their passion is the mere effect of what, in another portion of the poem, he calls " charms of look and limb." The fine speech which Giovanni makes over his brother's body is only a close paraphrase of that made by Sir Ector de Maris over the body of Lancelot, in Malory's " Morte d'Arthur." In later years he saw that he had made a mistake in the choice of his subject, but no one with a due sense of the feeling and execution of Dante's finest work could have taken that perfect cameo as the theme for a sprawling canvas. The gulf that separated him from the greater poets, and from Dante in particular, may be measured by his translation of one phrase. He renders Dante's " tutto tremente " by " all in a tremble."

Fail, however, as it does when judged by great standards, as a current poem of the time it is an important and meritorious piece of work. In the matter of versification it is a historical document. It was a determined and successful attack upon the serried ranks of the heroic couplet, which had been drilled into mechanical uniformity by Pope and his followers. The return to a freer versification and more natural phraseology had indeed been heralded by Wordsworth in the "Lyrical Ballads," but it was strongly aided by the man who had found in Chaucer a freshness, in Spenser a sweetness, and in Dryden a vigour, which he would fain reconquer for English verse.

He was able to capture some of the gentle simplicity of Chaucer, but the verve and virility of Dryden were beyond him. In endeavouring to vary the monotonous cadence of Pope he went to the opposite extreme, and sank to a slipshod measure which ambles along like a broken-kneed jennet, and is often little removed from doggerel. But he showed Keats and Shelley (and how many more!) the way to a freer treatment of the heroic couplet, and broke the neck of a convention which was sterilising English verse. In poetry, as in politics, he was a true liberator, and in both cases it was not he who was to reap the reward. He invented the instrument, but he had not skill to play upon it.

The poem underwent many alterations in the course of years. In the edition of his poems published by Moxon in 1844, he changed the scenery from English to Italian, and wrote a new ending for the fourth canto, making the tragedy end with the more authentic murder instead of the duel. In 1855 the duel reappeared in "Stories in Verse" (Routledge); and in the "Poetical Works" (Routledge) of 1860; the murder again closes the story, the duel being printed in a separate "fragment," called "Corso and Emilia."

As usual, Leigh Hunt is one of the best critics of his own work. He admits, in his Autobiography, that when he wrote "Rimini" he had not discovered "in what the subtler spirit of poetry consisted," that at that time he was not "critically aware that to enlarge upon a subject which had been treated with exquisite suffi- ciency, and to his immortal renown, by a great master, was not likely by any merit of detail to save a tyro in the art from the charge of presumption, especially one who had not studied poetical mastery itself, except in a subordinate shape ;" and in another place he implies the defects of his own heroics by praising "the lovely poetic consciousness" in the "Lamia" of Keats, "in which the lines seem to take pleasure in the progress of their own beauty, like sea-nymphs luxuriating through the water."

At the same time the plea that he was a tyro in the art is hardly to be accepted. He had already written a considerable quantity of poems, short and long, had spent years over "Rimini," and must have been twenty-seven when he started it. Moreover, many, if not all, its defects are observable in his later poetry. The use of strange words, or ordinary words in strange senses, the commonplaces which weary, the familiarities which jar, and above all, the faulty taste, as in his description of Francesca, with—

> " Her clipsome waist and bosom's balmy rise ; "

and of Paolo :—

> " So fine are his bare throat, and curls of black ;
> So lightsomely dropt in, his lordly back—
> His thigh so fitted for the tilt and dance."

All these defects he never outgrew. On the other
hand, the fresh, spring-like gaiety of the opening
verses, the movement and colour of the splendid marriage pageant in the first canto, and here and there a
sudden felicity of expression, as in the celebrated line
in which he describes the fall of the fountain as—

> " It shakes its loosening silver in the sun,"

might well have been taken as tokens of greater gifts
than he ever displayed in his later poems.

In the "Hero and Leander, and Bacchus and
Ariadne," published in 1819, he certainly showed no
advance in the management of heroic verse, nor
in the style of treatment adapted to great subjects.
A further proof of his limitations was given in
"The Nymphs," a poem contained in "Foliage," a
volume of verses, half original, half translated, which
appeared in 1818. This was dedicated to Sir John
Swinburne, and contained the lively epistles to his
friends Byron, Moore, Hazlitt, Barron Field, and
Charles Lamb, from which one or two quotations have
already been drawn ; and sonnets to Shelley, Keats,
Horace Smith, and B. R. Haydon. Here were also
printed his pretty but somewhat overpraised verses
"To T. L. H." and "To J. H.," written in prison to
his little sons Thornton and John ; sonnets to his wife
and her sister Elizabeth, and one to his three friends,
Henry Robertson, John Gattie (brother of Mrs. Ollier),
and Vincent Novello. Some of the sonnets must
rank amongst his best poems, especially "To the
Grasshopper and Cricket," and the still finer "To

the Nile," the former written in competition with Keats (December, 1816), the latter with Keats and Shelley (February, 1818).

But there was some difference between the Leigh Hunt of 1818 and the Leigh Hunt who came out of prison on February 3, 1815. During these years his intellectual powers were matured and his character became fixed. He ceased to be tentative, he ceased to be militant. His wide but promiscuous reading began to afford sufficient soil for the germination of his own thoughts, and he became less and less inclined to stroll outside the gates of that paradise of books which he had entered in his childhood. He had never really cared for the world or for politics, and he always hated strife. He had felt it a family duty to "stick up" against tyrants at school and afterwards, but he never had much of what is called "fight" in him. He would "dare" the bully and would not run away, but he took his punishment meekly, and that ended the matter. Two years in prison perhaps took the "martyr" spirit out of him ; at all events, though he might have nerved himself to be a martyr again if occasion called, the occasion did not call, and he did not seek the occasion again for himself. Circumstances had hitherto diverted him from his natural bent, but now they favoured his following it, and he did.

That bent was to shut himself up with his books, and let the devil, in the shape of all disagreeable things, including creditors, pipe to his own ; and he soon became a sort of literary sybarite, with benevolent intentions, and without any ambition but to secure a quiet corner where he could enjoy himself in his own way, communicate his pleasure to others by his writings, and make a name in literature. Never would there have been a man more happy or blameless than Leigh Hunt, if his earnings had always sufficed to pay his bills.

But he was not very happy when he first left prison, for he was weak in health and in a state of nervous depression, and for many months he could not leave home without a morbid wish to return—like a bird who had grown used to a cage. His first flight was across the road to the house of his friend Alsager, the commercial editor of the *Times*, whence he proceeded to lodgings in the Edgware Road, to be near his brother John. "When we met," he tells us, "we rushed into each other's arms, and tears of manhood bedewed our cheeks."

And here it may be as well to set down, as far as I have been able to ascertain, the different places in which he resided till he went to Italy. Even his father was scarcely more of a nomad. His next move (in the spring of 1816) was to the Vale of Health, Hampstead. In 1817 he was at 13, Lisson Grove North; in 1818 at 8, York Buildings, New Road; in 1820 at 13, Mortimer Terrace, Kentish Town; he was back at the Vale of Health, Hampstead, in March, 1821, and remained there till he set sail from London in the brig *Jane*, "bound direct to Leghorn;" but never to get there with Leigh Hunt on board of her.

His portrait at different periods of his life has been

drawn by many hands, and none more sympathetic than that of his son Thornton. From these we may gather that at the time with which we are now concerned, or, broadly speaking, "in his prime," Leigh Hunt was a tall, slight man, five feet ten and a half in height, straight as a dart, and with a "cheerful, almost dashing, approach." His sloping shoulders made his chest look narrower than it was, and the length of his body was rather out of proportion to his legs. His head was large, and crowned with straight, black hair, parted in the middle. His face was long and oval, but somewhat irregular in outline, and his complexion dark but warm. His forehead was high, upright, and flat ; his eyebrows black and firm ; his eyes (he was shortsighted) black also, and sparkling, " as gentle and brilliant as a gazelle's." His nose, which had no sense of smell, was long, and so was his upper lip ; his mouth was " large and hard in the flesh," and protruded rather ; while his chin was small and retreating. It is not easy to picture any face from a written description, and it seems to be more difficult than usual in the case of Leigh Hunt, especially as his portraits by pencil and paint have little resemblance to each other, and scarcely in any case tally with those by the pen. In this elusiveness his face is like the personality of the man. The elements are simple and distinct enough, but the whole effect of the composition is hard to realise. It is clear, however, that it was a strikingly intelligent and animated face, and bore distinct marks of creole blood.

One of the strongest testimonies to Hunt's personal

charm during this period is contained in the " Recollections of Writers," by Charles and Mary Cowden
Clarke, whose enthusiastic admiration for Leigh Hunt
was shared by the families of both. Clarke's father
(John Clarke, Keats' schoolmaster at Enfield), on his
first meeting Hunt at a theatre, was "deeply enthralled
by that bewitching spell of manner which characterised
Leigh Hunt beyond any man I have ever known."
His mother exclaimed after their first meeting : " He
is a gentleman, a perfect gentleman, Charles ! He is
irresistible." Of the Novellos' admiration for Leigh
Hunt their long intimacy testifies. Mary Victoria
Novello, the eldest daughter of Vincent Novello, and
afterwards Mrs. Charles Cowden Clarke, was a little
girl when her future husband first met her at Hunt's
cottage at Hampstead, and her " Recollections " do
not, therefore, begin so soon as her husband's, who
met him before his imprisonment, at a party, where
Hunt "sang a cheery sea-song with much spirit in
that sweet, small baritone voice which he possessed.
His manner — fascinating, animated, full of cordial
amenity, and winning to a degree of which I have
never seen the parallel—drew me to him at once,
and I fell as pronely in love with him as any girl
in her teens falls in love with her first-seen Romeo."
Some of the members of this party, amongst whom
were Charles Ollier, H. Robertson, and the brothers
Gattie, no doubt also formed part of the lively social
gatherings of which Leigh Hunt was the centre after
he left prison. Clarke describes with rapture " the
exquisite evenings at Vincent Novello's own house,

where Leigh Hunt, Shelley, Keats, and the Lambs
were invited guests ; the brilliant supper parties at
the alternate dwellings of the Novellos, the Hunts,
and the Lambs, who had mutually agreed that bread
and cheese, with celery, and Elia's immortalised
'Lutheran beer,' were to be the sole cates provided."
The same writer also speaks of the delightful meetings
at theatres, of evenings when Leigh Hunt's " almost
unequalled " dramatic readings were followed by Mrs.
Novello's famous elder wine and wassail, and of pic-
nics by appointment in the fields between Oxford
Street and Hampstead, where cold meat and salad
and Parmesan cheese (got by Novello specially for
Leigh Hunt, on account of his love for Italy) were
washed down with draughts of orange and ginger wine.
After reading these lively pages one seems to under-
stand better why Leigh Hunt was so charming. They
also perhaps account for some of his indigestion.

Charming as Leigh Hunt was at these innocent
orgies, he seems to have been still more delightful in
the morning, if we may trust Clarke.

" Leigh Hunt's simultaneous walk and talk were
charming ; but he also shone brilliantly in his after-
breakfast pacings up and down his room.  Clad in the
flowered wrapping-gown he was so fond of wearing
when at home, he would continue the lively subject
broached during breakfast, or launch forth into some
fresh one, gladly prolonging that bright and pleasant
morning hour.  He himself has somewhere spoken of
the peculiar charm of English women, as ' breakfast

beauties,' and certainly he himself was a perfect specimen of a 'breakfast wit.' At the first social meal of
the day he was always quite as brilliant as most company men are at a dinner party or a gay supper. Tea
to him was as exhilarating and inspiring as wine to
others, the looks of his home circle as excitingly
sympathetic as the applauding faces of an admiring
assemblage. At the time of which I am speaking
Leigh Hunt was full of some translations he was
making from Clément Marot and other of the French
epigrammatists, and as he walked to and fro he would
fashion a line or two and hit off some felicitous turn
of phrase, between whiles whistling with a melodious,
soft little birdy tone in a mode peculiar to himself of
drawing the breath inwardly instead of sending it
forth outwardly through his lips. I am not sure that
his happy rendering of Destouches' couplet epitaph on
an Englishman—

> " 'Ci-gît Jean Rosbif, écuyer,
> Qui se pendit pour se désennuyer,'

into—

> " ' Here lies Sir John Plumpudding of the Grange,
> Who hung himself one morning, for a change,'

did not occur to him during one of those after-break-
fast lounges of which I am now speaking. Certain
am I that at this time he was also cogitating the
material for a book which he purposed naming
'Fabulous Zoology'; and while this idea was in
the ascendant his talk would be rife of dragons,
griffins, hippogriffs, minotaurs, basilisks, and 'such
small deer' and 'fearful wild fowl' of the genus

monster, illustrated in his wonted delightful style by
references to the classic poets and romancists."

The following extract shows even more clearly the
position which Leigh Hunt held as the amiable oracle
of a devoted circle of young men and women who sat
at his feet in these days :—

" Unlike most eager conversers, he never interrupted. Even to the youngest among his colloquists
he always gave full attention, and listened with an air
of genuine respect to whatever they might have to
adduce in support of their view of a question. He was
peculiarly encouraging to young aspirants, whether
fledgling authors or callow casuists, and treated them
with nothing of condescension, or affable accommodation of his intellect to theirs, or amiable tolerance for
their comparative incapacity, but, as it were, placed
them at once on a handsome footing of equality and
complete level with himself. When, as was frequently
the case, he found himself left master of the field of
talk by his delighted hearers, only too glad to have
him recount in his felicitous way one of his 'good
stories' or utter some of his 'good things,' he would
go on in a strain of sparkle, brilliancy, and freshness
like a sunlit stream in a spring meadow. Melodious
in tone, alluring in accent, eloquent in choice of words,
Leigh Hunt's talk was as delicious to listen to as rarest
music."

This is the testimony of one who was perhaps too

much "in love" with Leigh Hunt to be accepted as an unbiassed witness, but it is fairly supported by others who were by no means so entirely devoted— by Hazlitt, for instance, and Haydon, both of whom saw his weaknesses plainly enough. Hazlitt tells us in his paper on Charles Lamb's evenings :—

"Leigh Hunt goes there sometimes. He has a fine vinous spirit about him and tropical blood in his veins, but he is better at his own table. He has a great flow of pleasantry and delightful animal spirits, but his hits do not tell like Lamb's ; you cannot repeat them the next day. He requires not only to be appreciated, but to have a select circle of admirers and devotees, to feel himself quite at home. He sits at the head of a party with great gaiety and grace ; has an elegant manner and turn of features ; is never at a loss—*aliquando suffliminandus erat ;* has continual sportive sallies of wit and fancy ; tells a story capitally ; mimics an actor or an acquaintance to admiration ; laughs with great glee and good-humour at his own or other people's jokes ; understands the point of an equivoque or an observation immediately ; has a taste and knowledge of books, of music, of medals ; manages an argument adroitly ; is genteel and gallant ; and has a set of by-phrases and quaint allusions always at hand to produce a laugh. If he has a fault, it is that he does not listen so well as he speaks, is impatient of interruption, and is fond of being looked up to, without considering by whom. I believe, however, that he has pretty well seen the folly of this."

Haydon, writing to Wilkie, says :—

"Though Leigh Hunt is not deep in knowledge, moral, metaphysical, or classical, yet he is intense in feeling, and has an intellect for ever on the alert. He is like one of those instruments on three legs which, throw it how you will, always pitches on two, and has a spike striking for ever up and ever ready for you. He 'sets' at a subject with a scent like a pointer. . . . As a man, I know none with such an affectionate heart, if never opposed in his opinions. He has defects, of course ; one of his great defects is getting inferior people about him to listen, too fond of shining at any expense in society, and a love of approbation from the darling sex bordering upon weakness."

Charles Lamb said of him in his famous letter to Southey : "He is the most cordial-minded man I ever knew, and matchless as a fireside companion."

From these and other contemporary but slightly conflicting pictures we are enabled to gather something like a true portrait of the man as a social being in this the noonday of his life. At once open-minded and opinionated, with a singularly clear but not very deep mind; full of playfulness and effusive in sentiment ; self-complacent, self-centred, yet diffident and sympathetic; accepting homage like the air, but ever most ready to appreciate the merits of others; with an intellect charged with abundant miscellaneous but unmethodical reading ; having half a dozen shafts ready for another's one, but never quite hitting the mark ; full of pleasantry not quite amounting to wit, of feeling seldom warming into passion, of learning which stopped short of knowledge, and sagacity which failed of wisdom, he was a flashing and fascinating personality, which, in spite of all its shortcomings, asserted itself even in the most brilliant society by its varied charm and persistent vigour.

So, though he might be weak enough to enjoy the position of a Triton among the minnows, he had the power to attract by his writings, political and poetical, and to fascinate by his company, men of high attainments and genius. Among them were the three great poets, Byron, Keats, and Shelley.

# CHAPTER VII.

BYRON'S acquaintance Hunt had made, as we know, while in prison, and Byron was one of the most frequent visitors at the lodgings in Edgware Road, where Hunt took up his abode after leaving Horsemonger Lane. Of his landlord at these lodgings, and of the visits of Byron, he has left us an amusing description. Byron had then been married a few months, and looked particularly "fine" and "noble." He used to ride on a large rocking-horse which had been given to Leigh Hunt's children, and chat with Hunt whilst Lady Byron (to whom Hunt was never introduced) went on in her carriage to a nursery garden to get flowers, calling for her husband on her return. Leigh Hunt had a study decorated with green and white, "like a box of lilies," which looked over the fields to Westbourne, then a sequestered spot embowered in trees ; and here one morning his dressing-gown caught fire, and he was "extinguished" by his wife's cousin, Miss Virtue Kent. Here also he received a visit from Wordsworth, who came to thank him for advocating the cause of his genius. In the revised edition of the "Feast of the Poets" (published in 1814, second edition 1815) he had reversed his verdict about Wordsworth. Instead of driving him from his presence in scorn, Apollo, after reading him a lesson, admits him to his table with the highest honours; and, in the notes, Leigh Hunt, while contending that Wordsworth abuses his genius, admits that he is the "greatest poet of the present," and "capable of being at the head of a new and great age of poetry." Wordsworth does not appear to have made a favourable impression on Hunt. His solemn vanity, and his disparagement of all other living poets, were peculiarly uncongenial to a man so light-hearted and generous as Hunt. They did not meet again for thirty years.

For some time Leigh Hunt could not shake off the ill-health and consequent hypochondria resulting from his imprisonment, and it was not till his removal to the Vale of Health, Hampstead, in the spring of 1816, that he was able to return the visits of his friends. He found Byron separated from his wife, "jaundiced with bile," and with an execution in the house. At that time Byron took the blame of the separation on himself, and told Hunt that Lady Byron liked "Rimini," "and had compared his temper to that of Giovanni, the heroine's consort." It was at the Vale of Health that he renewed his acquaintance with Shelley and formed that of Keats.

Keats was introduced to Leigh Hunt some time after February, in the spring of 1816, by Charles Cowden Clarke. Like Shelley, Keats had a great admiration for Hunt as the editor of the *Examiner*. The paper had been lent to him by Charles Cowden Clarke, and, long before they met, he had written his "Sonnet on the day Leigh Hunt left prison," which was included in the collection of his works published in 1817. They immediately took a liking to one another, but it appears to have been based mainly upon literary sympathy, and never to have reached the pitch of brotherly fellowship which subsisted between Hunt and Shelley. "I could not love him," said Leigh Hunt, "as deeply as I did Shelley. That was impossible. But my affection was only second to the one which I entertained for that heart of hearts." Nevertheless Keats soon spent a great part of his time (he was then a dresser at Guy's Hospital and lodging in its neighbourhood) at Hunt's cottage in the Vale of Health, where there was always a bed for him in the library; and Hunt promptly showed his appreciation of Keats's literary gifts by publishing his sonnet "O Solitude, &c.," in the *Examiner* of May 5th. At Hunt's house Keats met Shelley and John Hamilton Reynolds, and the poetical promise of the trio formed the subject of an article called "Young Poets" in the *Examiner* for December 1st, when Keats' sonnet on Chapman's Homer first appeared in print. It was on the 30th of December in the same year that Keats and Hunt composed together their sonnets on "The Grasshopper and Cricket." Clarke, who was the only other present, has described the incident delightfully, both poets being equally modest as to their own performance and generous in recognition of the other's merits.

This was the sonnet by Keats :—

" The poetry of earth is never dead :
   When all the birds are faint with the hot sun,
   And hide in cooling trees, a voice will run
   From hedge to hedge about the new-mown mead.
   That is the grasshopper's—he takes the lead
   In summer luxury—he has never done
   With his delights, for, when tired out with fun,
   He rests at ease beneath some pleasant weed.
   The poetry of earth is ceasing never :
   On a lone winter evening, when the frost
   Has wrought a silence, from the stone there shrills
   The cricket's song, in warmth increasing ever,
   And seems, to one in drowsiness half lost,
   The grasshopper's among some grassy hills."

And this was the sonnet by Leigh Hunt :—

" Green little vaulter in the sunny grass,
   Catching your heart up at the feel of June,
   Sole voice that's heard amidst the lazy noon,
   When even the bees lay at the summoning brass ;
   And you, warm little housekeeper, who class
   With those who think the candles come too soon,
   Loving the fire, and with your tricksome tune
   Nick the glad silent moments as they pass ;
   O sweet and tiny cousins, that belong,
   One to the fields, the other to the hearth,
   Both have your sunshine ; both, though small, are strong
   At your clear hearts ; and both seem given to earth
   To ring in thoughtless ears this natural song—
   Indoors and out, summer and winter, Mirth."

As sonnets, Hunt's is the better composition of the two, but Keats's first line is worth the whole of it. Hunt recognised its beauty instantly.

Hunt introduced Keats to Horace Smith [1] and also

---

[1] Horace Smith, as well as Shelley, made Hunt a " princely offer," and, like Keats, had a place in his heart next to Shelley.

to Haydon, whose relations with Hunt were becoming somewhat strained. The light manner in which the Christian creed was treated by the Hunts and their freethinking coterie shocked Haydon, who warned Keats against Hunt's vanity and light-mindedness. Keats probably owed also to Hunt his introduction to the brothers Ollier, who, to their lasting credit but immediate loss, undertook the publication of Keats's first volume of poems, which appeared in March, 1817, with a dedication to Leigh Hunt, and was reviewed with warm appreciation and just discrimination in the *Examiner* of June 1st, and July 6th and 13th. The subsequent intercourse between the two seems to have been somewhat intermittent until May, 1820, when Keats went to live in Wesleyan Place, Kentish Town, in order to be near the Hunts, who were then residing in Mortimer Street. In the following month Keats had a severe attack of hemorrhage of the lungs, and the Hunts took him into their house and nursed him. Down to this time there had never been any serious disturbance of the friendship, though it was liable to chills on Keats' side, through the influence of Haydon, and Keats' own morbid suspicions as to Hunt's sympathy and sincerity. Now, however, when Hunt had just published (August 2nd and 9th) two papers in the *Indicator* warmly eulogising his last volume, and was showing him the tenderest personal care, an unfortunate incident occurred which put a stop for ever to their intercourse in this world. A letter from Fanny Brawne was put into Keats's hands with its seal broken and two days late. He left the Hunts' house suddenly on August 12, 1821. On September 12th he left England with Severn, and on the 23rd of the following February he died in Rome.

From beginning to end of their acquaintance of over four years, Hunt seems to have shown nothing but kindness to Keats. He detected his genius from the first, and published it to the world in the *Examiner* before the poet had printed a line elsewhere. He opened his house to him, and, as each volume of his poems appeared, reviewed him with never-failing kindness and insight. The debt in this case (not a pecuniary one, for apparently there was no question of this kind between them) was not on Hunt's side. Hunt's poetical influence may not have been wholly good ; a few of Keats's less important verses may have, as Mr. Sidney Colvin well expresses it, some of Hunt's "jaunty colloquialism," but he gave material help in the development of Keats's genius. On the other hand, the unjust and malevolent attacks, which if they did not hasten Keats's end, certainly saddened his existence, were the result not of the defects of his poetry, but of his connection with Hunt. If it had not been for Hunt those articles on "The Cockney School of Poets" (*Blackwood*, 1818) would never have appeared, nor yet the notorious article in the *Quarterly* (April, 1818, but not published till September). But for this the blame does not rest with Hunt. How tenderly he thought of Keats during their last separation is told in the beautiful letter which he wrote to Severn at Rome. It is dated nearly a fortnight after Keats's death, the news of which does not appear to have then reached him ; for those were days before railways and telegrams.

"VALE OF HEALTH, HAMPSTEAD,
               "*March* 8, 1821.

"DEAR SEVERN,—You have concluded, of course, that I have sent no letters to Rome, because I was aware of the effect they would have on Keats's mind ; and this is the principal cause ; for, besides what I have been told about letters in Italy, I remember his telling me upon one occasion that, in his sick moments, he never wished to receive another letter, or ever to see another face, however friendly. But still I should have written to you, had I not been almost at death's door myself. You will imagine how ill I have been, when you hear that I have but just begun writing again for the *Examiner* and *Indicator*, after an interval of several months, during which my flesh wasted from me with sickness and melancholy. Judge how often I thought of Keats, and with what feelings. Mr. Brown tells me he is comparatively calm now, or rather quite so. If he can bear to hear of us, pray tell him ; but he knows it already, and can put it into better language than any man. I hear that he does not like to be told that he may get better ; nor is it to be wondered at, considering his firm persuasion that he shall not survive. He can only regard it as a puerile thing, and an insinuation that he shall die. But if his persuasion should happen to be no longer so strong, or if he can now put up with attempts to console him, of what I have said a thousand times, and what I still (upon my honour) think always, that I have seen too many instances of recovery from apparently desperate cases of consumption not to be in hope to the very last. If he still cannot bear this, tell him—tell that great poet and noble-hearted man—that we shall all bear his memory in the most precious part of our hearts, and that the world shall bow their heads to it, as our loves do. Or if this, again, will trouble his spirit, tell him that we shall never cease to remember and love him; and that, Christian or infidel, the most sceptical of us has faith enough in the high things that nature puts into our heads, to think all who are of one accord in mind and heart are journeying to one and the same place, and shall unite somewhere or other again, face to face, mutually conscious, mutually delighted. Tell him he is only before us on the road, as he is in every-thing else; or, whether you tell him the latter or no, tell him the former, and add that we shall never forget that he was so, and that we are coming after him. The tears are again in my eyes, and I must not afford to shed them. The next letter I write shall be more to yourself, and more refreshing to your spirits, which we are very sensible must have been greatly taxed. But whether your friend dies or not, it will not be among the least lofty of your recollections by and by that you helped to smooth the sick bed of so fine a being. God bless you, dear Severn.

" Your sincere friend,

" LEIGH HUNT."

It was one day in November, 1816, that Shelley

renewed his acquaintance with Leigh Hunt. Four years had elapsed since they had met, and meanwhile they had both passed through strange experiences. Hunt had been imprisoned for two years, and Shelley had married and left his first wife, and had been living with Mary Godwin for over two years. Shelley had recently returned from abroad, when Harriet committed suicide in the Serpentine. It was to seek consolation from Leigh Hunt that he now made his appearance at the Vale of Health, Hampstead.

There was perhaps no one living more capable of giving it. Different as they were in many ways, they had much in common. Both had gone to first principles for their rule and criticism of life, and both had found the established order of things so little in accordance with their ideals that they had risen in revolt against it. Both had resisted tyranny at school, and entered the world to fight for freedom—political, domestic, and religious. Both also had suffered greatly in the struggle. In all those qualities which Hunt prized most, Shelley was pre-eminent. He was single-minded, enthusiastic, generous, capable of great sacrifices for the sake of principle or the interests of humanity. These would have been of themselves powerful credentials to the sympathy of Leigh Hunt when Shelley came to him strongly agitated with the terrible end of his first experiment in love. However wrongly or weakly he may have acted, it was not the time to cast stones ; and Leigh Hunt had no stones to throw, for Shelley's conduct towards Harriet seemed to him venial compared to that which society condoned in other men towards other women. This, of course, was no excuse for Shelley, but it was an excuse for Leigh Hunt's ready sympathy, which soon deepened into the warmest friendship which he ever felt for any human being. From this moment till Shelley left England for the last time, in the spring of 1818, their intercourse was frequent and intimate. In March, 1817, Hunt paid Shelley a visit at Marlow, and after this Shelley was a frequent visitor at Hunt's home at Hampstead.

There is no doubt that the value of Hunt's services to Shelley was very great. He cheered, encouraged, and sympathised with him with persistent tenderness, at a time when he was most in need of such friendly offices. He proclaimed his genius as a poet to the world, and made the *Examiner* his champion when he was deprived of the custody of his children. These matters belong rather to the history of Shelley than of Leigh Hunt, and may be passed over here without detail ; but they yet deserve to be mentioned emphatically as a sufficient cause for the deep-rooted and unfailing affection for Leigh Hunt which was felt by Shelley during his life, and by his wife during hers. However severely Leigh Hunt may be condemned by others for the unscrupulous manner in which he sponged upon Shelley, it is clear that neither Shelley nor his wife thought his conduct blameworthy, or that there was any obligation on his side.

"Had I known," Shelley wrote, in dedicating "The Cenci" to Leigh Hunt, May 27, 1819, "a person more highly endowed than yourself with all that it becomes a man to possess, I had selected for this work the ornament of his name. One more gentle, honourable, innocent, and brave ; one of more exalted toleration for all who do and think evil, and yet himself more free from evil ; one who knows better how to receive and how to 'confer a benefit, though he must ever confer far more than he can receive ; one of simpler, and in the highest sense of the word of purer life and manners, I never knew, and I had already been fortunate in friendships when your name was added to the list."

Leigh Hunt took £1,400 from Shelley in one year, an amount considerably exceeding Shelley's income at that time, and he knew that he put him to great inconvenience to raise the money. Hunt had not even the excuse that this amount would clear him from debt. And, what is more, he increased his pecuniary obligation to Shelley afterwards, and never paid him a penny. Such conduct, judged by ordinary British standards, is not to be pardoned on the plea that the victim was willing. The only excuse is that Hunt was abnormal also, and that if the positions had been reversed he would probably have done for Shelley what Shelley did for him. For if Hunt was careless to a fault, he was never mean. He helped the still more careless and impecunious Haydon with money, though the latter characteristically complains that "poor Hunt" could not spare it long enough to be of use. No one probably ever felt more thoroughly that it was more blessed to give than to receive, though the circumstances of his life made it more convenient to accept the lesser beatification.

The letters (1818–1821) which passed between the Shelleys and the Hunts, after the former left England again, till the Hunts set out to join them in Italy, show that they were all (the women as well as the men) on terms of affectionate intimacy, and that the separation was keenly and continuously felt on both sides. For Mrs. Shelley, Hunt has pet names—"Marina mia," and "the nymph of the sidelong glances" ; he writes of her baby (Percy, the late baronet, born at Florence, November 12, 1819) as "Marina's new work," and playfully transforms Shelley's name into "Conchiglioso." He gives accounts of all his family, not omitting the new arrivals, first Percy, and then Swinburne, who was born about the same time as Shelley's Percy. He uses Mrs. Shelley's little green writing-case, and Shelley's pen-knife. He sends Shelley his portrait, by Wildman, and asks for one in return. The deaths of the Shelleys' children, Clara and William, and the long depression from which Mary Shelley suffered after-wards, call forth his tenderest sympathy, and he is always thinking "what it would be to be with Shelley in Italy, or to have him but in London."

This correspondence, though intermittent, throws much light on Hunt's life, domestic and literary, during this time. The "Parnaso Italiano" had made Italy the home of Hunt's imagination, and he discusses the merits of Ariosto, Pulci, and Bojardo, and concludes that "Petrarch, Boccaccio, and Dante, are the night, morning, and noon, of the great Italian day." He projects "Specimens of the Italian Poets from Dante to Metastasio," and translates Tasso's "Amyntas," "that

delightful compromise of art with nature" (published
1820). He bids Shelley tell him of Italian painters,
especially of Julio-Romano, in whom he, for some
reason, takes an exceptional interest, while he depre-
ciates the "heavy-built dreams, neither natural nor
supernatural," of Michael Angelo. He is busy on a
tragedy called "The Cid" (never published, and
apparently lost), which is finished in February, 1819,
and rejected at both Drury Lane and Covent Garden.
He makes translations from the Greek Tragedians
which he thinks "divine," and intends to publish them
(though he never did), with "Hero and Leander."
Shelley's "Prometheus Unbound" (published 1819)
nips in the bud his own project for a "Prometheus
Throned," and with his usual generosity and just
estimation of his own powers, he declares that he is
glad the subject is in better hands, as he is "rather the
son of one of Atlas's daughters than of Atlas himself."
Of the "Cenci" (published 1819) he writes (April 6,
1820), "what a noble book, Shelley, have you given us!
What a true, stately, and yet affectionate mixture of
poetry, philosophy, and human nature, and horror,
and all-redeeming sweetness of intention, for there is an
undersong of suggestion through it all, that sings, as it
were, after the storm is over, like a brook in April."
The violent attacks of the press on himself and Shelley
also come under occasional notice, and Gifford is still
the subject of his special aversion. He praises Hazlitt's
trenchant letter to the editor of the *Quarterly* (1819)
as masterly ; but two years later he has to refer to
the attacks of that capricious genius on Shelley and

himself. He longs to castigate Gifford, but he refers to Hazlitt with his usual tolerance and good-nature. "You may have heard also," he writes (July 11, 1821), "that Hazlitt, after his usual fashion towards those whom he likes and gets impatient with, has been attacking Shelley, myself, and everybody else, the public included, though there his liking stops. I wrote him an angry letter about S——, the first I ever did ; and I believe he is sorry ; but this is his way. Next week, perhaps, he will write a panegyric upon him. He says that Shelley provokes him by his going to a *pernicious* extreme, on the liberal side, and so hurting it. I asked him what good he would do the said side by publicly abusing the supporters of it, and caricaturing them ? To *this* he answers nothing. I told him I would not review his book, as I must quarrel with him publicly if I did so, and so hurt the cause further. Besides I was not going to give publicity to his outrages. I was sorry for it on every account, because I really believe Hazlitt to be a disinterested and suffering man, who feels public calamities as other men do private ones ; and this is perpetually redeeming him in my eyes.

Of other friends these letters also tell—of Hogg and Peacock, of the Novellos and the Lambs, of Alsager and Charles Lloyd—and in March, 1819, he records making "a very pleasant acquaintance in a young man of the name of Procter [Barry Cornwall], who was a little boy at Harrow when Lord Byron was there, and who wrote the verses in the *Pocket Book* signed P. R." This Pocket Book was " The Literary Pocket

Book" (1819–1822), an annual memorandum-book with
verses contributed by Leigh Hunt, Shelley, Procter,
and Keats. It contained also a poem by Mrs. Leigh
Hunt, to which Hunt refers as " Marianne's Dream "
in a letter of November, 1818.

Not the least noteworthy passage in this, the most
interesting series of letters which Leigh Hunt ever
wrote, is that which relates to the *Indicator*, a
periodical which contains the flower of Hunt's work
as an essayist.

" I have now (September 20, 1819) a new periodical
work in hand, in addition to the *Examiner*. My
prospectuses come out in a week or two, and the first
number follows the week after. [The first number
appeared October 13, 1819.] It is to be called the
*Indicator*, after a bird of that name who shows people
where to find wild honey, and will, in fact, be nothing
but a collection of very short pieces of remark,
biography, ancient fiction, &c.; in short, of any
subjects that come to hand, and of which I shall
endeavour to extract the essence for the reader. It
will have nothing temporary whatsoever in it, political
or critical, and indeed will be as pleasant labour to
me as I can have, poetry always excepted. Will you
throw me a paragraph or so now and then, as little
startling at *first* as possible to vulgar prejudices? It
will come out every Thursday, price twopence—an
accomplished specimen, you see, of the *Twopenny
Trash*. If it succeed, it will do me great service,
being my sole property ; and I am weary with writing
every day, and making nothing of it to put an end

to my straitnesses, though the *Examiner* increases
too."

These straightnesses, notwithstanding the £1,400
he had had from Shelley, were still troubling him.
It is said that when all had been paid, the expenses of
the trial and the fine had cost the brothers £1,000
a-piece, or double the fine ; and, according to his own
account, he had been very careless of expenditure while
he had been in prison, and he probably remained so
for some time after he came out of it.

Her son, Thornton, says that about the year 1821
Mrs. Hunt fell into a confirmed state of ill-health, and
that this deprived her husband of " his trusted agent
in domestic affairs " ; but these affairs were already in
a deplorable state. Nevertheless, the Hunts seem to
have made efforts to increase income and restrict
expenditure. In March, 1819, he writes to Mrs.
Shelley of "that noble action " (probably the gift
or loan of £1,400) and of difficulties still pelting
upon him, though he thanks God " the storm is
pretty well over," and adds that both his economy
and resources have been " increasing," and that he is
" writing like a dragon." He sold the copyright of
his " Literary Pocket Book " to Ollier for £200.
They left off giving dinners. Finally he started the
*Indicator*, and worked at it with desperate energy
from the autumn of 1819 to the beginning of
1821.

Musing sadly in after years over this period of his
life, with its carelessness in money matters, and "most
inconsiderate habit of taking books for the only ends

in life," which conspired to make him " so ridiculous,"
he writes :—

"Let me console myself a little by remembering
how much Hazlitt and Lamb, and others, were pleased
with the *Indicator*. I speak most of them because
they talked most to me about it. Hazlitt's favourite
paper (for they liked it enough to have favourite
papers) was the one on 'Sleep' (perhaps because there
is a picture in it of a sleeping despot), though he
repeated, with more enthusiasm than he was accustomed to do, the conclusion about the parent and the
bride. Lamb preferred the papers on 'Coaches and
their Horses,' that on 'Deaths of Little Children,' and
(I think) the one entitled 'Thoughts and Guesses on
Human Nature.' Shelley took to the story of the
'Fair Revenge'; and the paper that was most liked
by Keats, if I remember, was the one on a hot
summer's day, entitled 'A Now.' He was with me
while I was writing and reading it to him, and contributed one or two of its passages. Keats first
published in the *Indicator* his beautiful poem 'La
Belle Dame sans Mercy,' and the 'Dream after
reading Dante's Episode of Paolo and Francesca.'
Lord Holland, I was told, had a regard for the
portraits of the 'Old Lady' and the 'Old Gentleman,'
&c., which had appeared in the *Examiner ;* and a
late gallant captain in the navy was pleased to wonder
how I became acquainted with seamen (in the article
entitled 'Seamen on Shore'). They had sat to me
for their portraits. The common sailor was a son of

my nurse at school, and the officer a connection of my own by marriage."

In the *Indicator* Leigh Hunt earned a right to be included among the most delightful writers of playful and sentimental essays. They have not the intellectual grasp, the trenchant vigour, or the eloquence of Hazlitt ; they have not the inimitable drollery, the quaint turns of thought, the exquisite fitness of phrase, the lightning touch of Lamb, but in their way they are almost as unique. "No man," says James Russell Lowell, "has ever understood the delicacies and luxuries of language better than he ; and his thoughts often have all the rounded grace and shifting lustre of a dove's neck." The easy colloquial style—if that can be called "style" which is as free and flexible as running water—was suited to his matter. He talks to you—tells you his thoughts as they arise in his mind ; we follow their meanderings as those of a stream, now broad now narrow, now breaking into sparkles of gentle merriment and now falling, but only for a moment, into a somewhat deeper pool—and the sun is always shining, and the water is always clear ; there are no torrents or spates in Leigh Hunt's brook, but it is never dry.

It is impossible here to give fair samples of the varied beauties of Leigh Hunt's best essays ; but one passage seems doubly desirable in this place, for its beauty and personal interest. It is from " Deaths of Little Children " (*Indicator*, April 5, 1820), and refers to his mother's grave in Hampstead Churchyard :—

"We are writing at this moment just opposite a spot which contains the grave of one inexpressibly dear to us. We see from our window the trees about it and the church spire. The green fields lie around. The clouds are travelling overhead, alternately taking away the sunshine and restoring it. The vernal winds, piping of the flowery summer time, are nevertheless calling to mind the far-distant and dangerous ocean, which the heart that lies in that grave had many reasons to think of. And yet the sight of this spot does not give us pain. So far from it, it is the existence of that grave which doubles every charm of the spot ; which links the pleasures of our childhood and manhood together ; which puts a hushing tenderness in the winds, and a patient joy upon the landscape ; which seems to unite heaven and earth, mortality and immortality, the grass of the tomb and the grass of the green field ; and gives a more maternal aspect to the whole kindness of Nature. It does not hinder gaiety itself. Happiness was what its tenant, through all her troubles, would have diffused. To diffuse happiness, and to enjoy it, is not only to carry on her wishes, but realising her hopes ; and gaiety, freed from its only pollutions, malignity and want of sympathy, is but a child playing about the knees of its mother."

Under the united strain of the *Examiner* and the *Indicator*, Leigh Hunt's health thoroughly broke down. Throughout the pages of the latter there are many signs of overwork. He was unable to keep up the weekly supply of original essays. Sometimes he would substitute an extract from a book he had been reading, or reprint papers (like those on Charles Lamb) which had previously appeared in the *Examiner*, or give a makeweight in the shape of "Scenes from an Unfinished Drama," which lay handy in his portfolio. But it was all of no use; the *Indicator* had to be given up, and Leigh Hunt was fairly stranded. The year 1821 found him almost incapacitated for work of any kind, and though he revived enough about August to attend again to the *Examiner*, the hope of recovering his health was no doubt one of the strongest inducements to accept Shelley's repeated invitation to come to Italy. "Put your music and your books on board a vessel," Shelley wrote, "and you will have no more trouble."

Shelley made the arrangements, and borrowed the necessary money (£200) from Byron, who, through Shelley, seconded the invitation to Leigh Hunt. The proposal was to found a quarterly magazine, to which Byron and Shelley would contribute. The scheme appears to have been very vague, and one of the wildest that ever entered the heads of three men of understanding. But it was as a floating straw to the drowning Hunt, and his brother John (who was in prison again) consenting, Leigh Hunt, with his wife and seven children, his music, and his books (including the "Parnaso Italiano") went on board the brig *Jane*, Captain Whitney, at Blackwall, November 15, 1821, and set sail the following morning direct for Leghorn.

But here began a chapter of accidents fully narrated in the Autobiography. The weather was so rough that they did not pass the Nore till the 19th, and lay at Ramsgate for three weeks. They then encountered a series of violent gales, and reached Dartmouth with great difficulty December 22nd. Thence they went to Plymouth, and took lodgings at Stonehouse, Mrs. Hunt being so ill that she had to keep her bed the whole time, and lost a great deal of blood. Here he received much hospitality, and was presented with a silver cup by some friends of the *Examiner*.[1] It was not till May 13, 1822, that they sailed again, this time to reach their destination.

[1] Now in the possession of his grandson, Mr. Walter Leigh Hunt.

# CHAPTER VIII.

A S if to make amends for its long unkindness, the weather prospered the voyage of the *David Walter*, and at two o'clock on June 15, 1822, Leigh Hunt for the first time "entered an Italian harbour and heard Italian words." At last he had reached his Promised Land : troubles, sickness, all were forgotten in excitement and expectation. His frame of mind is well reflected in the following extract from the Autobiography : "' Va bene,' said the pilot in a fine open voice, and turned the head of the boat with a tranquil dignity. ' Va bene,' thought I, indeed. ' All goes well. The words are delicious and the omen good.'"

He wrote at once to the Shelleys, telling of his arrival. "I embrace you both," the letter runs, "a hundred times, each one warmer than the last." And Shelley replies in a day or two that " wind and waves, he hoped, would never part them more."

Shelley was then at the Villa Magni at Lerici, having left his house at Pisa for the summer months ; Byron was also in *villeggiatura* at Monte Nero, but the Hunts were bound for Pisa, where Shelley had already furnished for his accommodation the ground floor of Byron's house—the Casa Lanfranchi, on the bank of the Arno. They did not sail from Genoa till the 28th, reaching Leghorn on the 1st of July. During the passage they experienced a violent thunderstorm, which Hunt calls the "completest" he ever saw.

"The lightning fell in all parts of the sea like pillars, or like great melted fires suddenly dropped from a giant torch. Now it pierced the sea like rods; now fell like enormous flakes or tongues, suddenly swallowed up. At one time it seemed to confine itself to a dark corner of the ocean, making formidable shows of gigantic and flashing lances (for it was the most perpendicular lightning I ever saw); then it dashed broadly at the whole sea, as if it would sweep us away in flame; and then came in random portions about the vessel, treading the waves hither and thither like the legs of fiery spirits descending in wrath."

At Leghorn Hunt found neither Shelley nor Byron, but Trelawny was there on board Byron's yacht, the *Bolivar*, and Hunt at once proceeded to pay the "noble bard" a visit at Monte Nero, which was within a half-hour's ride. "Upon seeing Lord Byron," he says, "I scarcely knew him, he was grown so fat; and he was longer in recognising me, I had grown so thin." Hunt found the household in a state of great agitation as the Guiccioli's brother, Conte Piero Gamba, had just been wounded when interfering in a servants' quarrel, and the culprit was keeping watch outside, vowing he would assault the first person who issued forth.

"It was a curious moment for a stranger from England. I fancied myself pitched into one of the scenes in the 'Mysteries of Udolpho.' Everything was new, foreign, and vehement. There was the lady, flushed and dishevelled, exclaiming against the *scelerato;* the young Count, wounded and threatening ; and the assassin waiting for us with his knife. Nobody, however, could have put a better face on the matter than Lord Byron did ; composed and endeavouring to compose : and as to myself, I was so occupied with the whole scene that I had no time to be frightened. Forth we issue at the house-door, all squeezing to have the honour of being first, when a termination is put to the tragedy by the man's throwing himself on a bench, extending his arms, and bursting into tears. His cap was half over his eyes ; his face gaunt, ugly, and unshaved ; his appearance altogether more squalid and miserable than an Englishman would conceive it possible to find in such an establishment. This blessed figure reclined weeping and wailing, and asking pardon for his offence ; and, to crown all, he requested Lord Byron to kiss him."

Shelley, with his friend Williams, soon came in their boat, scudding into the harbour of Leghorn, and they, with the Hunts, proceeded to Pisa, where Byron joined them. On the following Monday, July 8th, the little boat *Don Juan* started off again for Lerici, carrying Shelley and Williams—to "solve the great mystery."

Of what passed in the few days Hunt and Shelley spent together at Pisa we know very little. Hunt

records only "one delightful afternoon (this was
Sunday the 7th) spent with him wandering about
Pisa and visiting the cathedral." We know that the
organ was playing, and that Shelley assented warmly
to the opinion expressed by Hunt, that a truly Divine
religion might be established if charity were really
made the principle of it instead of faith. Hunt's
eldest son remembered Shelley reading aloud some
passages of Plato to his father. We hear of Shelley's
last fragment of verse (unfortunately lost)—a welcome
to Hunt, in which he compared his friend to a firefly.
We know from the testimony of Trelawny and
Williams that these last days were shadowed by the
rude reception which Byron gave the Hunts, but
this is all, or nearly all, we know of what took place
at Pisa in that something less than a week of companionship which preceded the "dreadful interval"
between the departure of Shelley and the discovery of
his body near the town of Via Reggio, with Hunt's
copy of Keats's last volume in his pocket.

It was not only Shelley and his companions that went
down with the *Don Juan*, but the main hope of Hunt's
life. He was never quite the same man again, although
he bore the loss with fortitude, and his famous "animal
spirits" came to his rescue. There was only one
Shelley, and, except Mrs. Shelley, there was probably
no one in the world who loved him as Hunt loved
him. It is doubted by Trelawny whether Hunt ever
fully appreciated Shelley's genius as a poet. He rose
to heights where perhaps Hunt, with all his affection,
could scarcely follow him, but there is no doubt that

Hunt worshipped Shelley's soul as the purest and noblest in the world, and that he thought him, as he called him, " divine." The sincerity of the following passage is as undeniable as its beauty—

" He was like a spirit that had darted out of its orb, and found itself in another world. I used to tell him that he had come from the planet Mercury. When I heard of the catastrophe that overtook him, it seemed as if this spirit, not sufficiently constituted like the rest of the world to obtain their sympathy, yet gifted with a double portion of love for all living things, had been found dead in a solitary corner of the earth, its wings stiffened, its warm heart cold ; the relics of a misunderstood nature, slain by the ungenial elements."

The body was not found till the 18th, or ten days after the catastrophe, and the cremation took place on August 15th. Each of the principal persons present—Byron, Hunt, and Trelawny—has given an account of this ceremony. Byron's is very short ; Trelawny's is the fullest, as he made all the arrangements, and the calmest, as his nerves were proof, but Hunt's is the most poetical, and is the only one which would be in place here.

" The ceremony of the burning was alike beautiful and distressing. Trelawny, who had been the chief person concerned in ascertaining the fate of his friends, completed his kindness by taking the most

active part on this last mournful occasion. He
and his friend Captain Shenley were first upon
the ground, attended by proper assistants. Lord
Byron and myself arrived shortly afterwards. His
lordship got out of his carriage, but wandered
away from the spectacle, and did not see it. I remained inside the carriage, now looking on, now
drawing back with feelings that were not to be
witnessed. None of the mourners, however, refused
themselves the little comfort of supposing, that lovers
of books and antiquity, like Shelley and his companion,
Shelley in particular with his Greek enthusiasm, would
not have been sorry to foresee this part of their fate.
The mortal part of him, too, was saved from corruption ; not the least extraordinary part of his history.
Among the materials for burning, as many of the
gracefuller and more classical articles as could be
procured — frankincense, wine, &c. — were not forgotten ; and to these Keats' volume was added. The
beauty of the flame arising from the funeral pile was
extraordinary. The weather was beautifully fine.
The Mediterranean, now soft and lucid, kissed the
shore as if to make peace with it. The yellow sand
and blue sky were intensely contrasted with one
another : marble mountains touched the air with
coolness ; and the flame of the fire bore away towards
heaven in vigorous amplitude, wavering and quivering
with a brightness of inconceivable beauty. It seemed
as though it contained the glassy essence of vitality.
You might have expected a seraphic countenance to
look out of it, turning once more before it departed,

to thank the friends that had done their duty. Yet, see how extremes can appear to meet even on occasions the most overwhelming ; nay, even by reason of them ; for as cold can perform the effect of fire, and burn us, so can despair put on the monstrous aspect of mirth. On returning from one of our visits to this sea-shore, we dined and drank—I mean, Lord Byron and myself ; —dined little, and drank too much. Lord Byron had not shone that day, even in his cups, which usually brought out his best qualities. As to myself, I had bordered upon emotions which I have never suffered myself to indulge, and which, foolishly as well as impatiently, render calamity, as somebody termed it, 'an affront, and not a misfortune.' The barouche drove rapidly through the forest of Pisa. We sang, we laughed, we shouted. I even felt a gaiety the more shocking, because it was real and a relief."

Their regard for Shelley was almost the only bond between this exceedingly ill-matched pair, who had now to live together under the same roof. With Shelley's death the only chance (if, indeed, there was ever one at all) of the success of the new quarterly was at an end. Hunt and Byron had no scheme, and could not have worked it out together if they had had one. Byron's sole notion appears to have been to find a channel for the publication of anything he chose to write ; Hunt's only thought was to fire off a succession of squibs in the face of John Bull and Mrs. Grundy, mixed with poems and translations. He no doubt relied greatly on the powerful assistance of

Byron and Shelley, but especially of Byron, whose name commanded a large market ; but he also relied a great deal too much upon himself. Even if three such men as Byron, Shelley, and Leigh Hunt had all put their shoulders to the same wheel, they would have needed an editor with much greater tact and a much longer head than Leigh Hunt. The death of Shelley not only removed one of the triumvirate, but it so strained the relations between the other two as to put anything like co-operation out of the question.

It is impossible not to pity both Byron and Hunt for the exceedingly trying position in which they now found themselves. No doubt it was partly the result of their own imprudence—to use no stronger term. Hunt ought never to have agreed to a proposal which entailed the saddling of Shelley with the support of himself and his family for an indefinite period ; Byron ought never to have countenanced a project so little trusted by himself, and so fraught with danger to his friends. It is scarcely worth while, at this distance of time, to examine minutely into the motives of either Hunt or Byron. Hunt, however selfish and inconsiderate, never harboured a design against Shelley's happiness. Byron, though he may have thought the magazine would be useful to him, and may have reckoned on the support of the *Examiner* (though this is doubtful), certainly wished to please Shelley and to help Hunt. The motives on either side, if mixed (and what motives are not ?), were not (even the worst of them) evil, and their divergence from ideal purity was at least well punished by the situation produced through the unforeseen death of Shelley, the blameless cause of all the trouble.

Byron had probably repented of the share he had taken in inducing Leigh Hunt to come to Italy, long before the arrival of that gentleman, his wife, and seven children. The alliance was not pleasant to his Tory friends, and Moore had advised him strongly against it. Moore's advice was good, and he had the cleaner hands in giving it, as he himself had refused a somewhat similar offer from Byron (see Byron's letter to Moore, Ravenna, December 25, 1820). "I heard," some days ago," writes Moore, "that Leigh Hunt was on his way to you with all his family ; and the idea seems to be that you and he and Shelley are to conspire together in the *Examiner*. I deprecate such a plan with all my might. Partnerships in fame, like those in trade, make the strongest party answer for the rest. I tremble even for you with such a bankrupt company ! You must stand alone." Of these and other "faithful" words from his friends, Byron had probably thought much during the long time which elapsed between his invitation to Hunt, through Shelley, and the arrival of the family at Leghorn. Other matters of more pressing interest, and of greater excitement, had increased his indifference to the project. His *liaison* with Countess Guiccioli, and the subsequent difficulties with the Government of Tuscany ; dreams of a future—now pastoral in South America, now warlike in Greece ; fresh cantos of "Don Juan," and other projects—filled his restless soul and teeming brain with ferment, when Leigh Hunt knocked at the door, so to speak, by appointment, and asked for board and lodging for himself, his wife, and seven children—until such time as the success of their projected periodical should enable him to pay his own score. It was probably the intention neither of Shelley nor of Byron that the latter should be saddled with all Hunt's expenses ; but Byron did not wait for Shelley's death to show his feeling. In his last interview with Shelley he was irritable on the subject of his promises to Leigh Hunt. Williams, in his last letter to his wife, expresses his opinion that Byron had treated Hunt vilely, and says that they (Shelley and Hunt) can do nothing with his lordship, " who actually said as much as that he did not wish (?) his name to be attached to the work, and of course to theirs." He adds, "Lord B.'s reception of Mrs. H. was—as S. tells me—most shameful. She came into his house sick and exhausted, and he scarcely deigned to notice her ; was silent, and scarcely bowed. This conduct cut H. to the soul."

The friction thus set up between them at the outset was not lessened by the death of Shelley. Byron had no one to share his burden, Hunt had no one to sympathise with him or to conciliate Byron. Never were a pair less suited to live, to say nothing of working, together. "There was not a single subject on which Byron and Hunt could agree," says Trelawny, to whom Byron had observed before Hunt came, " You will find Leigh Hunt a gentleman in dress and address ; at least, he was so when I last saw him in England, with a taint of cockneyism." This " taint

of cockneyism" Byron could tolerate—at a distance.
It did not prevent him from thinking highly of Hunt's
talents, or praising his goodness as a man, but it
certainly did not tend to relieve the tension of the
present situation. Though he at times would bear
witness to Hunt's gentlemanly qualities, at others he
called him not only " a Cockney," but a vulgar coxcomb. On the other hand, Hunt had his ideal of a
" gentleman," to which Byron, in spite of his birth
and title, did not at all correspond. He was violent,
rude even to ladies, wanting in ease and self-possession,
he swaggered, he posed. In other words, neither could
tolerate the other's defects in character and manners.

And it was much the same with their minds as with
their manners. Byron was consistent enough in
praising " Rimini," though he objected to its style and
vocabulary, but he could not stand Hunt's other poems.
This is what he wrote to Moore about " Foliage " on
June 1, 1818 :—

" He sent out his ' Foliage ' by Percy Shelley . . .
and, of all the ineffable Centaurs that were ever
begotten by Self-love upon a nightmare, I think this
monstrous Sagittary the most prodigious. *He* (Leigh
H.) is an honest charlatan, who has persuaded himself
into a belief of his own impostures, and talks Punch
in pure simplicity of heart, taking himself (as poor
Fitzgerald said of *himself* in the *Morning Post*) for
*vates* in both senses, or nonsenses, of the word. Did
you look at the translations of his own which he
prefers to Pope and Cowper, and says so? Did you

read his skimble-skamble about Wordsworth being at the head of his own *profession* in the *eyes* of *those* who followed it ?   I thought that poetry was an *art*, or an *attribute*, and not a *profession*—but be it one, is that . . . at the head of *your* profession in *your* eyes ? I'll be curst if he is of *mine*, or ever shall be.   He is the only one of us (but of us he is not) whose coronation I would oppose.   Let them take Scott, Campbell, Crabbe, or you, or me, or any of the living, and throne him—but not this new Jacob Behmen, this . . . whose pride might have kept him true, even had his principles turned as perverted as his *soi' disant* poetry.   But Leigh Hunt is a good man and a good father—see his Odes to all the Masters Hunt ; a good husband—see his Sonnet to Mrs. Hunt ; a good friend —see his Epistles to different people ; and a great coxcomb and a very vulgar person in everything about him.   But that's not his fault, but of circumstances."

Hunt, on the other hand, only half-realised the power of Byron, and was out of sympathy with his style.   Trelawny says, that "at that time Hunt thought highly of his own poetry, and underestimated all other ;" that " Shelley soared too high for him, and Byron flew too near the ground."   He adds that Hunt did not conceal that his estimate of Byron's poetry was not exalted, and we have Hunt's own admission that he did not manifest the admiration due to Byron's genius, or read the manuscripts Byron showed him with a becoming amount of thanks or good words.

Then there was the serious difficulty of the ladies. Hunt's freely-spoken opinions about marriage and the relations of the sexes, prevented him from expressing, perhaps, from feeling, any objection to taking up his abode with Byron and his mistress; but it was very different with Mrs. Hunt, whose opinions were not so "advanced" as her husband's. To tolerate the Guiccioli would have been hard enough, but to tolerate the tolerance of her father and brother! Though compelled to live under the same roof with this strange family party, and to eat the bread of Byron, Mrs. Hunt kept to her own apartments, her ill-health affording an efficient excuse. Professor Nichol says that she does not seem to have been a very judicious person. "Trelawny here," said Byron one day, "has been speaking against my morals." "It is the first time I ever heard of them," she replied. This may have been injudicious, but it was well-deserved, and is about the only healthy utterance to be found in the records of this miserable episode in Hunt's life.

As if all these elements of disagreement were not enough, there was the pecuniary one, the basest and most potent of all. All Hunt's troubles at this time were intensified by the memory of Shelley. He could not help comparing Byron with this lost ideal, and the comparison, always to the disadvantage of Byron—was never more so than as a creditor. What a change from the more than brother who would cheerfully borrow hundreds of pounds on post obits in order to defray your debts, to the unwilling almsgiver who doled out small sums through his steward! How delightful to be indebted to a man, who gave money as though its acceptance was a favour, and his only regret that he could not give more! It made borrowing a luxury, almost a duty to your wife and children. But Byron was quite an ordinary creditor ; he did not pretend to like the position ; he showed no desire to advance more than was necessary ; he seemed to think that the obligation was on Hunt's side ; he did not go out of his way to sweeten the bread of dependence. For the first time in his life Hunt was made to feel that he was a sponge.

If we add to all this that Hunt was very ill, and that his wife was very ill, we may conclude that the Casa Lanfranchi was to Hunt (or at least would have been to any one else), a doleful dwelling-house indeed.

# CHAPTER IX.

THE situation would seem to have been devised to bring out the very worst qualities of the two men. Poor Hunt cut the most pitiful figure, but Byron was the most to blame, for he was powerful and Hunt was helpless—moreover, now that Shelley was gone, it was Byron who was responsible for the situation, and he should have faced it with more energy, with more generosity. Having no faith in the success of the proposed review, and no intention of putting his shoulder to the wheel in order to make a fair trial of it, it would have been better to have abandoned it at once, and put Leigh Hunt on his legs to start again. This would, at least so it appears to us now, have been the most just solution of the difficulty and probably the cheapest; for the cost of his alliance with the Hunts is estimated at about £500. But Byron chose to let things drift until the *Liberal* had run its fated course; and the Hunts were cut adrift with their expenses paid to Florence, and memories in their hearts which rankled for years. In justice to Byron it should be added, that he tried in vain to induce Moore to write for the *Liberal*, that he supplied Hunt's wants,

if not in the most considerate manner, at least without
grumbling, that he was far more ready to be friendly
with Hunt than Hunt was with him, and from first to
last spoke and wrote about Hunt sincerely, consistently,
and on the whole kindly, if not always in language
which was pleasant for Hunt to hear.

All parties being agreed to set the *Liberal* afloat,
Hunt seems to have set to work manfully, in spite of
ill health and distress of mind. The name was a matter
of debate. Byron at first suggested the *Hesperides*,
but the *Liberal* was ultimately determined upon, and
the first number appeared in September, which was
pretty quick work considering all things. What fresh
labour there was in it, was all Leigh Hunt's. Byron's
contributions were (with the exception of some brutal
epigrams on Castlereagh), " old stock," which Murray
and other publishers had declined to issue with their
names on the title-page. One of these was the
immortal " Vision of Judgment," of which Byron had
written to Moore in March : " The Quevedo (one of
my best in that line) has appalled the Row already,
and must take its chance in Paris if at all "—the other
was the famous " Letter to the Editor of My Grand-
mother's Review," which had been put into type by
Murray, but never issued. They were both pieces
of extraordinary literary merit ; but far more fitted
to arouse animosity than to float the new review
into public favour. It also contained Shelley's fine
translation of Goethe's " Walpurgis Nacht," another
example of good matter in the wrong place. All the
rest, or nearly all, was contributed by Hunt, and com-

prised a letter from Pisa, giving an Italian story, a
long translation from Ariosto, shorter ones from other
Italian poets, and a paper called " Rhyme and Reason,"
in which he contended, with a special hit at the Poet
Laureate, that of much modern poetry the whole of
the reason was contained in the rhymes.  In short, the
first number of the new review which was to rival the
*Quarterly* and the *Edinburgh*, was half academical,
half polemical, and addressed itself mainly to students
of foreign poetry, and the enemies of Southey.  Yet
this first number was by far the best of the four,
although the next contained Byron's " Heaven and
Hell," Shelley's exquisite song "I arise from Dreams
of Thee," and a tirade against Monarchy by Hazlitt.
To the third number Hazlitt contributed his delightful paper on " My First Acquaintance with
Poets ;" Byron, "The Blues" (which he called in 1821
" a mere buffoonery, never meant for publication ")
Shelley's " Lines to a Critic," were also published in
this number.  Then came the fourth and last, with
Byron's fine translation of the first canto of the
"Morgante Maggiore" of Pulci, and Hazlitt's paper
on "Pulpit Oratory—Chalmers and Irving."  With the
exception of a few other papers by Hazlitt and Mrs.
Shelley, and a few more by other hands, Hunt wrote
the rest of the *Liberal* himself.  He was not proud of
these contributions in after days, and, indeed, he had
no cause to be, for most of them were of a quality very
inferior to his best work.  This is certainly the case
with those which were unmistakably written in Italy.
His preface and notes were couched in quite the old

tone of defiance and self-complacency ; and he showed an extraordinary want of tact and taste in writing two long satirical poems, called " The Dogs," and " The Book of Beginnings," in the style and metre of " Don Juan." It was certainly imitation, it looked like rivalry, and to challenge a comparison between himself and Byron, especially in a style in which Byron was supreme, could only render himself ridiculous in the eyes of the public, and increase the contempt of his "noble friend." It shows among other things how greatly he at this time overestimated his own powers in comparison with those of Byron, and how utterly impossible it was for the two to pull together.

His " Letters from Abroad," in which he conveyed his first impressions of Italy, though interesting from a biographical point of view, were unenlivened even by his usual " animal spirits." They are wanting in acute observation, they are full of common-place reflection, they are pieced with quotations from other writers. A great part of them might have been written quite as well at Hampstead with the aid of a few books. Italy (the real country and its real inhabitants), even its ancient art and its architecture, interested him little and inspired him not at all. His account of the former, is one series of disadvantageous comparisons with England, and he was too ignorant of the latter to make his comments of much value. There are few sayings of his about Italy half so good as that of his wife's, that the " olive trees looked as if they only grew by moonlight." He took his Italy about with him in the " Parnaso Italiano," and found nothing in the real country which would compare with it. His best contributions to the *Liberal* were purely literary, like the amusing article on the "Giuli Tre" of Casti, and a few of his own poems like "Lines to a Spider" and "Mahmound."

Roughly speaking, Leigh Hunt was three years in Italy—one year of which was spent at Pisa and Genoa with Byron, during which he devoted himself principally to the *Liberal*—and the other two at Florence writing for the *Literary Examiner* and other periodicals.

His chief correspondent during all this time was his sister-in-law, Elizabeth Kent, to whom, in spite of some infirmities of temper, of which we hear too much, he was warmly attached. He addresses her as "Bebs mine," and "Dearest Bessy mine," and assures her that next to his wife and family, there is no one he loves so much. He no sooner arrived at Leghorn than he wrote her a long letter (July 2, 1822), pressing her to come out, painting Italy in rose colour, and signing himself with "*Mille baci, mille e mille volte,* your ever friend of friends. L. H." On the 8th (the day that Shelley left never to return), he writes still in excellent spirits, describing the household as though it were a most eligible one for an unmarried English lady. "We are all quietly housed here ; ourselves on the ground floor, and he and his fair friend (a Countess Guiccioli, who is separated from her husband, and is handsome, and I daresay amiable) in the rooms above us. The Gambas, owing to a late notice of the Tuscan Government (for they are ex-revolutionists and exiles) have gone to Lucca for the present ; otherwise they reside with him, and Madame Guiccioli is their daughter and sister,—so you see how lightly the Italians think of certain heavy English matters. Indeed the difference altogether on these points is great and most good-natured. They do not like *profligacy* and a certain worldliness of proceeding ; but they draw distinction (*sic*) with great kindness and philosophy." Unfortunately, one's good-nature (and even one's philosophy) is liable to be affected by circumstances. Before long Leigh Hunt was drawing distinctions certainly not good-natured, if philosophical, respecting the relations of Byron and his mistress. Byron's behaviour to the Guiccioli appeared to him wanting in sentimental tenderness and did not even attain to his ideal of refined sensuality.

On the way from Pisa to Genoa whither the two widows had preceded them, they met Lord Byron and Trelawny at Lerici, where there was an earthquake, and Byron was delayed by illness for some days. Hunt took away some myrtle leaves from the Villa Magni, some of which he kept for his sister-in-law Elizabeth. From Lerici they went to Sestri by water, the Hunts in a felucca by themselves, and thence over the Maritime Apennines to Albaro, a suburb of Genoa, where Mrs. Shelley had already found them accommodation— Lord Byron in the Villa Saluzzo, and the Hunts in the Casa Negrotto, where she herself was. This arrangement was more comfortable for all parties. Byron had no longer the seven "not very tractable" children of Hunt playing on his staircase, and Hunt

had the society and sympathy of Mary Shelley. Moreover, Byron and Hunt did not meet so often, which
was better, at least for Hunt, who was suffering in
temper and character from the strain of the situation.

To Byron the *Liberal* was only one of the least
interesting of many projects, and Leigh Hunt was
only a poor devil whom he wished to help ; but wished
more to be handsomely rid of. To Hunt the success
of the *Liberal* was a question almost of life and death,
and he himself was a person of much consequence,—as
a man, a poet, and a politician, accustomed to be treated
with the most tender and admiring regard by all around
him. Now he was utterly at a discount, and his state
of mind made him morbidly sensitive to anything
which could be interpreted into a slight, and ready to
impute the meanest motives to everything Byron said
or did.

The *Liberal* proved, what Byron from the first
prophesied it would, an abortion. At first there was
some glimmer of life : even Byron spoke to Hunt cheerfully about it ; but then the sale fell off, and poor John
Hunt was prosecuted and fined for publishing " The
Vision of Judgment," so that altogether it must have
been a genuine relief to both Leigh Hunt and Byron
when the *Liberal* was finally abandoned and the
partnership between them dissolved. Byron departed
for Greece July 13, 1823, and shortly afterwards Hunt
left Genoa for Florence, with his wife and family, now
increased to eight by the birth of a son (Vincent) at
Albaro. They were never to meet again, and when
less than a year afterwards, Hunt heard of Byron's

death he wrote thus coldly to Elizabeth Kent : "I could not help feeling emotion at the news of Lord Byron's death, strange as his conduct was. Poor fellow ! he was the most spoilt of men ; and I do believe was naturally good."

The *Liberal* being at an end, why did not Leigh Hunt return to England ? There is but one answer to this—he could not afford it, and it was one of those things which most rankled in his mind, that Byron had, as he called and thought it, "deserted" him, with only enough money to pay for his removal from one part of Italy to another. The change, however, was beneficial to him. Although he was still "disconsolate," and the health of both himself and his wife was very bad, and he was so poor that he had to take his turn in nursing the baby, his spirits and his mental energy revived in some degree. He first lived in the Via delle Belle Donne, at Florence, and then in the Piazza Santa Croce, but, "agreeably to his old rustic propensities," he soon left the city to live at Maiano, in the Villa Morandi, where he remained till his return to England. In Florence and its neighbouroood he was in what he calls " the Italy of books." He cared for Santa Croce, not so much for the treasures of art that it contained, as for the ashes of the great men who were buried there. He says, "The Church of Santa Croce would disappoint you as much inside as out, if the presence of the remains of great men did not always cast a mingled shadow of the awful and the beautiful over one's thoughts. Any large space, also, devoted to the pur- poses of religion disposes the mind to the loftiest of speculations. The vaulted sky out of doors appears small compared with the opening into immensity represented by that very inclosure—that larger dwelling than common, entered by a little door. The door is like a grave, and the enclosure like a vestibule of heaven." He derived some amusement at Maiano from the manners and customs of the peasantry, but he tells us that the greatest comfort he experienced in Italy, next to writing "Christianism," was living in a neighbour-hood which Boccaccio loved, and thinking of him as he walked about. The comparative freedom from worry, the composition of this book, and essays for the *Examiner*, and elsewhere, in the old style of the *Indicator*, all tended to restore his mind to its normal condition, and to make his stay at Maiano the most pleasant part of his exile. He had more society there also—Charles Armitage Brown, the old friend of Keats, Walter Savage Landor (who wrote, "over a bottle," his quatrain on one of the hairs of Lucrezia Borgia which Byron had given to Hunt), Lord Dillon, and Kirkup, an English artist of independent means. But in spite of all this he was homesick. His frame of mind is mirrored in the following extract from his Autobiography :—

"At Maiano, I wrote the articles which appeared in the *Examiner*, under the title of the ' Wishing Cap.' . . . The title was very genuine.

"When I put on my cap, and pitched myself in imagination into the thick of Covent Garden, the pleasure I received was so vivid,—I turned the corner of a street so much in the ordinary course of things, and was so tangibly present to the pavement, the shop-windows, the people, and a thousand ageeeable recollections which looked me naturally in the face,—that sometimes when I walk there now, the impression seems hardly more real.  I used to feel as if I actually pitched my soul there, and that spiritual eyes might have seen it shot over from Tuscany into York Street, like a rocket. . . . I not only missed 'the town' in Italy; I missed my old trees—oaks and elms. Tuscany, in point of wood, is nothing but olive-ground and vineyard. . . . Then, there are no meadows, no proper green lanes (at least, I saw none), no paths leading over field and stile, no hay-fields in June, nothing of that luxurious combination of green and russet, of grass, wild flowers, and woods, over which a lover of Nature can stroll for hours with a foot as fresh as the stags; unvexed with chalk, dust, and an eternal public path; and able to lie down, if he will, and sleep in clover. In short (saving, alas! a finer sky and a drier atmosphere, great ingredients in good spirits), we have the best part of Italy in books; and this we can enjoy in England. Give me Tuscany in Middlesex or Berkshire, and the Valley of Ladies between Harrow and Jack Straw's Castle. . . . The proud names and flinty ruins above the Mensola may keep their distance.  Boccaccio shall build a bower for us out of his books, of all that we choose to import; and we will have daisies and fresh meadows besides."

As he had once pined for Italy and Shelley, so he

now pined for Hampstead and all the loving circle of friends he had left behind, who still kept him his place in their hearts. His sister-in-law Bebs was still apparently his main correspondent, through whom he communicated messages to others. While at Florence, the great question, whether or not she should come out to them, still filled their letters to one another. Now she should, and now she should not. That question of her temper was debated over and over again. A question also of the revival of a mysterious " calumny " in regard to her and him, is taken into consideration. At last Hunt pretty plainly intimates that he is so ill, and his wife is so ill, that they cannot bear anything that would increase the strain of existence, and that unless she is quite sure that her presence will not introduce an element of strife, she had better not come. Then he repents having suggested such a possibility, and bids her consult her friends on the subject of the " calumny," and it all ends by her not coming.

All through this correspondence with Elizabeth Kent there runs an undoubted strain of strong affection. Though she sends him money to Genoa, he will not take it. The *Liberal* will soon supply him with funds, he can draw on his brother for £100, he is in no present need. So her bankbill goes back to her.

And this should be noted by any one who wishes to thoroughly solve the curious problem of Leigh Hunt's conscience in pecuniary matters. He will take money, and glory in it, from a true friend like Shelley ; he will take it, though not willingly, but without any sense of obligation from Byron, because he thinks it only his due under their compact ; and he will refuse it from his sister-in-law because she is poor and he loves her.[1] He not only sends her back her money, but he tries to help her in making more.   He gives her advice about her book (" Flora Domestica "), suggests mottoes, and books for consultation, and sends her translations from Latin and Greek poets.   Here is a paraphrase from Meleager, perhaps the prettiest of all his efforts of the kind.   It is contained in a letter from Albaro.

> " A flowery crown will I compose,
>     I'll weave the crocus, weave the rose ;
>     I'll weave narcissus, newly wet,
>     The hyacinth and violet ;
>     And myrtle shall supply me green,
>     And lilies laugh in light between :
>     That the rich tendrils of my beauty's hair
> May burst into their crowning flowers, and light the painted air."

" This delicious little Greek poem," he says, " is one of those which I always seem to scent the very odour of, as if I held a bunch of flowers to my face."

Altogether it is to be gathered that some of his happiest hours in Italy were spent in writing to Elizabeth Kent, and that his mind was never so tranquil or healthy as when it was set towards those he had left behind in England.   No doubt they did not forget him, but in his published correspondence there are few letters except those which he himself wrote.   The exceptions are, however, notable.   Mrs. Shelley writes : " You must know that Southey has attacked Elia's religion in the *Quarterly*, and whined over the fate of T. L. H.

[1] He also refused money from Trelawny.

(my favourite child) " [this, of course, was Thornton Hunt, to whom Lamb had written verses] " for not having better religious principles installed into him. This roused Lamb," &c. Then follows a full account of Lamb's famous " Letter of Elia to Robert Southey, Esq." (published in the *London Magazine*, October, 1823). Mrs. Shelley's letter must have been a great pleasure to Hunt, and it must have been a delightful day which brought to Florence from Mrs. Novello the account of a grand meeting at their house to celebrate his birthday (1823). " Miss Kent " was not in town, but there was Mrs. Shelley and Mrs. Williams, and the Gliddons and Charles Cowden Clarke, E. Holmes, H. Robertson, and others.

" Our room is decked, I know, to your taste, and worthy of him who taught us to enjoy the pleasures within our reach ; for though I always loved flowers, yet I was not easily pleased but with the finest, until you taught me the value of green boughs. We had bay in honour of our poet, laurustinus, Cuba japonica, &c. Our friends were with us at one in the day, excepting those who were at Smith Street, and who joined us between five and six. Then our day fairly began ; your name ran through the room like a charm, and your spirit seemed to animate them all, as though they could not better manifest their devotion, an universal spirit of enjoyment broke loose ; puns, good and bad—badinage, raillery, compliments ; but, above all, music was triumphant. We began with some of the most delightful motetts—Mozart, Haydn, Handel,

Beethoven . . . finishing with 'Connoscete,' until nearly midnight.  You may imagine the merry supper that succeeded, further aided by a dozen of champagne (British), which C. C. and E. H. sent in to assist the gaiety and to drink your health worthily.  Your health *was* drunk *con amore ;* and by this time, being pretty well elated with so many excitements, they sang round the table 'Beriamo,' 'How sweet is the Pleasure,' and many other musical merriments ; in short, they were in 'excellent fooling,' and declared unanimously that such an evening had never been spent before. Indeed, it only rates second to the Twelfth-night, and much reminded us of that meeting ; yet so closely allied, as you well know, are pleasures and pain, that several times, particularly during the singing of ' Ah, Perdona,' many tears were shed by friendly eyes.  Our cordial visitors are now journeying homewards.  My cavaliers are all gone to bed, and I am delightfully employed, endeavouring to give you an idea of our pleasure.  I wish you could get this to-morrow morning ; but at such a distance, as Mr. Lamb says in his letter to Barron Field, the spirit and unction of the thing quite evaporates.  I was haunted so constantly with your image during the evening, that I was almost tempted to believe in the theory, that what we earnestly and intently desire becomes realised.  Is there any chance of seeing you corporally among us again ? Mrs. Shelley playfully tells us we do not love you, or we should go to you. . . . "

No wonder he longed to go to them, but he had to

wait some two years yet, during which time he never
wrote so well as when he wore that " Wishing Cap,"
which gave the name to his papers in the *Examiner*.
His only other compositions of any importance be
longing to this period were his satire on Gifford (1823),
called " Ultra-crepidarius," which, however deserved,
was in bad taste and clumsy, and his very vigorous
translation of Redi's " Bacco in Toscana " (1825),
which was dedicated to his brother John.

The " Wishing Caps " afterwards formed part of his
volumes called " The Town," and " Men, Women, and
Books," and belong to the class of literary work most
congenial to him—a class to which he was hereafter
to devote himself mainly for the rest of his life—the
essays of a literary Epicure ; criticism of books, reflections, moral and sentimental, suggested by or quoted
from books ; gossip historical and topographical culled
from books—flowers, in a word, from the garden of
books.

# CHAPTER X.

WHAT were the sources and extent of Hunt's
supplies during his residence in Maiano,
history sayeth not ; but his financial affairs were as
usual an anxiety not only to himself, but to his friends,
and Mr. C. A. Brown, about September, 1824, drew
up a complete statement of them, and sent it to his
friend Novello.   He speaks in one letter of his
" annuity " of £100, which was possibly from his
brother on account of the *Examiner*, and he made
something by his papers in Colburn's *New Monthly
Magazine*, and the "Wishing Caps " in the *Examiner*.
But after a while his brother refused to publish the
latter weekly, and their fraternal relations became
strained by a dispute about Leigh Hunt's proprietary
rights in the paper.   This led to arbitration, ultimately
decided in favour of Leigh Hunt, and a lamentable
estrangement between the two brothers, which lasted
for some years.

But by the middle of 1825 the difficulty of finding
funds to return to England was solved by Colburn the
publisher, and on September 8th Leigh Hunt left
Maiano, and turned his face homewards again.   His

friend Novello seems to have assisted in the negotia-
tions with Colburn, which, as will be seen by the
following letter, were very satisfactory to Hunt :—

"FLORENCE, *June* 16, 1825.

"MY DEAR NOVELLO,—This is excellent !—I shall,
then, see you all shortly ! I shall drink tea in the
garden ! I shall hear Clarke's grinding and Holmes's
yearning ! I shall have dear Wilful [Mrs. Novello]
shaking her head, but not her heart, to me, and giving
infinite little laughs ! Sultana the saucy will come,
with 'dear Mr. Arthur !' and, as Mary says, there will
be no stopping the Babel but with music. In fine, I
shall have *mud*. No disrespect to my friends, but you
cannot imagine the reverent idea I entertain of a good
large weltering road full of right English mud, savage
and slush. I require it to take the hot dusty taste of
Italy out of my mouth, as the Irish chieftain used to
roll himself in a quagmire, to get rid of the fever of his
wine. I rattle away, but my delight is deep, dear
Novello, and my gratitude as much so. Colburn has
done all, and more, than I expected ; and I am glad of
the polite and cordial manner in which he behaved. . . .
I shall set him down as the most *engaging* of publishers. What I mean to do for him is infinite, but
I cannot yet speak with regard to theatricals till I
ascertain whether going to the theatre will injure my
health. Pray make my compliments to him, expressing my proper sense of his readiness to accommodate
me ; and say I shall be anxious to make my appearance
in Burlington Street. . . ."

The journey home was unattended by any memorable incidents, but Hunt appears to have enjoyed it. He made a bargain with a *vetturino* to take his party to Calais for eighty-two guineas. This party consisted of himself, wife, and eight children, a number which he characteristically states at "*about* ten," as if he was really not quite certain to a fraction. For this they were provided with a carriage with three horses, occasionally assisted by mules, with two meals a day, five beds at night, and four days of rest when and where Leigh Hunt chose, without further expense. They went by Bologna, Modena, Parma, and Turin, where Hunt saw De' Martini, "the finest dancer I had ever seen." At Chambéry he went to the house where Rousseau and Madame de Warens had lived, and picked a slip of evergreen for "Dearest Bebs." They did not get a sight of Mont Blanc till they had passed Lyons, when at a turning it appeared suddenly behind them, looking "like a turret in the sky, amber-coloured, golden, belonging to the wall of some ethereal world. This, too, is in our memories for ever—an addition to our stock—a light for memory to turn to when it wishes a beam upon its face."

For a while after his return to England he lived at Highgate, near to his beloved Hampstead, and thoroughly enjoyed his old habits.

"I used to stroll about the meadows half the day, with a book under my arm, generally a 'Parnaso' or a Spenser, and wonder that I met nobody who seemed to like the fields as I did. The jests about

Londoners and Cockneys did not affect me in the least, as far as my faith was concerned. They might as well have said that Hampstead was not beautiful, or Richmond lovely ; or that Chaucer and Milton were Cockneys when they went out of London to lie on the grass and look at the daisies. The Cockney school of poetry is the most illustrious in England ; for, to say nothing of Pope and Gray, who were both veritable Cockneys, 'born within the sound of Bow Bell,' Milton was so too ; and Chaucer and Spenser were both natives of the city. Of the four greatest English poets, Shakespeare only was not a Londoner."

Of the bright circle of men of genius whom he had known in England, the three stars, Shelley, Keats, and Byron, were all dead. There was still Lamb just released from his long servitude at the Indian House, and Hazlitt, a more uncertain visitor, and Coleridge, whom he often encountered in his walks, and Procter. There were also a number of other old friends, like the Novellos, who were true as steel, and at Highgate he was near the Gliddons, and Mathews the actor, but nothing could bring back the old days. In leaving the *Examiner*, he had resigned his position as a public man, and with it his importance and his power. In Shelley he had lost the best friend—indeed, the only perfect friend—of his life. His wife was a confirmed invalid. He had nothing to do except to fulfil his engagements to Colburn, and little interest in life outside his books, which became more and more to him. A fit of apathy seems to have come over him, and so long as Colburn's money lasted he enjoyed the rest and freedom from anxiety, wrote little or nothing, but let himself drift without an effort to shape his course.

A reference to the Bibliography will show that he published nothing between the "Bacchus in Tuscany," of 1825, and "Lord Byron and his Contemporaries," which appeared in 1828. During this period he chewed the cud of reflection, of which too much was bitter, and what work he did was of a retrospective kind. At last his conscience, aided no doubt by hints from Colburn, spurred him to complete the latter book ; the full title of which was "Lord Byron and his Contemporaries, with recollections of the Author's Life, and of his visit to Italy." The "recollections" form the major part of what was afterwards published as the Autobiography. It seems that his first engagement with Colburn was only for a selection from his writings, preceded by a biographical sketch, and that the account of Lord Byron was an afterthought, to "enlarge and enrich" a work which had been paid for, and was much overdue. It was not a case in which second thoughts were best, except, perhaps, for the publisher. The book rapidly reached a second edition, but it aroused such a storm of indignation against the author, mingled with reproaches of so painful a character, that it probably caused him more suffering than all the former attacks of the *Quarterly*, *Blackwood*, and other enemies put together.

I have already dealt at length with the relations of

Leigh Hunt and Byron in Italy, and their demora-
lising effect upon Hunt's character.  I am glad of this
excuse to pass over somewhat summarily what is
allowed, even by Hunt's most zealous friends, to have
been the most lamentable mistake of his life.  After a
lapse of some five years, all the slights, sufferings, and
injuries, real or imaginary, which he had endured
during those bitter months spent at Pisa and Albaro,
still rankled in his mind—that mind which was generally so elastic and so tolerant.  His unusual powers
of palliation and forgiveness failed him at this time of
trial, and the image of Byron became fixed in his
memory as that of an unfaithful partner, a false friend,
a very monster of selfishness and insincerity.  Though
he and his large family had been to a great extent
dependent on Byron for the best part of two years, he
would not admit that he was under any obligation to
him, and though he had lived as a friend under
Byron's roof, he made no scruple of publishing to the
world the secrets of his *ménage*, and the unlovely
details of his daily life.

The worst note of these " revelations " is not their
supposed " ingratitude," nor even their " ungentle-
manliness," for Leigh Hunt had, perhaps, some
excuses for both of these ; it is rather the pettiness
of the spirit which pervades them throughout.  Their
whole tenour is to make Byron an object of contempt
by means of ignoble aspersions and small stabs.

Although Leigh Hunt attempted to justify himself,
and when he ultimately expressed regret, sturdily
defended his rectitude and sincerity, there is ground

for thinking that even from the first he had doubts whether he was acting from quite such good motives as he professed. His strong asseveration of the purity of these motives in his preface to the first edition, and his evident anxiety throughout it to forestall criticism, are signs of a not too easy conscience.

Our pity for Leigh Hunt, however, for this " blot in his career " should rise above our blame, for it is plain that he was disqualified by nature or circumstance from looking at the matter from the right point of view. His admission that " he wrote in anger, but is angry no longer," is accompanied by a plea as to the lapse of time which had occurred between his connection with Byron and the publication of his book—a plea which would to other people have seemed an aggravation of the offence. Another of his excuses is even worse. " Though I have told nothing but the truth, I am far from having told all the truth, and I never will tell it all. *Common humanity will not let me.*" The humanity of this insinuation is fortunately not common, but there is no doubt that he was sincere in urging both these pleas, and thought them to his credit—all which goes to prove that he appraised the shame of certain actions at a very different rate to that usually accepted. He had a moral code of his own, and on the whole a high one, to which he adhered throughout life with great persistency, and in spite of much temptation and suffering, and to judge him rigidly by the ordinary code of society from which he always expressed his strong dissent, is not altogether just.

Greatly as the publication of this book is to be regretted, its effect with regard to himself may be regarded as salutary. It was a relief. It worked off, so to speak, the poison, or most of it, which had for years preyed upon his kindly nature, and left his heart and intellect free again to expand with genial warmth. Henceforth, though he was still to suffer from some misrepresentation, from impecuniosity, from family troubles, his life was spent in work which was con-genial, mainly directed by his own taste, and actuated by the desire to please and instruct his fellow-creatures.

He abandoned polemics, political and literary ; he abandoned, to a great extent, his ambition, especially as a poet. He settled into the literary man pure and simple. As a poet, he never, excepting in one or two pieces (the celebrated " Abou Ben Adhem " being certainly one of them), excelled his earlier efforts ; as an essayist he wrote little on a par with the best papers in the *Indicator*, but his criticism became more mature, and he developed his power of pleasant gossip about places and their histories till he made his work of this order a fine art and a model for future generations. In such amiable labours playing truly the part of the bird from which the *Indicator* took its name, he spent the rest of his life, till all animosity against him was out-worn, and he became a patriarch of letters, as much loved and honoured by men of all shades of opinion, as he had once been hated and abused by a powerful clique.

In spite of this, or should it not rather be said on account of it, this part of his life is comparatively

barren of material for the biographer.  If it is treated
here with apparent insufficiency, an example, if not an
excuse, may be found in his own Autobiography, where
the last thirty-five years of his life occupy but one-
ninth of the whole.  Fortunately, however, his correspondence and the recollections of others afford means
for spacing out to some degree this meagre record.

As an antidote to the acrimony of the Byron discord,
let us print here some extracts from a letter in which
he plays the far more congenial and characteristic *rôle*
of the peacemaker.  Of the nature of the wound
which it attempted—and with success—to heal, we are
but imperfectly informed, but we know that the occasion which suggested the effort at reconciliation was a
very sad one, the death of his son Swinburne.  It is to
his mother-in-law and her second husband, Mr. and
Mrs. Hunter, that he writes :—


"HIGHGATE, *September* 25, 1827.
"You know what took place on Saturday last with
my little boy.

"I think, if you could see his little gentle dead
body, calm as an angel, and looking wise in his inno-
cence beyond all the troubles of this earth, you would
agree with me in concluding (especially as you have
lost little darlings of your own) that there is nothing
worth contesting here below, except who shall be
kindest to one another.

"There seems to be something in these moments by
which life recommences with the survivors :—I mean,
we seem to be beginning, in a manner, the world

again, with calmer, if with sadder thoughts : and
wiping our eyes, and readjusting the burden on our
backs, to set out anew on our roads, with a greater wish
to help and console one another.  Pray, let us be very
much so, and prove it by drowning all disputes of the
past in the affectionate tears of this moment.  We
cannot be sure that an angel is not now looking at us,
and that we shall not bring a smile on his face, and a
blessing upon our heads, by showing him an harmonious
instead of a divided family.  It is the only picture we
can conceive of heaven itself.  He was always for
settling disputes when he saw them.  He showed this
disposition to the last ; and though in the errors and
frailties common to us all, we may naturally dislike to
be taught by one another, we can have no objection to
be taught by an angelic little child.

"For God's sake, let us say no more of these unhappy disputes, be the mistakes whose they may.  I
speak as one who am out of the pale of them, which
enables me to be calmer than those who are in it : and
if this will leave me without any merit in trying to
put an end to them, compared with those who will
agree to do so (as I am heartily sure it would), the
honour which the others will do themselves will be
only so much the greater.  But what signify such
words among friends and fellow-creatures ?  The question is, not who can have most honour, not even who
has been most right, but who can agree that there
shall be no more question at all. . . .

"When a trouble takes place, of any sort, the best
way is to try and turn it into a good, and make greater

peace than there was before. The question is not of merit or demerit, on which, perhaps, all the circumstances of life being considered, all persons are equal ; but we can be more or less kind to one another."

It is a pity that such Christian sentiments did not animate " Byron and his Contemporaries," which was published after this beautiful letter was written ; but the letter shows his normal nature, the book a transitory disease from which he was slowly but surely recovering.

# CHAPTER XI.

"FOR some time after the return from Italy," says Thornton Hunt, " the family had to undergo a frequent change of residence, leaving Highgate in 1828, and proceeding almost in each year to some fresh abode —at Epsom, at Old Brompton, St. John's Wood, and back to a house within three doors of the old room in the New Road." While at Highgate Hunt commenced a weekly publication called the *Companion*, which was similar to the *Indicator*, and contained amongst other charming papers, " Specimens of British Poetesses," afterwards reprinted in " Men, Women, and Books," and the first of his series of critical selections from the poets. The close of " Walks Home by Night " betrays the fact that he lived on the very top of Highgate Hill.

"But we approach our home. How still the trees ! How deliciously asleep the country ! The watchman and patrols, which the careful citizens have planted in abundance within a mile of their doors, salute us with their 'good-mornings' ; not so welcome as we pretend, for we ought not to be out so late ; and it is one of the assumptions of these fatherly old fellows to remind us of it. *A few strides on the level;* and *there* is the light in the window, the eye of the warm soul of the house—one's home. How particular, and yet how universal is that word ; and how surely does it deposit every one for himself in his own nest."

At Epsom he tells us that "Sir Ralph Esher," his solitary novel, was composed. It is not properly described as a novel, for the story is without coherence and the characters are mere dummies ; it is only a series of clever pictures of the time of Charles II. strung on the threads of two fictitious autobiographies, showing much reading of Pepys and Evelyn, and a faculty for description, but little else of any value.

The *Companion* ran its course from January 9 to July 23, 1828, and after about two years, most of which seems to have been spent in the composition of " Sir Ralph Esher," he started another periodical called the *Chat of the Week.* Its life was short, commencing on June 5, 1830, and ending on August 28th of the same year. At first its price was sixpence, but its success tempted Hunt to enlarge it and increase the price to sevenpence. The Government then insisted on its being stamped, which he could not afford. So he stopped it, and in wrath set up a daily paper called the *Tatler* in its stead. Of this he tells us :—

" I tilted against governments, and aristocracies, and kings and princes in general ; always excepting King William, for whom I had regard as a reformer, and Louis Philippe, whom I fancied to be a philosopher. I also got out of patience with my old antagonists the

Tories, to whom I resolved to give as good as they brought; and I did so, and stopped every new assailant. A daily paper, however small, is a weapon that gives an immense advantage; you can make your attacks in it so often. However, I always ceased as soon as my antagonists did."

So ended for awhile his rest from literary warfare, but this was the last blaze of his old polemical spirit. The price of the *Tatler* was twopence, and it lasted from September 4, 1830 to February 13, 1832. The wonder is that it lasted so long. It consisted of four folio pages only, but he says:

"I did it all myself, except when too ill; and illness seldom hindered me either from supplying the review of a book, going every night to the play or writing the notice of the play the same night at the printing office. The consequence was, that the work, slight as it looked, nearly killed me."

It probably injured his health permanently, and it reduced him to a condition of poverty and indebtedness which must have painfully reminded him of the old days of his childhood. It is to the time shortly after the cessation of his connection with the *Tatler* that the following piteous extract belongs. The letter is dated May 1, 1832, and was addressed to "the friend, who of all others, had most actively worked to mitigate difficulties and surmount them."

*May* 1, 1832.

" . . . You know how many children I have. They are constantly beside me, without my having the least hope of leaving them a penny. All I pray for is to be able to work for them till my last moment.

"My state of health is so bad, that I do not tell my nearest connections how much I suffer from it. I have constantly a bad head, often a bad side, always a leg swollen and inflamed, in consequence (I am told) of the side, and often while I am entertaining others in company, such a flow of melancholy thoughts comes over me, that their laughter if they knew it, would be changed to tears. I never hear a knock at the door, except one or two which I know, but I think somebody is coming to take me away from my family. Last Friday, I was sitting down to dinner, having just finished a most agitating morning, when I was called away by a man who brought an execution into my house for forty shillings. It is under circumstances like these that I always write. I have great *family* sufferings apart from considerations of fortune. One or two of my children, in temper and understanding unlike the rest, perplex me to a degree you have no conception of, and often make me ill and incompetent when other causes of trouble are giving me a respite.

" And I have more troubles and great ones. If you ask me how it is that I bear all this, I answer, that I love nature and books, and think well of the capabilities of human kind. I have known Shelley, I have known my mother. I know my own good intentions, which of course millions partake, and I have other friends who partake of Shelley's kindness, though they have not his means, and who console me for disappointments from others I thought such. And so, dear ——, pardon and think the best of me and my sorry letters, and come and advise me as soon as you can. Ever truly, your obliged and affectionate

"L. H."

It is not stated who this good friend was, but now as always Hunt had many good friends. One of the best of them was John Forster, who, among other kindnesses and notes of appreciation, sent him a copy of the original numbers of Steele's *Tatler*, and printed privately, at his own expense (1832), the manual of domestic devotion, "Christianism," already mentioned, which Hunt had written in Italy, and wrote a preface to it. Seventy-five copies only were printed. Amongst other friends who came to his assistance at this time were Procter (Barry Cornwall), who apparently sent him gratis contributions, Bentham, Dr. (afterwards Sir John) Bowring, and Colonel Thompson, who as leaders of the *Westminster Review* offered to bind up his advertisements without charge in the *Review*. Laman Blanchard and Sheridan Knowles were also among his friends and admirers, and it is pleasant to find that Wordsworth and Moore were among the subscribers to a volume of his collected poems, which was projected in 1831, and published for his benefit in 1832. Wordsworth wrote a letter also (December 19, 1831), in which he trusted that "the consideration of Mr. Hunt, being a man of genius and talents in distress," would prevent the proposal from being taken "as a test of opinion, and that the benevolent purpose will be promoted by men of all parties." The time was coming when such a regard for Leigh Hunt without "test of opinion" was to be general, and this and a letter from Macaulay may be looked upon as its harbingers. The latter wrote, "I do not know Mr. Leigh Hunt by sight; I dissent from many of his opinions; but I admire his talents—I pity his misfortunes—and I cannot think without indignation of some part of the treatment which he has experienced."

Unknown admirers in the shape of subscribers turned up in all parts of the kingdom; but little permanent benefit appears to have resulted. Once, shortly after writing the letter last quoted, his needs were so pressing, that he thought of parting with his dear "Parnaso Italiano," but we are glad to feel that this sacrifice was not made, for when William Bell Scott made his acquaintance a few years afterwards, it was still upon his shelves. He was then living at 4, Upper Cheyne Row, Chelsea, whither he had moved in 1833. "It was unquestionably during this period in Leigh Hunt's life," writes his son, "that he experienced the greatest pressure of difficulty. His embarrassments had been increasing in 1832, while he was in the New Road, but bad as they were then, they became infinitely worse after he had moved to Chelsea." His friends gave him pecuniary help, and an attempt was made by Dr. Bowring and others to procure him a pension, the result being a grant of £200 out of the Royal Bounty. His affairs at this time seem to have been a matter of special care to three friends,[1] alluded to in the following extract as the

[1] Probably Forster, Procter, and Talfourd.

triumvirate ; but his son, who prints it in the Correspondence, does not tell us to whom the letter was written. It belongs to 1835.

" . . . Pray show this letter both to P. and Talfourd, and let me tell the latter in the most private corner of your triumvirate ear (for none but such as you three must know such things), that I have at length got a coat to my back, and can have the face to join his friends. Himself of course I should not fear ; but it takes much nice criticism both of head and heart to judge properly of the public appearance of a threadbare coat ; and it makes me basely uneasy among strangers."

After the breakdown of his health over the *Tatler*, harassed as he was by debts and family troubles, it is no wonder that the next years were comparatively unproductive. In 1832–3 he published in Bull's *Court Magazine*, eight papers called " A Year of Honeymoons," by Charles Dalton, Esq. (reprinted in Professor Knight's " Tales from Leigh Hunt ") ; in 1833 papers in the " *True Sun* " *Daily Review* which have never been reprinted, and six more " Wishing Caps " in *Tait's Magazine*. In 1834 he commenced in partnership with Charles Knight, *Leigh Hunt's London Journal*, a periodical after his own heart. " They say it is to make me rich ! " he wrote to Mr. Hayward. " This is a novelty at any rate."

If it did not bring him wealth it brought him pleasure. For the first time he was able to expand his own best loved self—the self of literary benevolence

free from all ties, political or polemical—to extend
from his library hearth, his right arm with his heart
upon the sleeve, and his right hand open for the clasp
of humanity.  In other words, his delightful personality
had at last free play.  The *London Journal* of Leigh
Hunt has been called the "princeliest" of periodicals,
it was certainly the most personal, the most literary,
the most benevolent of them.  The most personal
because everything in it was of his choice, nearly all
the original matter of his own composition.  The
most benevolent because its object was purely to please
and benefit everybody, including himself; the most
literary because it was pure literature from beginning to end, entirely composed of essay, story, poem,
extracts and accounts of books ; even the advertisement sheet being before long dispensed with in
order that he might chat more freely with his correspondents.  Here and there a touch of science, a few
grains of philosophy, and some drops of moral and
religious tincture, gave variety to the mass, but only
sufficiently to enhance its pleasure to the palate.
It was composed mainly of quotations.  Every week
appeared a preliminary essay, a column or so on
"The Week," and a small "leader" or two, all by
Leigh Hunt, but even these were full of quotations.
He discoursed, in his own pleasant and playful vein of
learned garrulity, on bed, and breakfast, and sleep, on
the last book he had read, on himself, on the Journal,
on dancing and poetry, on belief in spirits and fabulous
animals, on every subject in earth or out of it that
customarily employed his thoughts, touching them all

with playfulness and tender sentiment, with sportive
wit and gay reflection, as the mood came. In "The
Week" he chatted of flowers and birds, and other
matters appropriate to the seasons, sprinkling his
thoughts between abundant extracts of prose and
verse ; and gave slight sketches of great men on the
anniversaries of their births. The other matter was
made up principally of extracts, "Specimens of Celebrated Authors," "Romances of Real Life" (mainly
derived from the "Lounger's Commonplace Book"),
"Passages" from new books, paragraphs called
"Table Talk." In the later numbers he incorporated
Hazlitt's "Characters of Shakespeare's Plays." All
these were, in fact, reprints, selected indeed, edited
sometimes, and accompanied with more or less
(generally very little) of head and tailpiece, and
comment. Such elements, with a few poems "original
or select," and a few original essays by other hands,
notably by the brilliant, but short-lived Egerton
Webbe, constituted *Leigh Hunt's London Journal*,
which was indeed Leigh Hunt himself gossiping and
musing in his library, reading passages from his
favourite authors, and occasionally obliging the company with a recitation of his own works.

The book is such a mine of pleasant reading, and
the spirit that pervades it is so kind and gentle, so
learned and urbane, so interesting and human, and
the essays and comments and notes by the editor are
so full of mild wisdom and sweet thought felicitously
expressed, that its large and friendly folio is still a joy
to the possessors, and has roused one of them to such

enthusiasm, that he has devoted a whole (if rather a thin) volume to its glory. In this book—" Characteristics of Leigh Hunt "—Mr. Lancelot Cross has regarded the journal as a kind of epitome of Leigh Hunt, and rightly so, as it contains the best of him as a man, his best qualities, if not his finest work as an author, and gives us such a complete view of him as is not to be found elsewhere in one volume.

He was fifty years old. He had still twenty-five years to live, but he had reached the summit of life, and could look back calmly on the battlefields of the past. His domestic troubles, indeed, were not over, and his pecuniary embarrassments were still with him, but he had buried the hatchet, and his enemies were fast burying theirs. One of the worst, Professor Wilson, not only expressed privately to him his regret for the injustice he had done him, and invited him to write for *Blackwood* (an offer which was declined), but publicly retracted his old slanders in the pages of " Maga " (August, 1834), and spoke of him in the highest terms. This paper contained the famous sentence : "The animosities are mortal, but the humanities live for ever." His hopes and his faith were as strong as ever, and his charity overflowed. He probably never felt any joy without wishing to impart it to others, and this was certainly the case with his literary joys—the most abundant of all in his life. Even when a boy at school, he could not refrain from giving away the precious sixpenny volumes of Cooke's Poets, and now in the *London Journal* he found full scope for the same kind of charity. He tells us in the first column that "he proposed to furnish ingenuous minds of all classes with such help as he possesses towards a share in the pleasures of taste and scholarship," and, in the second, that "Pleasure is the business of this journal."

"Pleasure is the business of this journal: we own it : we love to begin it with the word : it is like commencing the day (as we are now commencing it) with sunshine in the room. Pleasure for all who can receive pleasure ; consolation and encouragement for the rest : this is our device. But then it is pleasure like that implied by our smile, innocent, kindly, we dare to add, instructive and elevating. Nor shall the gravest aspects of it be wanting. As the sunshine floods the sky and ocean, and yet nurses the baby buds of the roses on the wall, so we would fain open the largest and the very least sources of pleasure, the noblest that expands above us into the heavens, and the most familiar that catches our glance in the homestead. We would break open the surfaces of habit and indifference, of objects that are supposed to contain nothing but so much brute matter or common-place utility, and show what treasures they conceal. Man has not yet learnt to enjoy the world he lives in ; no, not the hundred-thousand-millionth part of it ; and we would fain help him to render it productive of still greater joy, and to delight or comfort himself in his task as he proceeds. We would make adversity hopeful, prosperity sympathetic, all kinder, richer, and happier. And we have some right to assist in the endeavour, for there is scarcely a single joy or sorrow within the experience of our fellow-creatures, which we have not tasted ; and the belief in the good and beautiful has never forsaken us. It has been medicine to us in sickness, riches in poverty, and the best part of all that ever delighted us in health and success."

Now he began at last to reap the fruit of this charity of heart which had animated him through life, and the founder of the *Indicator* and the *Tatler*, while he indicated and tattled to his heart's content in the pages of the *London Journal*, received expressions of good-will, appreciation, and respect from all sides. In the fourth number he was able to print a long congratulatory letter from one who, if he had been of a less generous nature, might have been inclined to entertain anything but friendly feelings towards the new journal and its editor. This was Mr. Robert Chambers, who, with his brother, had started their famous *Edinburgh Journal* about two years before. In this letter he states, as the chief of his reasons for addressing him, Hunt's " kind nature," as exemplified in his writings, which prove him " the friend of all mankind."

But the circulation of the *Journal*, though promising at first, was doomed to wane before long, like that of all Leigh Hunt's literary periodicals. In his Autobiography he says that the note which it struck was " of too æsthetical a nature for cheap readers in those days." It is also probable that it was too entirely literary ; too much composed of quotations ; too much, in spite of its variety, permeated with the spirit of an individual. At the same time it should be noted that in a letter to Mr. Thomas Weller (Jan. 16, 1836) he attributes its termination to "some mysteries of partnership" which he cannot explain, and proposes to renew it under a similar title ; a project which was attempted, with little success, in 1850. But though the *Journal* came to an end in August, 1835, after less than seventeen months of existence, it was not all labour in vain, for it contained the principal matter of several of his most popular books, notably "The Seer" (1840–41) ; "Imagination and Fancy" (1844) ; "Wit and Humour" (1846) ; and "The Town" (1848), most of which was published in the supplement of the *Journal* under the title of "The Streets of London."

Though it was too late in his life for fresh influences to have much effect on his character or his writings, he still had his eyes clear to detect fresh talent, and his heart open for new friendships. In the *Journal* he had detected the genius of the author of the "Revolution-ary Epic," and had brought to notice the brilliant talent of Egerton Webbe, and welcomed Hugh Miller's "Legends and Scenes of the North of Scotland" as the work of a man who "will infallibly be well known." The reproduction from *Fraser* of Carlyle's tribute to the memory of Irving, if not to be reckoned as one of his discoveries of genius, shows at least his impar-tiality, as *Fraser* was numbered among his enemies ; and it also marks his friendship with Carlyle, which is principally associated with the Chelsea days, though it began a little before either he or Carlyle lived there. Hunt sent him a copy of "Christianism" in February,

1832, and they met in London for the first time on the 20th of the same month. Here also he appears to have made the acquaintance of Robert Browning. The Correspondence of this period contains some interesting letters from Talfourd, Egerton Webbe, and Walter Savage Landor, who was helping him in the editorship and contributing to the pages of the *Monthly Repository*, a magazine which was conducted by Leigh Hunt for a short time in 1837–8. Among his other correspondents were John Forster, Charles Ollier (of course), and two apparently new literary friends, Mr. J. G. de Wilde and Mr. J. W. Dalby. To the latter he writes (June 29, 1836), "Thank God, my pen never felt stronger for prose or verse (such as they are)—never so strong, I think, for the latter. Pardon this vanity ; but with certain kinds of friends one thinks out loud."

His poems of the period scarcely justify such complacency, if we except the remarkable verses on Paganini ("the pale magician of the bow"), which appeared in his *London Journal*, and the charming *rondeau* (so-called), "Jenny kissed me," which was first printed in the *Morning Chronicle* in November, 1838. As he penned the passage just quoted he was probably thinking not so much of such minor efforts as of the "Blue Stocking Revels," which he composed about this time, and published in the *Monthly Repository*, and of "Captain Sword and Captain Pen," a contrast between Peace and War, full of terrible pictures of the battle-field, which had been published in 1835, with a dedication to Lord Brougham. He appears to have had a. particular fondness for both these compositions, as he devotes several pages to them in his scant account of his later years. " The latter," he says, " gave him a sense of his advance in imaginative culture," but its composition was attended by such distress of mind that nothing but a sense of duty could have enabled him to persist in writing it. He adds with characteristic frankness, both as to his mind and body: " I have implied this before ; but I will now state, for reasons which may be of service, that I was several times forced to quit my task by accesses of wonder and horror so overwhelming, as to make me burst out in perspirations (a thing very difficult in me to produce), and that nothing but the physical relief thus afforded me, the early mother-taught lesson of subjecting the one to the many, and perhaps the habit of thinking the best in worst, and believing that everything would, somehow or other, come right at last, could have given me courage enough to face the subject again."

Truly the child is father to the man. Could any other individual have ever thus associated perspiration with his mother's moral teaching, except this same Leigh Hunt, who looked upon his bilious attacks with affection because they were inherited from the same parent (see p. 23). He tells that there were three passages in particular which tried him in a degree almost unbearable :—

" One was that in which the shriek of the horse is noticed ; another, the description of the bridegroom lying by the ditch, sabred, and calling for water ; and the third, the close of the fourth canto, where the

horriblest thing occurs, that maddens a taken city.
Men of action are too apt to think that an author, and
especially a poet, dares and undergoes nothing as he
peacefully sits by his fireside 'indulging his muse.'
But the muse is sometimes an awful divinity. With
truest devotion, and with dreadful necessity for patience,
followed by what it prayed for, were the last three lines
of that canto written :—

> "O God! let me breathe, and look up at the sky.
> Good is as hundreds, evil as one :
> Round about goeth the golden sun."

If he had written more lines like these Leigh Hunt
might have been reckoned among the great poets, but
unfortunately he did not, and the most abundant perspiration (even when difficult to produce) will not supply the place of another very similar word. Practised
versifier as Leigh Hunt was, and charming as many
of his poems are, he nearly always failed when he
attempted to convey strong emotion in verse. To
this rule "Captain Sword and Captain Pen" is no
exception, in spite of the sincerity of the feeling and
the strength of the language. The verse also, with
the exception of a few lines, is doggerel. Here, for
instance, is one of the passages which tried him "in a
degree almost unbearable"—and, it may be added, has
tried many a reader in a similar degree :—

> "Two noble steeds lay side by side,
> One cropped the meek grass ere it died ;
> Pang-struck it struck t'other, already torn,
> And out of its bowels that shriek was born."

No wonder many lovers of poetry and excellent critics, including Mr. Saintsbury, get little joy from Leigh Hunt's muse.

"Blue Stocking Revels" was a sort of female companion to the "Feast of the Poets," but, although sprightly, it was much inferior as a literary performance, and sadly defective in good taste. Leigh Hunt, indeed, deserved well of the ladies, for he was their constant friend and champion, claiming for them equal consideration with men as intellectual and social beings, in days when "women's rights" were generally ridiculed. He thought no pleasure, not even that of calm enjoyment of a beautiful view, complete without their society. We know that he was not only esteemed and loved, but even reverenced, by such women as Mrs. Shelley, Mrs. Browning, and Mrs. Cowden Clarke, to mention no more. But the ill-bred personalities, in which he too often indulges when writing about women, were apparently due to an inherent defect in taste, which no culture or experience could eradicate.

How blind Leigh Hunt was to this is shown by his defence of the following lines in the "Blue Stocking Revels," which relate to Lady Blessington :—

> " 'Lady Blessington !' cried the glad usher aloud,
> As she swam through the doorway, like moon from a cloud.
> I know not which most her face beam'd with,—fine creature !
> Enjoyment, or judgment, or wit, or good-nature.
> Perhaps you have known what it is to feel longings
> To pat buxom shoulders at routs and such throngings ;—
> Well,—think what it was, at a vision like that !
> A Grace after dinner !—a Venus grown fat."

Hunt says he had good reason to know that Lady
Blessington did not take them in an offensive light.
Possibly this is true, but then she knew it was "only
Leigh Hunt."

Though "nobody took any notice" of this *jeu
d'esprit*, he was pleased with it himself, and with a
remark of Samuel Rogers that it would have been
sufficient "to set up half a dozen young men about
town in a reputation for wit and fancy." He had
more reason to be pleased with his article on Lady
Mary Wortley Montagu, in the *Westminster Review*
(1837), his first contribution to one of the Quarterlies,
and still more with the success of another composition.

This was his best play, "The Legend of Florence,"
which was written (long before its appearance) in six
weeks, "in a state of delightful absorption, notwithstanding the nature of the story and the cares which
beset " him. When first written it was rejected, and
he wrote another, "The Secret Marriage," afterwards
called "The Prince's Marriage," with the same result.
"How pleasant it was," he records, long after its
production, " to find my rejected 'Legend' welcomed
and successful at another theatre (Covent Garden), in
February, 1840." He adds: "Here I became acquainted,
for the first time, with a green-room, and surrounded
with a congratulating and cordial press of actors and
actresses. But every step which I took into Covent
Garden Theatre was pleasant from the first. One of
the company, as excellent a woman as she was an
actress, the late Mrs. Orger, whom I had the pleasure
of knowing, brought me acquainted with the manage-

ment ; an old and esteemed friend was there to second
her, in the person of the late Mr. Henry Robertson,
the treasurer, brother too of our quondam young
society of " Elders," and every way harmonious
associate of many a musical party afterwards at the
Novellos', and at Hampstead. Mr. Charles Mathews
welcomed me with a cordiality like his own : Mr.
Planché, the wit and fairy poet of the house, whom
envy accused of being jealous of the approach of new
dramatists, not only contributed everything in his
power to assist in making me feel at home in it, but
added the applause of his tears on my first reading of
the play. To conclude my triumph in the green-room,
when I read the play afterwards to its heroine, Miss
Tree (now Mrs. Charles Kean), I had the pleasure of
seeing the tears pour down her glowing cheeks, and
of being told by her afterwards, that she considered
her representation of the character her best performance. And finally, to crown all, in every sense of
the word, loyal as well as metaphorical, the Queen did
the play the honour of coming to see it twice (to my
knowledge)—four times, according to that of Madame
Vestris, who ought to have known. Furthermore,
when her Majesty saw it first, she was gracious and
good-natured enough to express her approbation of it
to the manager in words which she gave him per-
mission to repeat to me ; and furthermost of all, some
years afterwards she ordered it to be repeated before
her at Windsor Castle, thus giving me a local memory
in the place, which Surrey himself might have envied."

The success of this play was all the more pleasant,

because, though he had always had a great inclination to write for the stage, he had a very poor opinion of his own dramatic faculty.   " The Legend of Florence " notwithstanding, this opinion of his own was true. It was the work of a man of great literary talent, of long experience of the theatre as a critic, and of a poet with an unusual gift for the expression of tender sentiment ; but without that grasp of character which alone can give individuality to the *dramatis personæ,* and breathe life into dialogue, it was impossible even for Leigh Hunt to make a great play.   It was again produced at Manchester in 1859, but in spite of many striking situations and pathetic passages it has not retained its hold on the stage.

# CHAPTER XII.

THE rest of Hunt's life was spent at Kensington and Hammersmith in comparative comfort. He received an annuity of £120 from the Shelley family in 1844, and another of £200 from the Civil List in 1847. He enjoyed all the consideration and honour due to a veteran in literature. His assistance was sought by editors of magazines, and he contributed to the *Edinburgh*, to *Ainsworth's Magazine, Household Words, Fraser*, the *Spectator*, and many other periodicals. Much of his time was spent in revising and re-editing former compositions, which were published in many volumes, the most important being collections of his "Poetical Works" in England (1844) and America (1857); "Imagination and Fancy" (1844), and its companion, "Wit and Humour" (1846); "Men, Women, and Books" (1847); "The Town" (1848); "The Religion of the Heart" (1853); and his Autobiography (1850). His life was cheered to the last by the companionship of such of his old friends as still survived, especially Charles Ollier, Bryan Procter, and his ever kind doctor, Southwood Smith. He made many new acquaintances among the younger generation of literary men and women, the most distinguished of whom were Dickens, Thackeray, Mrs. Gaskell, and the Brownings. To the latter he gave the lock of Milton's hair, which had been given to him by an M.D. (see Sonnet published in "Foliage," p. cxxxi), and an intimacy sprung up at once, which is testified by the long and affectionate letters which passed between them (see Correspondence, vol. ii., *Athenæum*, 1883, 2. 15, and *Cornhill Magazine*, May, 1892). His recognition of the genius displayed in Aurora Leigh is not the only instance in which he showed that his eye for literary power and beauty was undimmed. He had the gratification of knowing that he was greatly appreciated in America. Mr. S. Adams Lee made to him friendly and generous overtures, which resulted in the American edition of his poems, and the compilation of his "Book of the Sonnet" (partly edited by Lee), which appeared after Hunt's death (1867). Nathaniel Hawthorne visited him, and William Story, and James Russell Lowell, who has left one of the most eloquent descriptions of his style. Another incident of some interest in this period is a brief but friendly renewal of acquaintance with his West Indian relations. But the time was also marked by two severe bereavements—the deaths of his son Vincent and his wife.

In 1840 Hunt removed from Chelsea to Kensington, a district so well known in connection with him as "The Old Court Suburb." He took a house in Edwardes Square, No. 51, and settled down for over ten years. In the same square, at No. 45, lived his

eldest daughter, Mrs. Gliddon, and her husband, and
his eldest son Thornton and his wife. He arrived
(says this son) " flushed with the success of the 'Legend
of Florence,'" and about this time he had another
cause for self-congratulation in the article by Macaulay
on his first essay at editing an English classic ; if the
plays of "Wycherley, Congreve, Vanbrugh, and Far-
quhar" can be called by so severe a name. In this
year he also wrote a preface to Moxon's Edition of
"Sheridan," and contributed two papers to Kenny
Meadows' "Heads of the People."

In 1841 appeared "The Seer," a title which was
intended to mean "See-er," and not "Prophet." It
bore as motto, "Love adds a precious seeing to the
eyes," and had the following preface, characteristic in
all except its brevity : "Given at this our suburban
abode, with a fire on one side of us, and a vine at the
window on the other, this 19th day of October, one
thousand eight hundred and forty, in the very green
and invincible year of our life the fifty-ninth.—L. H."
The book was a collection of papers from the *London
Journal*, the *Liberal*, the *Monthly Repository*, the
*Tatler*, and "The Round Table." His contributions
to "Poems of Chaucer Modernised"[1] belong to this
year, as well as his "Notes of a Lover of Books," in
the *Monthly Chronicle*, and his first article (that on
the Colman Family) in the *Edinburgh Review*.

His engagement to write in this *Review* was one of
his many debts to Macaulay—a debt which was soon

[1] Edited by R. H. Horne, who has left one of the best accounts
of Leigh Hunt in " A New Spirit of the Age."

increased by his services as a peace-maker between the editor and his contributor.   After the article was published a correspondence ensued with regard to further contributions, and Macvey Napier, the editor, who held strong views as to the "style" demanded to sustain the dignity of the *Review*, wrote Hunt a letter, at which even a less sensitive man might well have taken offence.   It applied the word "vulgar" to some of Hunt's modes of expression, and suggested that the new article should be "gentlemanlike."   At this crisis, feeling that he had been insulted, but not wishing to quarrel, he did the wisest thing he could—he appealed to his "big brother" Macaulay, who arranged the difficulty with the finest tact, without the least insincerity to either of his friends, and without compromising the dignity of either.   Room must be found for one admirable passage in Macaulay's letter to Hunt, which indeed puts the whole matter in a nutshell.

 " His [Napier's] taste in composition is what would commonly be called classical,—not so catholic as mine, nor so tolerant of those mannerisms which are produced by the various tempers and trainings of men, and which, within certain limits, are, in my judgment, agreeable.   Napier would thoroughly appreciate the merit of a writer like Bolingbroke, or Robertson ; but would, I think, be unpleasantly affected by the peculiarities of such a writer as Burton, Sterne, or Charles Lamb.   He thinks your style too colloquial ; and, no doubt, it has a very colloquial character.   I wish it to retain that character, which to me is exceedingly pleasant. But I think that the danger against which you have to guard is excess in that direction. Napier is the very man to be startled by the smallest excess in that direction. Therefore I am not surprised that, when you proposed to send him a *chatty* article, he took fright, and recommended dignity and severity of style ; and care to avoid what he calls vulgar expressions, such as *bit*. The question is purely one of taste. It has nothing to do with the morals or the honour."

So the matter was arranged, and Leigh Hunt went on contributing to the *Edinburgh Review*, where his articles on " The Colman Family " (already referred to), " Pepys' Memoirs," " Life and Letters of Madame de Sevigné," and " George Selwyn and his Contemporaries," appeared in the years 1841-44.

Hunt's desire for peace and reconciliation was also shown by a letter he addressed (June 8, 1841) to Thomas Moore, who had republished some old verses which attacked him.

About this time Southey was not expected to live, and Macaulay thought that Leigh Hunt might succeed him as Poet Laureate. The proposition no doubt pleased Hunt greatly. Wordsworth had sunk again in his estimation, and there was no other living poet of his own generation whose rivalry he need have feared. It would have been pleasant also to have taken Southey's place. His estimation of his own poetry had gradually become more and more modest, but he had never fallen so low in his own opinion as to rate himself below Southey. Here he drew always a most decided line.

He would have had no scruple in accepting the post
on political grounds, for he was never violently opposed
to monarchy as an institution, still less to the acceptance of patronage. He had now received two grants
from the Royal Bounty of £200 each, one from William
IV. and the other from Queen Victoria. Even towards
George IV. his feelings became kindly, and with the
latter's death all personal hostility to the occupants of
the throne had ceased. Towards Queen Victoria his
feelings had grown very warm since her visits to
Covent Garden to see the " Legend of Florence," and
he had celebrated her birthday in 1840, and the birth
of the Princess Royal, in verses loyal and tender, but
familiar and patronising (*Morning Chronicle*, May 28
and November 25, 1840). " Blest be the Queen," he
sang—

> " Blest when the sun goes down;
> When rises, blest. May love line soft her crown.
> May Music's self not more harmonious be,
> Than the mild manhood by her side, and she.
> May she be young for ever—ride, dance, sing,
> 'Twixt cares of state carelessly carolling,
> And set all fashions healthy, blithe, and wise,
> From whence good mothers and glad offspring rise.
> May everybody love her. May she be
> As brave as Will, yet soft as Charity ;
> And on her coins be never laurel seen,
> But only those fair peaceful locks serene,
> Beneath whose waving grace first mingle now
> The ripe Guelph cheek and good straight Coburg brow,
> Pleasure and reason."

The familiarity of this poem is nothing to that of
the other, which is very pretty notwithstanding. In

1842 he sent to the Queen a copy of his new poem, "The Palfrey," a long story in verse, founded on an old French *conte*, readable and lively, but of no great literary merit. Except another poem, "A Rustic Walk and Dinner," in the *Monthly Magazine*, he seems to have done little or nothing in this and the next year, beyond editing the "Hundred Romances of Real Life," which was published in 1843.

The year 1844 was in every way more busy and important. He received what he called "a nice little windfall (say rather a heaven-fall)," in the shape of an allowance from the Shelley family of £120 a year, which he enjoyed till his death. A volume of his poems was published by Moxon, containing "The Legend of Florence," "The Palfrey," "Abou Ben Adhem," and several other pieces not included in previous collections, and another collection, called "Rimini and Other Poems," was published in Boston. In this year also appeared "Imagination and Fancy," a collection of his characteristic papers on British poets. The book is made up of choice extracts, accompanied with critical notices, and explanatory notes, in which the opinions of others are quoted, perhaps more frequently than his own, but the whole of it is pervaded by his exquisite taste in selection, and delight in literary beauty. Of his long-loved Spenser he tells us that "his versification is almost perpetual honey." Of him and Marlowe he declares that "they were the first of our poets who perceived the beauty of words as a habit of the poetic mood, and as receiving and reflecting beauty through the feeling of the ideas." Of Shakespeare he says, "His 'wood - notes wild' surpass Haydn and Bach. His wild roses are twenty times double." He praises Coleridge as "the sweetest of all our poets," and the greatest master of pure poetry of his time. "If you could see it [his poetry] in a phial, like a distillation of roses (taking it, I mean, at its best), it would be found without a speck." Of Keats's "Eve of St. Agnes," he writes, "It is young, but full-grown poetry of the rarest description ; graceful as the beardless Apollo." This volume is prefaced by an essay called "An Answer to the Question, What is Poetry?"—the most valuable of his contributions to the science of criticism. His mind was unsuited to argument, almost incapable of concentrated thought ; but this was a subject which had engaged his attention all his life, and he brought to bear upon it all such powers as he possessed of definition and analysis, with a result not only delightful but of real value. In distinguishing the elements of poetry he employs great care, and clothes his conclusions in choice and beautiful language. In his definition of Fancy, he describes admirably the quality in which, not only his own poetry, but his own prose, chiefly excelled. "Fancy," he says, "is a lighter play of imagination, or the feeling of analogy coming short of seriousness, in order that it may laugh with what it loves, and show how it can decorate it with fairy ornament."

It is to be remarked that in the essay on poetry he quotes the mighty description of "Nimrod" from Dante's "Inferno," which shows that he could appreciate even the sterner of Dante's creations. But he did not like them. He admits that in the infernal line "Shakespeare did nothing like him," but he adds, "it is not to be wished he had." In a letter to Landor he calls him "the great but infernal Dante, whom I am inclined to worship one minute, and send to his own devil the next!" All pictures of pain, all suggestions of punishment after death were always intolerable to him, since as a little boy he had refused to believe in damnation. He thought Dante "one of the greatest poets," but also "one of the most childishly mistaken men that ever lived." Milton's "Paradise Lost" also fell under his ban. While allowing that it includes that poet's noblest flights of imagination, he declares his preference for the verses written by Milton when he was "a happy youth, undegenerated into superstition."

This book, and the similar volume on "Wit and Humour" (published 1846), are justly described by Lord Jeffrey as "jewel cases," and the jewels are not all in the extracts. They show us what Hunt was to literature, "a taster," as James Hannay aptly says; though he might have added, "with a sweet tooth." They show us what literature was to him—a garden of sweet flowers, from which he sucked the honey, or, to amplify Jeffrey's image, a wide romantic shore, on which he wandered, searching with faultless eye for precious stones. All books were to him "Arabian Nights."

It was a story in the "Arabian Nights" that suggested the first of the chapters in the "Jar of Honey from Mount Hybla" (published with a dedication to Horace Smith at the close of 1847), but written for *Ainsworth's Magazine* in this year. Among other delightful things it contains some charming translations from Theocritus, and the "Legend of King Robert," one of those tales of moral sentiment clothed in picturesque fable, of which he was a master. For stories of character he had no vocation, but for an apologue he had no rival. Though in prose, it belongs to the same order as "Abou Ben Adhem," "Mahmound," "Giaffar," and "The Inevitable," all of which might have ranked with "Abou Ben Adhem," if that imp which seems to have been always lurking in his poetic brain had not spoilt them by some uncouth word or unhappy rhyme. To these should be added "Abraham and the Fire Worshipper," though its form is dramatic, and here no saving clause is needed, for it is throughout sustained by language almost biblical in its simplicity. Here is a specimen—

> " For if ever
> God came at nightime forth upon the world,
> 'Tis now the instant. Hark to the huge winds,
> The cataracts of hail, the rocky thunder,
> Splitting like quarries of the stony clouds
> Beneath the touching of the foot of God."

"Imagination and Fancy" and "Wit and Humour" were only two out of the five projected books of the same kind. The others were to have been "Narrative and Dramatic Poetry," "Poetry of Contemplation," and "Poetry of Song or Lyrical Poetry," and it is much to be regretted that they were never completed.

In 1845 he wrote a brief preface to Thornton Hunt's novel—"The Foster Brother";—and in the next year, under the "Catholic signature" of Adam Fitz Adam, he "hebdomadized Table Talk" for the *Atlas*, which his son was then editing. In August (1846) he was at Wimbledon, "on account of a cough of some years' growth." It was there that he received with astonishment and regret the news of the suicide of Haydon, his old estranged friend, who had broken the long silence between them by a hearty note of applause and congratulation on the success of the "Legend of Florence." "There were touches in your play" (he had written) "Shakespeare could not excel," and he told him how he had just written of him in his diary that "he was a man who would have died at the stake for a principle, though he might have cried out like a child from physical pain, and would have screamed still louder if he put his foot in the gutter! Yet not one iota of recantation would have quivered on his lips, if all the elysium of all the religions on earth had been offered and realised to induce him to do so. I suppose we shall meet again at some other epoch. Till then success to you."

In 1846 he made the acquaintance of Mr. Charles Kent. The friendship which sprang up between them lasted till Hunt's death, and has been since testified by a charming book of selections made by Kent from Hunt's works, and published, with an interesting biographical introduction, in Warne's Cavendish Library.

In 1847 his sole publication in book form was "Men, Women, and Books," a collection of some of his

most important essays and papers on all subjects and
from many sources, including the *Westminster* and
*Edinburgh* reviews.

For some time now his circumstances had been
easier. He says, in a letter dated the 10th of January,
which is inserted in the Correspondence (vol. ii. 74)
among the letters of 1855, and probably refers to a grant
from the Royal Bounty of £200, " I shall cherish the
hope of the play's [" The Secret Marriage " or " Lovers'
Amazements "] being only deferred ; which, indeed, is
possible, perhaps probable ; though Phelps leaves the
point in mysterious condition. But what a blessed
thing not to be so anxious about it as I was ! *and what
a beatitude to find myself, at last, actually paying as I
go, and incurring no more bills ! I hardly seem to
have yet recovered the delightful stunning of the security
and the silence !* I received yesterday another letter
from Lord John [Russell], most pleasant and friendly
—in reply to my final acknowledgments."

In February, 1846, he was able to write to Forster :—

" . . . I also want to talk with you very much about
all sorts of things, past, present, and prospective, *in esse*
and *in posse*, among others my hope of soon not having
a single debt undischarged ; and meantime, such as I
have, are most kind and would never press me.

" I have only one remaining to an ordinary creditor,
and he too treats me like a thorough gentleman. Upon
the strength of all this I found myself enabled yesterday to give a few shillings to a poor man in charity, a
luxury that I have not had—God knows how long, and
I seemed in consequence to sit on my chair taller and

nobler. Such tendencies have human beings to mount on little molehills."

It is somewhat disappointing to find, after all this, that he was still £200 in debt on the next New Year's day, but this year brought healing on its wings. On June 22, 1847, he was granted a Civil List pension of £200 a year. This welcome and substantial addition to his income was no doubt greatly due to the exertions of his friends, Macaulay not least, who, however, told him that he owed it entirely to Lord John Russell. At the time when this pension was granted, Dickens had already set on foot a project for the performance of "Every Man in his Humour," for Hunt's benefit. In this scheme, Dickens, Forster, Frank Stone, Augustus Egg, John Leech, George Cruikshank, Douglas Jerrold, Mark Lemon, Dudley Costello, and George Henry Lewes, were associated. Talfourd supplied a prologue for Manchester, Sir E. Bulwer Lytton another for Liverpool, and the performances came off with great success at those places on the 26th and 28th of July respectively. After paying expenses a sum of four hundred guineas remained, which was presented to Hunt. On Sept. 10 a dinner of congratulation was given to Hunt, at which Mr. W. J. Fox took the chair, and Douglas Jerrold and many other literary friends were present.

In 1848 appeared "The Town," the first of those agreeable *mélanges* of History, Literature, and Topography, in which both he and his readers delighted. He improved, if he did not invent, the art of learned, fanciful, and humorous gossip, of which "The Town,"

and "The Old Court Suburb" (1855) are examples
scarcely to be excelled.　The fare is not unsubstantial,
but it is treated with a light hand, and mingled with
a fine taste, like the pasty in Tennyson's "Audley
Court" :—

> " A pasty, costly-made
> Where quail and pigeon, lark and leveret lay,
> Like fossils of the rock, with golden yolks
> Imbedded and injellied ; "—

We learn from a letter dated Nov. 2, 1848, to Mr.
Robert Bell, that at this time he was hard at work at
his play of "The Secret Marriage," which appears to
have been accepted by Webster in 1850, but was never
produced.

In 1849 appeared the pleasant selections in prose and
verse called "A Book for a Corner ;" and in 1850 the
Autobiography, a book which is perhaps his greatest
achievement as a man and an author.　Most of it had
already been published in "Byron and his Contemporaries," and he now brought his recollections down
to date, and revised them in a spirit of universal
kindliness, excepting in regard to Gifford, the only
man whom he could never forgive.　Carlyle called it,
in a letter now in possession of Mr. Alexander Ireland,
the image "of a gifted, gentle, and valiant human
soul, as it buffets its way through the billows of the
time and will not drown, though often in danger,
*cannot* be drowned, but conquers and leaves a track
of radiance behind it."　So much of it has been
woven into this book that it is not necessary to say
more of it here.

The close of the year saw the commencement of Leigh Hunt's last effort as an editor of a periodical. *Leigh Hunt's Journal*, before referred to, began on Dec. 7, and ended on March 22 in the following year. In it appeared "Lover's Amazements," the second and last of Leigh Hunt's published dramas. This comedy, which should rather have been called "Lover's Confusions," is full of vivacious dialogue, but has no great merit as a play. It was produced at the Lyceum Jan. 20, 1858. Its reception gave Hunt great pleasure. He tells us, "The audience called for me with the same fervour as on the appearance of the 'Legend of Florence,' and I felt myself again, as it were, in the warm arms of my fellow-creatures, unmistaken, and never to be morbidised more." It is impossible not to regret that he did not have a greater share of pleasure like this, which he was so well fitted to enjoy, but his other plays were never acted. Three of them, "The Secret Marriage," or "The Prince's Marriage," as it was called in its final shape, "The Double," and "Look to your Morals," still exist in manuscript, and are described in the Autobiography, chapter xxv.

The close of his residence at Kensington was sadly marked by the loss of his dearest son Vincent. He moved from Edwardes Square to 2, Phillimore Terrace in 1851, part of which year was spent at Ewell for the benefit of Vincent's health. He himself was also ill—so ill that he was never able to go to the Great Exhibition, a sight which should have been specially delightful to him as an augury of that golden age of which he was always dreaming, when war should cease and all nations join hands in brotherly love. Mr. Francis H. Grundy, with whom he and Vincent were staying shortly before the latter's death, tells us that Vincent was the " too willing factotum, amanuensis, friend, son, and servant," of his father, and that his disease (consumption) was aggravated by his riding outside an omnibus or coach in bleak weather to make room for a woman. It is probably to this good-natured imprudence that his father alludes in the following passage :—

" He was just reaching his thirtieth year. He had not lived away from home during the whole time, with the exception of some nine or ten months. He was one of the most amiable, interesting, and sympathising of human beings, a musician by nature, modulating sweet voluntaries on the pianoforte—a born poet of the tender domestic sort, though in his modesty he had taken too late to the cultivation of the art, and left little that was finished to show for it ; and he was ever so ready to do good offices for others at his own expense, that I am not sure the first seeds of his distemper were not produced by an act almost identical with that which was the death of my mother, and aggravated by his first undergoing fatigue in assisting the wayfaring and the poor. For nearly two years I saw him fading before my eyes ; and a like time elapsed before he ceased to be the chief occupation of my thoughts. For nine months it was all but a monomania with me ; and I devoutly thanked Heaven for having twice in the course of my life undergone the like haunting of one idea, and so learnt to hope that it might terminate. I mention this to comfort such persons as have experienced the like suffering. My son's Christian name was Vincent. This is only the second time [written probably shortly before his own death] I have dared to write it. He died at the close of October, in the year 1852, and was buried in beautiful Kensal Green, my own final bed-chamber, I trust, in this world, towards which I often look in my solitary walks, with eyes at once most melancholy, yet consoled."

"The death of my brother Vincent," says Thornton Hunt, "had made a longer residence at Phillimore Terrace too painful," and so Leigh Hunt removed to the smaller house in Cornwall Road, Hammersmith (No. 7), where he was to spend the rest of his days.

In 1852, great annoyance was caused to Leigh Hunt and his friends by the general recognition of himself as the original of Harold Skimpole, in "Bleak House." Taken as a portrait of the man, it cast a slur upon the honesty of his character, which was unjust, and would have been unjustifiable if intended. Dickens's answer to the charge must be accepted as far as it goes. It amounted to this, that he had drawn certain agreeable parts of the character from Leigh Hunt, but never dreamed that the disagreeable parts would have been accepted as being drawn from him also. The plea that he only took the "light externals" from Hunt is not a good one, as Macaulay points out, and it is not even true. Here is a portrait of Leigh Hunt, drawn by himself in his last years :—

" Suppose he has had to work his way up through animosities, political and religious, and through such clouds of adversity as, even when they have passed away, leave a chill of misfortune round his repute, and make ' prosperity' slow to encourage him. Suppose, in addition to all this, he is in bad health, and *of fluctuating, as well as peculiar powers ; of a temperament easily solaced in mind, and as easily drowsed in body ; quick to enjoy every object in creation, everything in nature and in art, every sight, every sound, every book, picture, and flower, and at the same time really qualified to do nothing, but either to preach the enjoyment of those objects in modes derived from his own particular nature and breeding, or to suffer with mingled cheerfulness and poverty the consequences of advocating some theory on the side of human progress.* Great may sometimes be the misery of that man under the necessity of requesting forbearance or undergoing obligation ; and terrible will be his doubts, whether some of his friends may not think he had better have had a conscience less nice, or an activity less at the mercy of his *physique.* He will probably find himself carelessly, over-familiarly, or even superciliously treated, pitied, or patronised, by his inferiors ; possibly will be counted inferior, even in moral worth, to the grossest and most mercenary men of the world ; and he will be forced to seek his consolation in what can be the only final consolation of any one who needs a charitable construction ; namely, that he has given, hundreds of times, the construction which he would receive once for all."

The man pictured by himself in the words in italics was the man whom Dickens disfigured and debased in Harold Skimpole. It cannot be contended that Dickens took only his outward appearance and demeanour, his gaiety of spirits, his brilliant touch on the piano, his childishness in money matters, and other surface items from his model. The picture went deeper than this. Nor was Dickens unconscious of the fact that the resemblance was too close. He was warned of it by Forster, and, when "Bleak House" was in progress, he made many alterations in order to efface the likeness between Skimpole and Hunt. But this tells both ways. If it makes us wonder more at his blindness as to the probable effect of his own creation, it tends to exonerate him from any intention of holding up Leigh Hunt to public derision and contempt. It was only an excessive case of an error to which all creative artists are liable who take their models from living persons. When once done, the injury was irremediable, even by the personal expressions of regret which he hastened to offer, or the public apology which he published in *All the Year Round* after Hunt's death.

It is probable, however, that the incident caused more annoyance to Dickens than to Leigh Hunt, who, it is said, was almost the only person who did not recognise himself as the original of Skimpole, and the appearance in *Household Words* (1853-4) of the papers afterwards incorporated in "The Old Court Suburb" may be taken as a sign that the Harold Skimpole incident did not permanently affect the relations between Hunt and Dickens.

Some portion of this year was devoted to preparing the enlarged edition of "Christianism," which was published in 1853, under the title of "The Religion of the Heart." Hunt himself prized this work above all others for the help he hoped it would afford to the human race in their need for an undogmatic religion, which would narrow the limits of superstition. John Forster thought highly of it, and Hunt himself claims for it that it had been used by his family and others with good effect. It contains a sort of domestic service, and exercises and meditations of the religious character which he describes as Christianism, or, in other words, a creedless Christianity. He himself might be described as a "Christianist," taking the ethics of Christ for his guide, without recognition of Christ's Divinity, and ever hovering somewhere between agnosticism and atheism. The latter he never touched, preserving through life a vague but strong faith in the ultimate working of all things for good, under the guidance of a supreme and benevolent power. If we say that he had a strong belief that there was a God, and that God was good, we shall come perhaps as closely as possible to his religion and rule of life. This is preached throughout all his writings, and often with much more force and felicity of expression than in the volume specially intended for its promulgation. He was engaged in further enlarging this book to the close of his days, and the copy of it on which he was working is now in the British Museum. He proposed again to change its name, this time choosing "Cardinomia," a title under which it is often referred to in his later correspondence.

The following passage, which is inserted to show how, even to the last, Leigh Hunt could enjoy not only old, but new, books, begins with a short account of " The Religion of the Heart."

" One more book I wrote partly at Kensington, which I can take no pride in,—which I desire to take no pride in,—and yet which I hold dearer than all the rest. . . . With the occasional growth of this book, with the production of others from necessity, with the solace of verse, and with my usual experience of sorrows and enjoyments, of sanguine hopes and bitter disappointments, of bad health and almost unconquerable spirits (for though my old hypochondria never returned, I sometimes underwent pangs of unspeakable will and longing on matters which eluded my grasp), I passed in this and another spot of the same suburb by no means the worst part of these my latter days, till one terrible loss befell me. The same unvaried day saw me reading or writing, ailing, jesting, reflecting, rarely stirring from home but to walk, interested in public events, in the progress of society, in the ' New Reformation ' (most deeply), in things great and small, in a print, in a plaster-cast, in a hand-organ, in the stars, in the sun to which the sun was hastening, in the flower on my table, in the fly on my paper while I wrote. (He crossed words, of which he knew nothing ; and perhaps we all do as much every moment, over things of divinest meaning.) I read everything that was readable, old and new, particularly fiction, and philo-

sophy, and natural history ; was always returning to
something Italian, or in Spenser, or in the themes of
the East ; lost no particle of Dickens, of Thackeray, of
Mrs. Gaskell (whose 'Mary Barton' gave me emotions
that required more and more the consideration of the
good which it must do) ; called out every week for my
*Family Herald*, a little penny publication, at that time
qualified to inform the best of its contemporaries ;
rejoiced in republications of wise and witty Mrs. Gore,
especially seeing she only made us wait for something
newer ; delighted in the inexhaustible wit of Douglas
Jerrold, Thackeray, and his coadjutors, Tom Taylor,
Percival Leigh, and others, in *Punch*, the best-
humoured and best-hearted satirical publication that
ever existed ; wondered when Bulwer Lytton would
give us more of his potent romances and prospective
philosophies ; and hailed every fresh publication of
James. . . .

"Yet I could at any time quit these writers, or any
other, for men, who, in their own persons, and in a
spirit at once the boldest and most loving, dared to
face the most trying and awful questions of the time,—
the Lamennais and Robert Owens, the Parkers, the
Foxtons, and the Newmans,—noble souls, who, in these
times, when Christianity is coming into flower, are
what the first Christians were when it was only in the
root,—brave and good hearts, and self-sacrificing con-
sciences, prepared to carry it as high as it can go, and
thinking no earthly consideration paramount to the
attainment of its heavenly ends. I may differ with
one of them in this or that respect ; I may differ with

a second in another ; but difference with such men,
provided we differ in their own spirit, is more harmonious than accord with others ; nay, would form a
part of the highest music of our sphere, being founded
on the very principle of the beautiful, which combines
diversity with sameness, and whose ' service is perfect
freedom.' Nobody desires an insipid, languid, and
monotonous world, but a world of animated moral
beauty equal to its physical beauty, and a universal
church, embracing many folds."

Of his private life during his later years (1840–59)
Leigh Hunt himself tells us little, but we obtain many
glimpses of it from other sources—especially his Correspondence edited by his son Thornton. His family
troubles were many and deep. Some "not to be
told," as his son says, and over the rest a veil,
here at least, may well be drawn. Absorbed in his
books, he appears to have paid little more attention
to his children than to his accounts, but his letters
testify,—especially those to Vincent, and Jacintha
(Mrs. Cheltnam), and Walter Leigh Hunt,—to the
warmth of his affection as a father and a grandfather. He evidently did not go out much, became
more and more of " a closet man," living mainly in his
library, and taking his exercise by pacing a regular
number of times up and down the room, occasionally
going out to tea with an intimate friend like Ollier,
Procter, or Forster, or having a few friends to see him
in the evening. Some of the side-lights thrown upon
his *ménage* and manners are not altogether pleasant,

telling of weakness, and vanity, and questionable
taste.   Francis H. Grundy, in " Pictures of the Past,"
shows him to us sitting surrounded by adoring ladies
who stroked his long white hair.   Mrs. Carlyle tells of
still more tender caresses—"smacks" she calls them—
heartily administered to a lady, neither young nor
beautiful, who, after a very short acquaintance, had
dosed him with flattery (not that Mrs. Carlyle had
any right to be severe on this point if, as is said, she
was the Jenny of " Jenny kissed me ").   Carlyle himself has given some disagreeable glimpses of Hunt's
disorderly establishment at Chelsea, and his habit of
expecting loans.   In short, even his friends must
admit that he was a careless father, that his views of
meum and tuum were eccentric, and his customs not
always those ot May Fair.

   But we have pleasanter pictures of him than these,
some from the same hands, and many a trustworthy
witness to the kindness and honesty of his character,
to the purity and sweetness of his manners.   Bryan
Procter says (" Recollections of Men and Letters ") :
" During an intimacy of many [forty] years, I never
heard him utter an oath, although they were then
very common ;  and I never heard from him an
indelicate hint or allusion."   Charles Dickens bears
witness that he, " in all public and private transactions,
was the very soul of truth and honour " (*All the Year
Round*, December 24, 1859).   Carlyle averred that
he was " a man of the most indisputably superior
worth ; *a Man of Genius* in a very strict sense of that
word, and in all the senses which it bears or implies ;

of brilliant varied gifts, of graceful fertility, of clear-
ness, lovingness, truthfulness ; of childlike open character ; also of most pure, and even exemplary piivate
deportment." Other such testimonies are not wanting,
and will be found garnered in Mr. Alexander Ireland's
" List of the Writings of William Hazlitt and Leigh
Hunt, &c." To the portraits of Leigh Hunt already
given let us add two (in the Chelsea days), by that
incomparable portrait painter Carlyle, and another,
about 1855, a few years before his death, by Nathaniel
Hawthorne, who was not the less able to appreciate
him because he was an American.

In one of Carlyle's letters of 1834, printed in Froude's
" Carlyle," we are introduced to Hunt in his dirty, disorderly house, " a poetical Tinkerdom," where "the
noble Hunt receives you in the spirit of a king,
apologises for nothing, places you in the best seat,
takes a window-sill himself if there is no other, and
then folding closer his loose-flowing ' muslin cloud ' of
a printed night-gown in which he always writes,
commences the liveliest dialogue on philosophy and
the prospects of man (who is to be beyond measure
' happy ' yet) : which again he will courteously terminate the moment you are bound to go."

In Carlyle's " Reminiscences " we read :—

" Our commonest evening sitter, for a good while,
was Leigh Hunt, who lived close by, and delighted to
sit talking with us (free, cheery, idly melodious as bird
on bough), or listening, with real feeling, to her [Mrs.
Carlyle's] old Scotch tunes on the piano, and winding
up with a frugal morsel of Scotch porridge (endlessly

admirable to Hunt). . . . Hunt was always accurately
dressed these evenings, and had a fine, chivalrous,
gentlemanly carriage, polite, affectionate, respectful
(especially to her), and yet so free and natural. . . .
Dark complexion, . . . copious, clean, strong black
hair, beautifully shaped head, fine beaming serious
hazel eyes ; seriousness and intellect the main expression of the face (to our surprise at first) ; he would
lean on his elbow against the mantel-piece (fine, clean,
elastic figure, too, he had, five feet ten or more), and
look round him nearly in silence, before taking leave
for the night, ' as if I were a Lar,' said he once, ' or
permanent household god here ' (such his polite,
Ariel-like way). Another time, rising from this Lar
attitude, he repeated (voice very fine) as if in sport of
parody, yet with something of very sad perceptible,
' While I to sulphurous and penal fire ' . . . as the
last thing before vanishing."

This picture by Hawthorne is from " Our Old
Home " :—

" A slatternly maid-servant opened the door for us,
and he himself stood in the entry, a beautiful and
venerable old man, buttoned to the chin in a black
dress-coat, tall and slender, with a countenance quietly
alive all over, and the gentlest and most naturally
courteous manner. . . . I have said that he was a beautiful old man. In truth, I never saw a finer countenance,
either as to the mould of features or the expression,
nor any that showed the play of feeling so perfectly
without the slightest theatrical emphasis. It was like
a child's face in this respect. . . . But when he began

to speak, and as he grew more earnest in conversation, I ceased to be sensible of his age ; sometimes, indeed, its dusky shadow darkened through the gleam which his sprightly thoughts diffused about his face, but then another flash of youth came out of his eyes and made an illumination again. I never witnessed such a wonderfully illusive transformation, before or since ; and, to this day, trusting only to my recollection, I should find it difficult to decide which was his genuine and stable predicament,—youth or age. . . . His eyes were dark and very fine, and his delightful voice accompanied their visible language like music. . . . I felt that no effect upon my mind of what he uttered, no emotion, however transitory, in myself, escaped his notice. . . . On matters of feeling, and within a certain depth, you might spare yourself the trouble of utterance, because he already knew what you wanted to say, and perhaps a little more than what you would have spoken. His figure was full of gentle movement, though, somehow, without disturbing its quietude ; and as he talked, he kept folding his hands nervously, and betokened in many ways a fine and immediate sensibility, quick to feel pleasure or pain, though scarcely capable, I should imagine, of a passionate experience in either direction. There was not an English trait in him from head to foot, morally, intellectually, or physically. . . . In response to all that we ventured to express about his writings (and, for my part, I went quite to the extent of my conscience, which was a long way, and there left the matter to a lady and a young girl, who happily were with me), his face shone, and he manifested great delight, with a perfect, and yet delicate, frankness for which I loved him. He could not tell us, he said, the happiness that such appreciation gave him ; it always took him by surprise, he remarked, for—perhaps because he cleaned his own boots, and performed other little ordinary offices for himself — he never had been conscious of anything wonderful in his own person. And then he smiled, making all the poor little parlour about him beautiful thereby. . . . At our leave-taking he grasped me warmly by both hands, and seemed as much interested in our whole party as if he had known us for years. All this was genuine feeling, a quick luxuriant growth out of his heart, which was a soil for flower seeds of rich and rare varieties, not acorns, but a true heart, nevertheless."

In 1855 appeared Leigh Hunt's selections from " Beaumont and Fletcher ; " and a collection of his " Stories in Verse ; " in 1857 editions of his " Prose," and " Poetical Works " were published in America. The latter was revised by himself and edited by his American friend S. Adams Lee. It is the only volume which contains both his published plays. The reception of this book by the American public, and of his play of " Lovers' Amazements " by the London press, were two of the greatest pleasures of his last years. In 1857 he had also an article in the *National Magazine*, " Christmas Day divided between two worlds "—a fragment of a day-dream in the first heaven. And as if to show that all animosity was over, his old enemy Regina (*Fraser's Magazine*) which, by the hand of "bright broken" Maginn, had named him "Signor Le Hunto gran gloria di Cocagna," opened its columns in 1857 to two tales in verse in the manner of Chaucer, called "The Tapiser's Tale" and the "Shewe of Fair Seeming," and published, after his death, an article by him on "English Poetry *v.* Cardinal Wiseman."

At the beginning of this year Mrs. Leigh Hunt died at the age of sixty-nine. They had been married for more than half a century, and she had borne long years of adversity and ill-health without a murmur. Her loss made him feel "to belong as much to the next world as to this." This grief was now added to the melancholy which had tinged his life ever since Vincent's death, and though he still preserved his indomitable cheerfulness, his health was broken, and nothing more came from his pen till January 25, 1859, when the first of his last series of papers, called "The Occasional," was published in the *Spectator*. One of these contained an account of Charles Ollier, who died three months before himself; the last appeared on August 20th, and on the 28th he was dead. "The Occasional" was concluded by Edmund Ollier, the son of Charles, and with his words and those of Thornton Hunt, this account of the life of Leigh Hunt may fittingly come to a close :—

"His life was in several respects a life of trouble, but his cheerfulness was such that he was, upon the whole, happier than some men who have had fewer

griefs to wrestle with.　Death often stabbed him in
his tenderest affection ; and the loss of his youngest
son, Vincent, from consumption, in 1852, was a
calamity from which the father never recovered.
But his darkest clouds had more than a silver lining ;
they had the golden suffusion and interpenetration
of a quenchless sunlight.　In the two volumes of
' Correspondence,' edited in 1862 by his eldest son,
my friend Mr. Thornton Hunt, we see him as those
who knew him familiarly saw him in his everyday
life : sometimes overclouded with the shadow of afflic-
tion, but more often bright and hopeful, and at all
times taking a keen delight in beautiful things ; in
the exhaustless world of books and art ; in the rising
genius of young authors ; in the immortal language of
music ; in trees, and flowers, and old memorial nooks
of London and its suburbs ; in the sunlight which
came, as he used to say, like a visitor out of heaven,
glorifying humble places ; in the genial intercourse of
mind with mind ; in the most trifling incidents of
daily life that spoke of truth and nature ; in the
spider drinking from the water-drop which had fallen
on his letter from some flowers while he was writing ;
in the sunset lighting up his ' little homely black
mantelpiece,' till it kindled into ' a solemnly gorgeous
presentment of black and gold ; ' in the domesticities
of family life, and in the general progress of the world.
A heart and soul so gifted could not but share largely
in the happiness with which the Divine Ruler of the
Universe has compensated our sorrows ; and he had
loving hearts about him to the last, to sweeten all.

"The end reached him on the 28th of August, 1859, in the seventy-fifth year of his age. . . . His health had been failing for some time before, and he died, with entire tranquillity, at the house of his friend and relative, Mr. Charles Reynell at Putney." "It is an interesting incident," says his son, in a postscript to a second edition of the Autobiography (1860), "that his very last efforts were devoted to aid the relatives of Shelley in vindicating the memory of the friend who had gone so many years before him [in connection with the work entitled "Shelley Memorials"]. His death was simply exhaustion : he broke off his work to lie down and repose. So gentle was the final approach that he scarcely recognised it to the very last, and then it came without terrors. His physical suffering had not been severe ; at the latest hour he said that his only 'uneasiness' was failing breath. And that failing breath was used to express his sense of the inexhaustible kindnesses he had received from the family who had been so unexpectedly made his nurses, —to draw from one of his sons, by minute, eager, and searching questions, all that he could learn about the latest vicissitudes and growing hope of Italy,—to ask the friends and children around him for news of those whom he loved,—and to send love and messages to the absent who loved him."

He was buried as he wished in Kensal Green Cemetery, and a monument to his memory (originally proposed by Mr. S. C. Hall, and subscribed for by numerous friends and admirers) was erected over his grave.

It was designed by Joseph Durham, A.R.A., and bears on its front beneath a bust of Leigh Hunt, the appropriate line from " Abou Ben Adhem " :—

" Write me as one who loved his fellow-men."

Though Leigh Hunt's character was simple and his gifts distinct, he is not easy to class either as an author or a man. His literary pretensions were well summed up by Charles Lamb in the couplet—

" Wit, poet, proseman, party man, translator,
Hunt, thy best title yet is ' Indicator.' "

With a nature filled with poetry, but yet most faulty as a poet ; learned beyond the average, but hardly a scholar ; full of sweet thoughts, but no thinker ; vivacious and sportive to an extraordinary degree, yet falling short of supreme qualities as a humourist, . Leigh Hunt scarcely attained to the first rank of writers, except as a sentimentalist, an anthologist, and a gossip, yet he so nearly touched it at so many points, and there is such a special quality in almost everything he wrote, that one hesitates to set him in a duller circle.

When we consider his character similar difficulties beset us. Not quite a martyr, for his sufferings were too self-provoked ; far too self-indulgent to be wor-shipped as a saint ; with too little backbone for a hero, yet when seen in a kindly light, he had some touches of them all.

At least it can be said, as James Hannay said, that

he was the finest belles-lettrist of his day. Few writers have given more pleasure or worked harder in the cause of humanity, few men have shown such an example of truthfulness and cheerfulness under the most trying circumstances. For these reasons alone Leigh Hunt deserves to be honoured much and loved still more.

It was hard to take leave of Hunt when he was alive : it is hard to take leave of him now when he is dead, without at least wishing him well. In spite of all creeds we cannot entirely dissociate the happiness of lost friends from the pleasures in which they most delighted on earth, and in moments of unfettered fancy it is pleasant to think of him in some sweet Elysian field, dressed in a very clean and flowery dressing-gown, surrounded by "real English" trees, far from riot and arithmetic, just lifting his eyes from a book—his face beaming with love and literature.

THE END.

# INDEX.

———•—

16                                   241

S. A. Lee. 2 vols. Boston, 1866, 16mo.

Favourite Poems. Illustrated. Boston, 1877, 16mo.

The Poetical Works of Leigh Hunt, etc. London [1883], 8vo.
Part of "Moxon's Popular Poets."

The Poetical Works of Leigh Hunt and Thomas Hood. Edited, with introduction, by J. H. Panting. London [1889], 8vo.
One of "The Canterbury Poets."

Juvenilia; or, a Collection of Poems. Written between the ages of twelve and sixteen. London, 1801, 8vo.

—— Second edition. London, 1801, 8vo.

——[Third edition.] London, 1802, 8vo.

The Feast of the Poets, with notes, and other pieces in verse. By the Editor of the *Examiner*. London, 1814, 12mo.
Reprinted enlarged from the *Reflector*. Re-issued by Gale, Curtis, & Fenner in 1815.
A second edition appeared in vol. ii. of the "Poetical Works," 1815.

The Story of Rimini; a poem. London, 1816, 12mo.
The third edition appeared in vol. i. of "Poetical Works," 1819.

Foliage; or, Poems Original and Translated. 2 pts. London, 1818, 8vo.

Hero and Leander, and Bacchus and Ariadne. *See* "Poetical Works," vol. 2, 1819.

Ultra-Crepidarius; a Satire [in verse] on William Gifford. (Notes. Extracts from Mr. Hazlitt's letter to Mr. Gifford.) London, 1823, 8vo.

Bacchus in Tuscany, a dithyrambic poem, from the Italian of Francesco Redi, with notes original and select. By Leigh Hunt. London, 1825, 8vo.

Captain Sword and Captain Pen; a poem. With some remarks on war and military statesmen. London, 1835, 12mo.

——Third edition, with a new preface, remarks on war, and notes detailing the horrors on which the poem is founded. London, 1849, 16mo.

Blue Stocking Revels. London, no date, 12mo.
Mentioned in Lowndes. Appeared originally in the *Monthly Repository* for 1837, pp. 33-57.

The Palfrey; a love-story of old times. London, 1842, 8vo.

Rimini, and other poems. Boston, 1844, 8vo.

Stories in Verse. Now first collected. With illustrations. London, 1855, 8vo.

## II. PROSE WORKS.

Critical Essays on the performers of the London Theatres, including general observations on the practise [sic] and genius of the stage. London, 1807, 8vo.
Reprinted from the *News*.

An attempt to show the folly and danger of Methodism. In a series of essays, first published in the weekly paper called the *Examiner*, etc. London, 1809, 8vo.

Reformist's Reply to the Edinburgh Review. London, 1810, 8vo.
Mentioned in Lowndes.

The Prince of Wales v. The Examiner. A full report of the trial of John and Leigh

Hunt, proprietors of the *Examiner*, on the 9th Dec. 1812. To which are added observations on the trial by the editor of the *Examiner* [Leigh Hunt]. London, 1812, 8vo.

Musical Copyright. Proceedings on a trial—Whitaker v. Hime. To which are subjoined observations on the defence made by Sergeant Joy, by Leigh Hunt. London, 1816, 8vo.

The Months, descriptive of the successive beauties of the year. London, 1821, 12mo.

> Appeared originally in the *Library Pocket Book* as "Calendar of the Seasons."

Lord Byron and some of his Contemporaries; with recollections of the author's life and of his visit to Italy. London, 1828, 4to.

——Second edition. 2 vols. London, 1828, 8vo.

——Another edition. 3 vols. Paris, 1828, 12mo.

Christianism; or, Belief and Unbelief Reconciled: being exercises and meditations. [London, 1832], 8vo.

> Seventy-five copies were privately printed.

Sir Ralph Esher; or, Adventures of a Gentleman of the Court of Charles II. 3 vols. London, 1832, 8vo.

——Another edition. (*Standard Novels.*) London, 1850, 8vo.

The Indicator and the Companion, a miscellany for the fields and the fire-side. 2 vols. London, 1834, 12mo.

> Selections from the *Indicator*, published 1819-21, and the *Companion*, 1828.

The Seer; or, Common-Places

refreshed. 2 pts. London, 1840-41, 8vo.

> Consists of essays which had appeared in the *Liberal*, the *Monthly Repository*, *London Journal*, the *Tatler*, and the *Round Table*.

Imagination and Fancy; or selections from the English Poets illustrative of those first requisites of their art; with markings of the best passages, critical notices of the writers, and an Essay in answer to the question, "What is Poetry?" London, 1844, 12mo.

——Second edition. London, 1845, 12mo.

——Another edition. London, 1852, 12mo.

Wit and Humour, selected from the English Poets, with an illustrative essay, and critical comments. London, 1846, 12mo.

Stories from the Italian Poets; with lives of the writers. 2 vols. London, 1846, 12mo.

Men, Women, and Books; a selection of sketches, essays, and critical memoirs, from his uncollected prose writings. 2 vols. London, 1847, 8vo.

> Collected from *The Westminster Review*, *The Monthly Chronicle*, *Tait's Magazine*, *The New Monthly Magazine*, and *Ainsworth's Magazine*.

A Jar of Honey from Mount Hybla. Illustrated by Richard Doyle. London, 1848, 8vo.

> Originally appeared in *Ainsworth's Magazine*, in 1844.

The Town; its memorable characters and events. 2 vols. London, 1848, 8vo.

——New edition. London, 1859, 8vo.

The Autobiography of Leigh

Hunt, with Reminiscences of Friends and Contemporaries. 3 vols. London, 1850, 8vo.

——New edition, revised by the author, with further revision, and an introduction by his eldest son [Thornton Hunt]. London, 1860 [1859], 8vo.

Table Talk. To which are added Imaginary Conversations of Pope and Swift. London, 1851, 12mo.

"Table Talk" appeared originally in the *Atlas* and other periodicals.

The "Imaginary Conversations of Pope and Swift" formed part of a series entitled "The Family Journal" in the *New Monthly Magazine*, 1825.

The Religion of the Heart. A Manual of Faith and Duty. London, 1853, 8vo.

This is an expansion of "Christianism," published in 1832. A copy of this work is in the British Museum, which Leigh Hunt intended for a second edition. It bears a new title, "Cardinomia; or the Religion of the Heart," and has numerous MS. corrections by Leigh Hunt. Bound up with the volume is an autograph letter of Leigh Hunt's to Mr. Charles Reynell.

The Old Court Suburb; or, Memorials of Kensington, regal, critical, and anecdotical. 2 vols. London, 1855, 12mo.

——Second edition, revised and enlarged. 2 vols. London, 1855, 12mo.

——Third edition. London, 1860, 8vo.

A Saunter through the West End. London, 1861, 8vo.

These papers originally appeared in the *Atlas* newspaper in 1847.

The Correspondence of Leigh Hunt. Edited by his eldest son. With a portrait. 2 vols. London, 1862, 8vo.

## III. SELECTIONS, ETC.

A Tale for a Chimney Corner, and other essays. From the *Indicator*, 1819-1821. Edited [with an introduction and notes] by E. Ollier. London [1869], 8vo.

A Day by the Fire, and other papers, hitherto uncollected. [Edited by J. E. B.—*i.e.*, J. E. Babson.] London, 1870, 8vo.

The Wishing-Cap Papers, now first collected [by J. E. B.—*i.e.*, J. E. Babson]. Boston, 1873, 8vo.

Published also in London, 1874. These papers originally appeared in the *Examiner*, commencing March 23, 1824, and ending October 16, 1825.

Essays of Leigh Hunt. Edited, with introduction and notes, by A. Symons. London, 1887, 8vo.

Part of "The Camelot Classics."

Leigh Hunt as Poet and Essayist, being the choicest passages from his works, selected and edited, with a biographical introduction, by Charles Kent. London, 1889, 8vo.

Part of "The Cavendish Library."

Essays of Leigh Hunt. (Poems of Leigh Hunt. With prefaces from some of his periodicals.) Selected and edited by R. B. Johnson. With introduction, portrait by S. Lawrence and etchings by H. Railton. (Classified Bibliography.) 2 vols. London, 1891, 8vo.

One of the "Temple Library" series.

Tales by Leigh Hunt now first collected; with a prefatory memoir by William Knight, LL.D. London, 1891, 8vo.

## IV. DRAMATIC WORKS.

The Descent of Liberty. A mask.
London, 1815, 8vo.
  A new edition of this work
  appeared in vol. i. of "Poetical
  Works," 1816.
Amyntas, a Tale of the Woods;
  from the Italian of Torquato
  Tasso. London, 1820, 12mo.
A Legend of Florence. A play in
  five acts. London, 1840, 8vo.
Lovers' Amazements, or How will
  it end ?
  Printed in *Leigh Hunt's Journal*,
  January 4, 11, 18, 25 ; February 1, 8,
  15, 22 ; March 1, 1851.

## V. BOOKS, MAGAZINES, ETC., EDITED BY LEIGH HUNT.

### (a) BOOKS.

Classic Tales, serious and lively.
  With critical essays on the
  merits and reputation of the
  authors. 5 vols. London,
  1806-7, 12mo.
The Round Table. A Collection
  of Essays. By William Hazlitt
  [and Leigh Hunt]. 2 vols.
  Edinburgh, 1817, 12mo.
  Reprinted from the *Examiner*.
——Third edition, edited by [his
  son] W. Hazlitt. London,
  1841, 8vo.
——Another edition. London,
  1869, 16mo.
  One of "The Bayard Series."
——Another edition, edited by
  W. C. Hazlitt. London, 1871,
  8vo.
The Masque of Anarchy, a poem.
  By Percy Bysshe Shelley.
  Now first published, with a
  preface, by Leigh Hunt. Lon-
  don, 1832, 8vo.
The dramatic works of Wycherley,

Congreve, Vanbrugh, and Far-
  quhar. With biographical and
  critical notices, by Leigh Hunt.
  London, 1840, 8vo.
——New edition. London, 1849,
  8vo.
The Dramatic Works of Richard
  Brinsley Sheridan. With a
  biographical and critical sketch,
  by Leigh Hunt. London, 1840,
  8vo.
——Another edition. London,
  1846, 8vo.
The Poems of Geoffrey Chaucer,
  modernized [by R. H. Horne,
  Leigh Hunt, and others]. London, 1841, 8vo.
  The poems of Chaucer modernized
  by Leigh Hunt were "The Man-
  ciple's Tale," "The Friar's Tale,"
  "The Squire's Tale."
One Hundred Romances of Real
  Life ; selected and annotated
  by Leigh Hunt. London,
  1843, 8vo.
——Another edition. London,
  1888, 8vo.
The Foster Brother ; a tale of the
  War of Chiozza. A novel by
  Thornton Hunt. [Edited, with
  an introduction, by Leigh Hunt.]
  3 vols. London, 1845, 8vo.
A Book for a Corner; or selections
  in prose and verse from authors
  the best suited to that mode of
  enjoyment; with comments on
  each, and a general introduction. [Illustrated with eighty
  wood engravings from designs by
  F. W. Hulme and J. Franklin.]
  2 vols. London, 1849, 8vo.
——Another edition, illustrated
  with eighty wood engravings,
  from designs by F. W. Hulme
  and J. Franklin. (*Bohn's Illustrated Library*.) London [1858],
  8vo.

Readings for Railways ; or anecdotes and other short stories, reflexions, maxims, characteristics, passages of wit, humour, and poetry, etc. Together with points of information on matters of general interest. Collected in the course of his own reading. By Leigh Hunt. London [1849], 12mo.

Another series by Leigh Hunt and J. B. Syme appeared in 1853.

Beaumont and Fletcher ; or the finest scenes, lyrics, and other beauties of those two poets . . . with notes and preface by Leigh Hunt. London, 1855, 8vo.

Part of "Bohn's Standard Library."

The Book of the Sonnet. Edited [with an essay on the sonnet] by Leigh Hunt and [with an essay on American sonnets and sonneteers by] S. A. Lee. 2 vols. Boston, 1867, 8vo.

One hundred copies were printed on large paper.

The Poetical Works of Percy Bysshe Shelley. With a memoir by Leigh Hunt. 2 series. London [1871], 8vo.

(*b*) MAGAZINES.

The Examiner, a Sunday Paper on politics, domestic economy, and theatricals. [Successively edited by Leigh Hunt, A. Fonblanque, and others.] London, 1808, etc., 4to, and fol.

Edited by Leigh Hunt for thirteen years, and to which he largely contributed.

The Reflector, a collection of essays on miscellaneous subjects of literature and politics ; originally published as the commencement of a quarterly magazine, and written by the editor of the *Examiner* [Leigh Hunt], with the assistance of various other hands. 2 vols. London [1812], 8vo.

These essays appeared as a quarterly magazine, 1810-12.

The Literary Pocket - Book for 1819-1822. [Edited by Leigh Hunt.] London, 1819-22, 8vo.

The Indicator. [Edited by Leigh Hunt to No. 77 of vol. ii.] vol. i., ii. London, 1820-22, 8vo.

Began on the 13th October 1819, and continued to March 21, 1821, when Leigh Hunt's connection with it ceased. A new series commenced on March 28, 1821, and ended on October 13, 1821. Bound in 2 vols., with title-pages bearing dates 1820, 1822.

The Liberal: Verse and Prose from the South. [By Leigh Hunt, Lord Byron, and others.] 2 vols. London, 1822-23, 8vo.

The Literary Examiner : consisting of the Indicator, a Review of Books, and miscellaneous pieces in prose and verse. [Edited by Leigh Hunt.] London, 1823, 8vo.

The Companion. By Leigh Hunt. London, 1828, 8vo.

Commenced on January 9th, and discontinued July 23rd, 1828.

The Chat of the Week, or Compendium of all Topics of Public Interest, Original and Select. [Edited by Leigh Hunt.] Nos. 1-13, London, 1830, 8vo.

The title was changed in the 8th No. to "The Chat of the Week, and Gazette of Literature, Fine Arts, and Theatricals." After No. 13, Aug. 28, 1830, the publication was discontinued, and it was succeeded by the "Tatler."

The Tatler. A daily Journal of Literature and the Stage. [Edited by Leigh Hunt.] 4 vols. London, 1830-32, 8vo.
Commenced Sept. 4, 1830, and Leigh Hunt's connection with it ceased Feb. 13, 1832.

Leigh Hunt's London Journal, No. 1-61. [United with the Printing-Machine, and continued as:] Leigh Hunt's London Journal and the Printing Machine, No. 62-91. 2 vols. London, 1834-35, fol.

The Monthly Repository. Enlarged Series, edited by Leigh Hunt. London, 1837-38, 8vo.
Leigh Hunt's editorship commenced in July 1837, and ended in April 1838, when the work was discontinued.

Leigh Hunt's Journal; a miscellany for the cultivation of the memorable, the progressive, and the beautiful. [Edited by Leigh Hunt.] No. 1-17, London, 1850-51, 8vo.

## VI. CONTRIBUTIONS TO OTHER MAGAZINES, ETC.

*European Magazine.*—Lines on Melancholy, vol. 40, 1801, p. 448.

*Juvenile Library.*—Retirement, or the Golden Mean. By Master J. H. L. Hunt, aged 15: Late of Christ's Hospital, London; a poetical essay, vol. ii., 1801, pp. 118-121.

*Poetical Register.*—Several poems in the volumes for 1801, 1805, 1806-11.

*Traveller.*—Papers signed Mr. Town, junior, critic and censor general, 1804-05.

*The News.*—Theatrical Criticisms, 1805. Reprinted in book form in 1807.

*New Monthly Magazine.*—Contributed essays and poems from its commencement in 1821.—Series of Papers, "The Family Journal," by Harry Honeycomb.—Family of the Honeycombs, vol. 13 N.S., 1825, pp. 17-28.—Beautiful Offspring.—The Town, pp. 166-176.—The Country, pp. 276-282.—Love will find out a way, pp. 353-369.—April Fools.—Perukes of King Charles the Second's Time, pp. 419-424.—New May-day and Old May-day, pp. 457-466.—Conversation of Pope. Dinner of Apsley Honeycomb with him, pp. 548-555.—Swift's Mean and Great Figures, vol. 14 N.S., pp. 41-45.—Conversation of Swift and Pope, pp. 199-206.—A Country Lodging. Dialogue with a Sportsman, pp. 323-332.—The Human Beings killed by the Feathered Monster, pp. 429-431.—Keeping Christmas, pp. 514-518.—Criticism on Female Beauty, vol. 14 N.S., 1825, pp. 70-77, 140-159.—A man introduced to his Ancestors, pp. 343-345.—Specimens of a Dictionary of Love and Beauty, vol. 17 N.S., 1826, pp. 47-59, 136-149, 280-282, 425-432; vol. 19, 1827, pp. 48-54.—To May (poem), vol. 34, 1832, p. 456.—The Indicator, pp. 457-468.—To June (poem), p. 580.—On Giants, Ogres, and Cyclops, vol. 43, 1835, pp. 170-180.—Songs and Chorus of the Flowers (verse), vol. 47,

1836, pp. 17-20. — The Glove and the Lions (verse), p. 40.— The Nymphs of Antiquity and of the Poets, pp. 88-96.—The Fish, the Man, and the Spirit (verse), pp. 190, 191.—Reflections on some of the Great Men of the reign of Charles the First, pp. 207-218.—The Sirens and Mermaids of the Poets, pp. 273-282.—Three Sonnets to the Author of "Ion," p. 448.—A Visit to the Zoological Gardens, pp. 479-491. — Words for a Trio (verse), pp. 491.—Apollo and the Sunbeams, p. 498.— Wealth and Womanhood (verse), vol. 48, 1836, p. 19.—Æronautics, real and fabulous, pp. 49-61.—Our Cottage (verse), pp. 68-70.—Gog and Magog, and the Wall of Dhoulkarnein, pp. 178-181. — Translations from the Greek Anthology, p. 182. — Christmas, a song for good fellows, young and old, pp. 462, 463.—Lazy Corner; or, Bed *v.* Business. A poem from the Italian of Berni, vol. 75, 1845, p. 143. Included in the 1860 edition of "The Poetical Works."—The Inevitable (poem), vol. 88, 1850, pp. 1, 2. —Jaffàr (poem), pp. 143, 144. —Godiva (poem), pp. 285, 286. —The Bitter Gourd (poem), pp. 427, 428.—Ode to the Sun, vol. 89, 1850, pp. 1-3.—Death (poem), p. 143.—Wallace and Fawdon (ballad), pp. 269-271.

*The Keepsake.*—Pocket-Books and Keepsakes, 1828, pp. 1-18.— Dreams on the Borders of the Land of Poetry, pp. 234-241.

Reprinted in Symons' "Essays of Leigh Hunt."

*Court Magazine.*—A Year of Honeymoons. By Charles Dalton, Esq.; Introduction, vol. 1, 1832, pp. 273-277; January, vol. 2, 1833, pp. 37-41; February, pp. 91-94; March, pp. 174-179; April, pp. 250-253; May and June, pp. 304-309; July, vol. 3, pp. 33-35; August (the last paper), pp. 82-85.

Reprinted in Prof. Knight's "Tales from Leigh Hunt."

*"True Sun" Daily Review:* A series of Critical Notices of New Books, Magazines, etc. Commencing 16th August, and ending 26th December 1833.

*Tait's Magazine.*—Articles, being a New Series of "The Wishing Cap," Jan.-Sept. 1833.

*Westminster Review.*—Review of "The Letters and Works of Lady Mary Wortley Montagu," vol. 27, 1837, pp. 130-164.

Reprinted in *Men, Women, and Books.*

*National Magazine.* — Christmas Day divided between two worlds, vol. 1, 1837, pp. 195-197.

*Monthly Chronicle;* a National Journal of Politics, Literature, Science, and Art.

Five articles by Leigh Hunt appeared between October 1838 and February 1839, all of which, with the exception of one, were reprinted in *Men, Women, and Books,* 1847.

*Musical World.* — "Words for Composers"; "Musician's Poetical Companion," eight papers, January 10 to March 21, 1839.

The Romancist and Novelist's Library. Edited by William Hazlitt. 4 vols., London, 1839-40, 4to.

Contains several papers by Leigh Hunt.

*Morning Chronicle.*—To the Queen, May 28, 1840.—To the Infant Princess Royal, November 25, 1840.—Three Visions. On the Birth and Christening of the Prince of Wales, February 8, 1842.

*Heads of the People*, Kenny Meadows', 1840.—"The Monthly Nurse" and "The Omnibus Conductor," pp. 97-104 and 193-200.

*Edinburgh Review.* — Review of R. B. Peake's "Memoirs of the Colman Family," vol. 73, 1841, pp. 389-424.

——Review of "The Life, Journal, and Correspondence of Samuel Pepys, Esq. By the Rev. John Smith," vol. 74, 1841, pp. 105-127.
Reprinted in *Men, Women, and Books.*

——Review of "Madame de Sevigné and her Contemporaries," vol. 76, 1842, pp. 203-236.
Reprinted in *Men, Women, and Books.*

——Review of John H. Jesse's "George Selwyn and his Contemporaries," vol. 80, 1844, pp. 1-42.

*Monthly Magazine.* — Poem; A Rustic Walk and Dinner, vol. 96, 1842, pp. 233-240, 343-346.

*Ainsworth's Magazine.*—A Jar of Honey from Mount Hybla, January to December, 1844.
Reprinted in book form in 1848.

——The Fancy Concert (poem), vol. 7, 1845, pp. 93, 94.

*Atlas.*—Table Talk, March 14, 1846.—Liston, March 28, 1846.—Wild - Flowers, Furze, and Wimbledon, March 25, 1846.—Eclipses, Human Beings, and the Lower Creation, May 2, 1846.—Malice of Fortune, May 16, 1846.—"Table Talk," by Adam Fitz-Adam, Esq., 1846, reprinted in 1851.—"Streets of London," re-issued in book form as a *Saunter through the West End.*

*Leigh Hunt's Journal.*—"Lovers' Amazements" (a play), January 4, 11, 18, 25; February 1, 8, 15, 22; March 1, 1851.
Reprinted in the American edition of his poems.

*Household Words.* — Lounging through Kensington, etc., 7 papers, Aug. 6, 1853 to Feb. 25, 1854. Incorporated in *The Old Court Suburb.*

*Musical Times.*—Inexhaustibility of the subject of Christmas, vol. 5, 1853, pp. 295, 296. (A reprint from the *Monthly Repository*, Dec. 1837). — Twelfth Night, pp. 313-316.—An Effusion upon Cream, and a Desideratum in English Poetry, pp. 333-341.—On Poems of Joyous Impulse. A sequel to the "Effusion upon Cream," etc., pp. 393-396. — Eating Songs, vol. 6, 1854, pp. 37-39.—On the combination of grave and gay, pp. 91-93.—An Organ in the House, pp. 159-162, 207-210.

*Fraser's Magazine.*—Two poems—"The Tapiser's Tale, attempted in the manner of Chaucer," vol. 57, 1858, pp. 160-163; The Shewe of Faire Seeming in the manner of Spenser, pp. 602-610.—An article, "English Poetry *v.* Cardinal Wiseman," vol. 60, 1859, pp. 747-766.

*Spectator.*—The Occasional, a series of papers from January 15 to August 20, 1859.

*Temple Bar.* — "Men are but children of a larger growth," vol. 50, 1877, pp. 386-391.

*Athenæum.*—A long letter from Leigh Hunt to Robert Browning, July 7, 1883, pp. 15-18.


## VII. APPENDIX.

BIOGRAPHY, CRITICISM, ETC.

Carlyle, Thomas. — Letters of Thomas Carlyle, 1826 - 1835. Edited by C. E. Norton. 2 vols. London, 1888, 8vo.
> Numerous references to Leigh Hunt.

Clarke, Charles, and Mary Cowden. —Recollections of Writers. With letters of Charles Lamb, Leigh Hunt, etc. London, 1878, 8vo.
> Leigh Hunt and his letters, pp. 190-272.

Cross, Launcelot [*i.e.*, Frank Carr]. —Characteristics of Leigh Hunt, as exhibited in that typical literary periodical, *Leigh Hunt's London Journal* (1834 - 35). With illustrative notes. London, 1878, 8vo.

Dowden, Edward.—The Life of Percy Bysshe Shelley. 2 vols. London, 1886, 8vo.
> Numerous references to Leigh Hunt.

Dubost, Antoine. — Hunt and Hope. An appeal to the public against the calumnies of the Editor of the *Examiner* [J. H. Leigh Hunt]. London [1807], 8vo.

Fox, W. J.—Lectures addressed chiefly to the Working Classes. 4 vols. London, 1845-49, 8vo.
> Leigh Hunt, vol. ii., pp. 169-188.

Gilfillan, George.—A Second Gallery of Literary Portraits. London, 1850, 8vo.
> Leigh Hunt, pp. 344-352.

Grundy, Francis H.—Pictures of the Past : Memories of Men I have met, etc. London, 1879, 8vo.
> Leigh Hunt and his Family, pp. 162-170.

Hall, S. C.—A Book of Memories of Great Men and Women of the Age, etc. London, 1871, 4to.
> Leigh Hunt, pp. 241-254.

Hannay, James.—Characters and Criticisms. Edinburgh, 1865, 8vo.
> The Correspondence of Leigh Hunt, pp. 219-229.

Hawthorne, Nathaniel.—Our Old Home. 2 vols. London, 1863, 8vo.
> Leigh Hunt, vol. ii., pp. 175-184.

Hazlitt, William.—The Spirit of the Age. London, 1825, 8vo.
> Thomas Moore.—Leigh Hunt, pp. 387-405.

Horne, R. H.—A New Spirit of the Age. 2 vols. London, 1844, 8vo.
> William Wordsworth and Leigh Hunt, vol. i., pp. 305-332.

Howitt, William.—Homes and Haunts of the most eminent British Poets. 2 vols. London, 1847, 8vo.
> Leigh Hunt, vol. ii., pp. 347-367.

Hunt, John.—Report of the proceedings on an information filed against John Hunt and Leigh Hunt, proprietors of the *Examiner*, for publishing an article on military punishment, tried on Feb. 22, 1811. Stamford, 1811, 8vo.

Ireland, Alexander.—List of the Writings of William Hazlitt and Leigh Hunt, chronologically arranged. London, 1868, 8vo.

Liberal, The. — A critique on "The Liberal." London, 1822, 8vo.

M. J.—The true story of Lord and Lady Byron, as told by Lord Macaulay, Thomas Moore, Leigh Hunt, etc. London [1869], 8vo.

Macaulay, Thomas Babington.— Critical and historical essays, contributed to the *Edinburgh Review.* A new edition. London, 1850, 8vo.
A review of Leigh Hunt's "Dramatic Works of Wycherley, Congreve," etc., pp. 556-582.

Mitford, Mary Russell.—Recollections of a literary life, etc. 3 vols. London, 1852, 8vo.
Leigh Hunt, vol. ii., pp. 172-183.

Moir, D. M.—Sketches of the poetical literature of the past half century. Edinburgh, 1851, 8vo.
Leigh Hunt, pp. 209-215.

Moore, Thomas.—The life of Lord Byron, with his letters and journals. London, 1847, 8vo.
Numerous references to Leigh Hunt.
——Memoirs, Journal, and Correspondence. 8 vols. London, 1853-56, 8vo.
Numerous references to Leigh Hunt.

Oliphant, Mrs. M. O.—The Literary History of England, etc. 3 vols. London, 1882, 8vo.
Numerous references to Leigh Hunt.

Patmore, P. G.—My Friends and Acquaintance: being memorials, mind portraits, etc., of deceased celebrities of the nineteenth century. 3 vols. London, 1854, 8vo.
Numerous references to Leigh Hunt.

Procter, Bryan Waller (Barry Cornwall).—An autobiographical fragment and biographical notes, etc. London, 1877, 8vo.
Leigh Hunt and Keats, pp. 195-202.

Saintsbury, George. — Essays in English Literature, 1780-1860. London, 1890, 8vo.
Leigh Hunt, pp. 201-233.

Trelawny, Edward John.—Recollections of the Last Days of Shelley and Byron. London, 1858, 8vo.
References to Leigh Hunt.
——Records of Shelley, Byron, and the Author. 2 vols. London, 1878, 8vo.
Numerous references to Leigh Hunt.

Tuckerman, Henry T.—Thoughts on the Poets. Third edition. New York, 1848, 8vo.
Leigh Hunt, pp. 154-164.

MAGAZINE ARTICLES, ETC.

Hunt, Leigh.—Analectic Magazine, vol. 4, 1814, pp. 73-77.—Blackwood's Magazine, vol. 2, 1817, pp. 38-41.—Fraser's Magazine (with portrait), vol. 9, 1834, p. 644. — Southern Literary Messenger, by H. T. Tuckerman, vol. 7, 1841, pp. 473-477. —Tait's Edinburgh Magazine, by G. Gilfillan, vol. 13, 1846, pp. 655-660; same article, Littell's Living Age, vol. 11, pp. 368-372; and Eclectic Magazine (with portrait), vol. 9, pp. 384-390. — People's Journal (with

portrait), by M. Howitt, vol. 1, 1846, pp. 268-270.—American Review, vol. 4, 1846, pp. 17-26. —Democratic Review, by J. Savage, vol. 27 N.S., 1850, pp. 426-434.—American Whig Review, vol. 15, 1852, pp. 444-448.—Bentley's Miscellany, vol. 38, 1855, pp. 96-110; same article, Eclectic Magazine, vol. 36, pp. 701-709.—Littell's Living Age (from the Spectator), vol. 63, 1859, pp. 213-220.—Examiner, Sept. 3, 1859.—Spectator, Sept. 3, 1859.—Athenæum, Sept. 3, 1859.—North British Review, vol. 33, 1860, pp. 356-380; same article, Littell's Living Age, vol. 68, pp. 29-43.—Cornhill Magazine, vol. 1, 1860, pp. 85-95; same article, Littell's Living Age, vol. 64, pp. 421-427.—Methodist Quarterly, by W. H. Barnes, vol. 42, 1860, pp. 245-260.—North American Review, by G. M. Towle, vol. 97, 1863, pp. 155-180.—Art Journal, by S. C. Hall, 1865, pp. 317-321; same article, Eclectic Magazine, vol. 66, pp. 17-25.—Broadway, vol. 4, 1869, pp. 307, etc.—Western, by C. N. Gregory, vol. 7, pp. 365, etc.—Atlantic Monthly, by Louise I. Guiney, vol. 54, 1884, pp. 467-477.—Scribner's Magazine (with portrait), by Mrs. Fields, vol. 3, 1888, pp. 285-305. — Macmillan's Magazine, by George Saintsbury, vol. 59, 1889, pp. 426-438; same article, Littell's Living Age, vol. 181, pp. 487-496.
——*and B. R. Haydon.* St. James's Magazine. by S. R

Townshend Mayer, vol. 13 N.S., 1874, pp. 349-371.
——*and Charles Lamb.* Athenæum, 1889, pp. 344, 374, 403.
——*and Charles Ollier.* St. James's Magazine, by S. R. Townshend Mayer, vol. 14 N.S., 1875, pp. 387-413.
——*and Dr. Southwood Smith.* St. James's Magazine, by S. R. Townshend Mayer, vol. 14 N.S., 1875, pp. 76-99.
——*and his family.* Appleton's Journal, vol. 7 N.S., 1879, pp. 135-138.
——*and Lord Brougham.* Temple Bar, by S. R. Townshend Mayer, vol. 47, 1876, pp. 221-234; same article, Eclectic Magazine, vol. 24 N.S., pp. 164-172, and Littell's Living Age, vol. 130, pp. 239-247.
——*Art of Love.* Blackwood's Edinburgh Magazine, vol. 12, 1822, pp. 775-781.
——*as a Poet.* Fortnightly Review, by A. T. Kent, vol. 30 N.S., 1881, pp. 224-237; same article, Eclectic Magazine, vol. 34 N.S., pp. 550-557.
——*Autobiography.* North British Review, vol. 14, 1850, pp. 143-168. — Chambers's Edinburgh Journal, vol. 14 N.S., 1850, pp. 19-23; same article, Eclectic Magazine, vol. 21, pp. 247-253.—Dublin University Magazine, vol. 36, 1850, pp. 268-286.—American Whig Review, vol. 13, 1851, pp. 34-53.—Eclectic Review, vol. 28 N.S., 1850, pp. 409-424. — International, vol. 1, 1850, pp. 35, 36, 130-132.—Sharpe's London Journal, vol. 12, 1850, pp. 121-127.—Tait's Edinburgh Maga-

zine, vol. 17, 1850, pp. 563-572.—Spectator, Feb. 18, 1860.

——*Bacchus in Tuscany.* Blackwood's Edinburgh Magazine, vol. 18, 1825, pp. 155-160.

——*Book for a Corner.* Hogg's Instructor, vol. 3 N.S., 1849, pp. 103-112.

——*Correspondence.* Chambers's Journal, vol. 17, 1862, pp. 266-270.—Saturday Review, March 8, 1862.

——*Descent of Liberty.* Analectic Magazine, vol. 6, 1815, pp. 113-118.

——*Feast of the Poets.* Analectic Magazine, vol. 4, 1814, pp. 243-249.—Monthly Review, vol. 75 N.S., 1814, pp. 100-103.

——*Foliage.* Portfolio, vol. 7, fourth series, 1819, pp. 394-402.—Blackwood's Edinburgh Magazine, vol. 6, 1819, pp. 70-76.—Quarterly Review, vol. 18, 1818, pp. 324-334.—Eclectic Review, vol. 10 N.S., 1818, pp. 484-493.

——*Gossip about.* New Monthly Magazine, vol. 81, 1847, pp. 84-87.

——*Hero and Leander, and Bacchus and Ariadne.* London Magazine, vol. 2, 1820, pp. 45-55.

——*Imagination and Fancy.* British Quarterly Review, vol. 1, 1845, pp. 563-581.—Dublin University Magazine, vol. 25, 1845, pp. 649-655; same article, Eclectic Magazine, vol. 5, pp. 500-508.

——*Last Evening at Home.* Dublin University Magazine, vol. 58, 1861, pp. 610-613.

——*Legend of Florence.* Black-

wood's Edinburgh Magazine, vol. 47, 1840, pp. 303-318.

——*Letter to Robert Browning.* Athenæum, July 7, 1883; also in Littell's Living Age, vol. 158, pp. 315-320.

——*Letters to.* Blackwood's Edinburgh Magazine, vol. 2, 1818, pp. 414-417; vol. 3, pp. 196-201.

——*Life, Character, and Work of.* London Quarterly Review, vol. 67, 1887, pp. 331-354.

——*Literary Life of.* All the Year Round, vol. 7, 1862, pp. 115-120.—Littell's Living Age, vol. 73, pp. 585-591.

——*Literary Pocket Book.* Blackwood's Edinburgh Magazine, vol. 6, 1819, pp. 235-247; vol. 10, 1821, pp. 574-582.

——*Men, Women, and Books.* Dublin University Magazine, vol. 30, 1847, pp. 386-397.—Littell's Living Age (from the Examiner), vol. 14, 1847, pp. 188-191.

——*on the Pension List.* Tait's Edinburgh Magazine, by G. Gilfillan, vol. 14, 1847, pp. 522-526; same article, Eclectic Magazine, vol. 12, pp. 118-122.

——*on the Performers of the London Theatres.* Monthly Review, vol. 57 N.S., 1808, pp. 423-429.

——*Poems.* Southern Literary Messenger, by Henry C. Lea, vol. 10, 1844, pp. 619-629.—New Monthly Magazine, vol. 37, 1833, pp. 297-301.—Littell's Living Age (from the Saturday Review), vol. 66, pp. 125-127.—Tait's Edinburgh Magazine, vol. 2, 1833, pp. 630-636.—Macmillan's Magazine, vol. 6,

1862, pp. 238-245.—Monthly Repository, vol. 7 N.S., 1833, pp. 178-184.—Littell's Living Age (from the Examiner), vol. 1, 1844, p. 342.

——*Round Table.* Analectic Magazine, vol. 7, 1816, pp. 278-285.

——*Stories from the Italian Poets.* Foreign Quarterly Review, vol. 36, 1846, pp. 333-354.—Littell's Living Age (from the Spectator), vol. 8, 1846, pp. 481-483.

——*Story of Rimini.* Blackwood's Edinburgh Magazine, vol. 2, 1817, pp. 194-201. — North American Review, by W. Tudor, vol. 3, 1827, pp. 272-283.— Quarterly Review, vol. 14, 1816, pp. 473-481.—Edinburgh Review, by W. Hazlitt, vol. 26, 1816, pp. 476-491.—Monthly Review, vol. 80 N.S., 1816, pp. 138-147.

——*The Town.* Dublin University Magazine, vol. 32, 1848, pp. 669-683.

——*Ultra-Crepidarius.* Blackwood's Edinburgh Magazine, vol. 15, 1824, pp. 86-90.— Literary Examiner, Dec. 13, 1823.

*Wit and Humour.* Littell's Living Age (from the Examiner), vol. 12, 1847, pp. 97-100. —Westminster Review, vol. 48, 1847, pp. 24-59; same article, Littell's Living Age, vol. 15, pp. 344-359, and Eclectic Magazine, vol. 12, pp. 456-473.—Dublin University Magazine, vol. 29, 1847, pp. 74-80.—Fraser's Magazine, vol. 34, 1846, pp. 735-750.

——*Works.* Revue des Deux Mondes, by Eugène Forcade, Jan. 1, 1849, pp. 145-166.

---

## VIII.—CHRONOLOGICAL LIST OF WORKS.

THE WALTER SCOTT PRESS, NEWCASTLE-ON-TYNE.